"It's very warm in here, isn't it?"

"And getting warmer by the minute," he said.

Marshaling her composure, Mary Beth turned and tried to remember what they'd been talking about. Heating and cooling. Ductwork. She smiled, nervous. "Texas summers are always hot. What do you suggest?"

"It's always been my feeling that if you've got an itch, you ought to scratch it." He swiped his handkerchief over his chest. And over his navel.

Aware that her gaze had followed the handkerchief's path, she jerked her attention away again, her face fiery. "I was talking about heating and cooling the *apartment*."

"You can always pick up a couple of second-hand window units to use temporarily through the summer, but come winter, you'll have to think about keeping warm." He gave her a lopsided grin that told her he'd be happy to provide the warmth.

"J.J., stop that!"

Dear Reader,

This book is the first of three about the Outlaw family. I hope you'll enjoy them. The germ of the idea for the Outlaw brothers came when I remembered Jesse James—not Jesse James the Missouri outlaw, but Jesse James the Texas state treasurer who held office many years ago. Talk about name recognition! And how could you resist the irony of having a famous outlaw in charge of the state's money? He was reelected for years.

From that bit of history I created old Judge John Outlaw, a wily Texas politician who started the tradition of naming his sons after famous outlaws to give them a leg up in the world (name recognition) and pointing them in the direction of politics and public service. His grandsons, all charmers, have fulfilled his dream and are in law enforcement: a sheriff, a judge and a cop.

The series is set in Naconiche (NAK-uh-KNEE-chee), a fictitious small county seat in the east Texas area where I was born and still live as of this writing. Although there's a real Naconiche Creek, the town and colorful characters are from my imagination—but, trust me, they *could* be real. And the love stories…well, love is always real.

Join me on a bus trip to the Piney Woods, and we'll soon arrive at the town square of Naconiche, population 2438. We can stay at the Twilight Inn….

To love and laughter!

Jan Hudson

THE SHERIFF
Jan Hudson

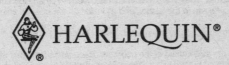

TORONTO • NEW YORK • LONDON
AMSTERDAM • PARIS • SYDNEY • HAMBURG
STOCKHOLM • ATHENS • TOKYO • MILAN • MADRID
PRAGUE • WARSAW • BUDAPEST • AUCKLAND

ISBN 0-373-75021-8

THE SHERIFF

www.eHarlequin.com

Printed in U.S.A.

To old friends
Tootie, Elizabeth, Wanda and Carol
for all the happy times and winning hands

Chapter One

When the Greyhound bus pulled to a stop at Wally's Feed Store, a ton of memories flooded Mary Beth Parker. This was the first time she'd been back to Naconiche, Texas, in twelve years—a lifetime ago, or so it seemed.

"Wake up, Katy," she whispered to her daughter, kissing the little blond head that nestled against her. "We're here."

Katy stretched and yawned, moving slowly, tired after the long trip from Natchez. Mary Beth had hated to put the four-year-old through the exhausting bus trip, but there simply wasn't enough cash to buy plane tickets—even if there had been an airport nearby. They had endured some rough times in the past two years, but their luck had finally changed. Just when she was starting to feel most desperate, Mary Beth had received word of an inheritance. A distant relative on her father's side had died and left everything to her—not a huge estate, the attorney had cautioned, but anything at all would be welcome to Mary Beth. She and Katy had been living off the kindness of friends.

Mary Beth struggled to her feet and got her crutches and her carry-on from the overhead bin. The blasted cast on her foot made moving in the cramped space awkward, and her leg ached from the long ride.

"Don't forget Penelope and your toy bag," she told Katy. Penelope, a worn, flop-eared stuffed dog, went everywhere with her daughter, including to bed at night.

Several passengers called goodbye as they moved down the aisle. With her bubbly personality, Katy had become the mascot of the group and had told anybody who would listen, "We're going to find our fortune in the town where my mommy was queen." Katy was quite precocious, but she hadn't learned the finer points of discretion yet.

The driver helped them off and unloaded their bags from the belly of the bus. "Good luck to you, ma'am. And to you, too, Katy."

"Thanks, Mr. Emmett." Katy waved merrily and turned to face the old courthouse across the street. "Where's the square, Mommy? The one where you rode when you were queen."

"That's it, sugarplum. See, the courthouse is in the middle and the streets make a square around it."

As the bus drove away, a tan sheriff's car pulled up. The door opened and a tall man in a black cowboy hat climbed out. Mary Beth thought his slow, deliberate movements seemed familiar. Broad-shouldered and ruggedly handsome, he walked as if he owned the place. When he started toward her, a big grin spread across his face.

Her heart almost stopped. It was the grin that she recognized—that Outlaw grin. The years had been kind to him; they had etched his face with character, changing him from a boy to a man.

Automatically her hand started to her hair, then she forced it back down. She looked as if she'd been pulled through a knothole backward and she knew it. She'd hoped to have time to prepare herself before running into him. Actually, she was hoping that he had moved to Houston or Topeka—somewhere far away so that she wouldn't have to face him in her humiliation. But there he stood, sexy as all get-out, and her looking like a frump in rumpled clothes with sleep in her eyes. There was nothing to do but keep her chin up and play it cool.

"Mary Beth Beams? Darlin', is that you?"

"J.J.?" she asked, as if she didn't know.

"In the flesh," he said, taking her into his arms in a bear hug.

The crutches made hugging him difficult, but she gave it her best shot. It felt so good to be in a strong, masculine embrace—so darned good. The years seemed to roll away. She was a girl again, secure in familiar arms.

"You look great," he said, "but what in the world happened to your foot?"

"I broke it. A really stupid accident."

She felt a tug on her jacket and looked down.

"Who's he?" Katy asked in a loud whisper.

Mary Beth stepped away, grateful that her daughter had pulled her back to reality. J.J. seemed happy to see her, but she was sure the man hadn't spent all this time pining for her. In fact, an old pain slashed through her as she recalled he hadn't even pined for her a full day when she'd broken up with him all those years ago. But those days were long past. He probably had a wife and four kids by now. "This is J. J. Outlaw, an old friend of mine. J.J., this is my daughter, Katy."

He grinned down at Katy, who was looking him over quite thoroughly, and tipped his hat. "Delighted to meet you, Miss Katy. Welcome to Naconiche."

Katy frowned, inched closer to Mary Beth and said, "Are you a *real* outlaw? Outlaws are bad guys."

J.J. chuckled. "My last name is Outlaw, but I'm one of the good guys. I'm the county sheriff."

"Is that why you have a gun?"

He nodded gravely. "For emergencies. In case I meet up with any real bad guys."

"Do you put people in the pokey? My daddy—"

Horrified at what her daughter was about to blurt out, Mary Beth clamped her hand over Katy's mouth. "You're the sheriff now? I thought your father would be sheriff forever."

J.J. laughed. "I was beginning to think that, too, but he retired last year, and I ran for his job and won the election."

"It's great to see you again," Mary Beth said, trying her best to act casual. Seeing J.J. again aroused a legion of conflicting feelings inside her, and her emotions were already stretched dangerously thin after a grueling seventeen-hour bus trip. He'd once been the love of her life.... She couldn't deal with him right now, she thought, looking around. "Mr. Murdock was supposed to meet us, but I don't see him. Where is his office?"

"On the other side of the square." J.J. motioned across the way. "But he's in court right now, and no telling when he'll be done. He asked me to meet you and get you settled."

Her heart hit the pavement. Since it seemed that there was no escaping him, she pushed all her memories and muddled emotions behind a thick door and locked it. Lifting her chin and giving him a perky smile, she said, "Why, isn't that sweet of you, J.J."

"No problem. Will you be staying at Ouida's Bed-and-Breakfast?"

Surprised by his question, Mary Beth said, "I—I don't know where we'll be staying. I had assumed that we could stay at the motel, but I suppose it might be full."

"The motel?"

"Yes, The Twilight Inn. I inherited it, you know. The motel and the restaurant next door. Marjorie Bartlett owned it, but she died a few months ago and left it to me. Well, she actually didn't leave it to me...or to anybody. She had Alzheimer's and had been in a nursing home for years, but she was my father's cousin and I'm the only relative left on his side of the family. On either side, really. Since my folks died, I'm it, except for some of my mom's cousins in Bremerton, Washington, and I've never met any of them. Truthfully, I barely remembered Cousin Marjorie, but I'm extremely thankful to have inherited her property." She laughed. "Sorry, I'm babbling, but I'm very tired. I'm eager to get settled at the motel and soak in a warm bath."

J.J. looked puzzled and was about to say something when Katy tugged her mother's jacket again and pointed. "Look, Mommy! There's a giant ice-cream cone in front of that store."

"The Double Dip," Mary Beth said, smiling. "Is that place still operating?"

"Sure is," J.J. said. "My mother runs it now."

"Do they sell ice cream? Could I have some, please, please, please?" Katy danced around as she pleaded.

J.J. hoisted Katy up into his arms, "'Course you can, Miss Katy. I'll treat you and your mother to ice cream while we wait for Mr. Murdock to finish his case. Is that okay, Mary Beth? Mama would love to see you."

"Please, Mommy. Please, please, please. Could I have chocolate with sprinkles?"

Mary Beth stroked a wayward curl from Katy's forehead and smiled. "Okay." She glanced at her luggage. "But what will we do with our bags?"

"Wally!" J.J. shouted, it seemed like to no one in particular. "Keep an eye on Mary Beth's stuff, will you?"

"Yep," a voice answered from behind a stack of feed sacks.

"This way, ladies," J.J. said, slipping his free hand under Mary Beth's elbow as she hobbled along the sidewalk. "Wait, I forgot about your foot. Should I drive you over?"

"Heavens, no. It's only half a block, and I'm tired of sitting. I need to stretch."

As they walked, slowly because of the crutches, Katy chattered a mile a minute—about their bus ride, about her dolls, about her best friend Emily in Natchez, but not, thank goodness, about her daddy. It was bad enough that the homecoming queen had returned practically penniless, but Mary Beth wasn't ready to announce to everyone in her old hometown that her ex-husband was in prison.

The pressure of J.J.'s hand was steady and secure. Steady. Secure. Rock solid. She could feel the staggering weight of two years of stress begin to ease.

Had it been two years? It seemed like a lifetime ago that the police had come for her husband and his name was plastered across the newspaper headlines. Shocked by Brad's subsequent indictment for embezzlement, she'd been quickly hit with the fact that they were in debt up to their eyebrows. Brad had always insisted on handling the finances and, like a fool, she'd trusted him. And like a fool she'd never questioned how he supported their lavish lifestyle and his gambling habit. He'd gone to prison, and the mortgage company had fore-closed on their beautiful home. Most of their assets had gone for attorney fees and toward restitution. She'd been left only with her car, part of the furniture that was paid for and her personal possessions—what she hadn't hocked to pay the utilities.

She and Katy had been left literally on the street. A friend had generously provided them a place to live, and after some of the bewilderment had worn off, Mary Beth had given herself a good talking-to. The time had come for her to stop acting like such a wuss and take control of her life. After searching want ads, asking around among the few friends still associating with her and going on endless interviews, she landed a job as an aerobics instructor. It wasn't much, but the deal was better than anything else she could find—and she was a darned good instructor. They were managing to get back on their feet, when Mary Beth had her accident. With no income and no insurance, the situation was bleak. As her meager bank balance dwindled, panic had set in. She had a child to feed and clothe. She had wept and prayed and cursed Brad Parker and her own stupid-ity for marrying him.

Now walking down this street in Naconiche, she wondered what would have happened if she hadn't moved away with her parents the summer after she graduated from high school? What would her life have been like if she'd stayed here and married J.J. instead of the scoundrel she'd chosen?

Yet, without Brad Parker there would have been no Katy. And Katy was worth every humiliation she'd endured.

What was done, was done and she was back now, starting over in the place she'd been so eager to leave.

The grass hadn't been greener on the other side of the fence, but it had taken her a long time to discover that. And she'd also learned that she couldn't trust a man— or anyone else—to provide for her or make her happy. She had to depend on herself, make it on her own. And, by damn, she was giving it her best shot.

Mary Beth took a deep breath and immersed herself in the sights and sounds of her old hometown.

Very little about Naconiche had changed. The familiar clicking of shuffling dominoes came from under the shade tree on the courthouse lawn, where old men met to play every day except Sunday. Roses still bloomed beside the bank, and the smell of sizzling meat and frying onions from the City Grill wafted by her.

As they stepped inside the Double Dip, the cold-sweet scents of chocolate and peppermint and strawberry took her back a dozen and more years. How many times had she sat on one of those red stools at the counter and eaten a banana split with extra pecans or a hot-fudge sundae with her friends? Her throat tightened and tears sprang to her eyes.

She was home.

"Mom," J.J. said. "Look who I found. Mary Beth Beams. And this is her daughter Katy."

"Mary Beth Parker, now." She smiled at the gray-haired woman who had taught her in third grade. "It's good to see you, Miss Nonie."

"Mary Beth!" Her arms open wide, Nonie Outlaw hurried to the front of the store and enveloped her former student in a hug. "How wonderful to see you! And Katy, what a beautiful young lady you are. You look just like your mother when she was your age. We were so excited when Dwight Murdock told us you were coming to town. Welcome home."

Another bit of tension gave way, and Mary Beth smiled. When she was seventeen, she could hardly wait to get away from the hick town where she'd grown up. Now that same town was her refuge.

Yes, she was finally home. Everything was going to be okay.

NONIE OUTLAW PLAYED with Katy, while J.J. and Mary Beth sat at one of the marble tables by the window. He felt himself grinning like an idiot as he watched Mary Beth dig into the banana split she'd ordered. She'd been a pretty girl the last time he saw her. Now she was a beautiful woman. He thought he'd forgotten her—but he hadn't. All the old feelings came barreling down on him. It was like being blindsided by Shorty Badder's log truck.

He'd been crazy about Mary Beth for as long as he could remember. He'd finally gotten up the nerve to ask her for a date when he was a senior in high school and she was a sophomore. From that moment on, they'd been a couple, even when he'd gone off to college in Huntsville the next year.

He thought of one of the last times he'd seen her. It was a week or two after she'd graduated from high school, and they had gone to a movie. He remembered her hiding her eyes against his shoulder during some of the scarier parts. Afterward, they had gone out to the overlook and parked.

He'd meant to propose to her that night—he had the ring in his pocket. But before he could ask her to marry him, she'd broken up with him. She told him that she and her family were moving to Dallas the next week— her father had gotten a sudden promotion—and besides, she'd be going off to college in the fall anyhow. She'd been accepted at some fancy school in Florida, one that he didn't even know that she'd applied to. But then, Mary Beth had always had highfalutin ideas about getting out of Naconiche and seeing the world.

It had damned near broken his heart.

No, not damned near. It had broken his heart. Devastated him.

Instead of telling her he loved her and asking her to marry him the way he'd planned, pride had made him brush her off and turn his attention to Holly Winchell the very next night. Holly was a hot little number who worked as a waitress at the restaurant next to The Twilight Inn, the one that Mary Beth now owned. She'd been a sorry substitute for Mary Beth and the fling hadn't lasted long. He couldn't remember the name of the restaurant then—it had gone through several changes through the years—or what happened to Holly. In its heyday the old Twilight Inn had been a thriving business, but it had gone from bad to worse before it finally closed down about four or five years ago.

J.J. was afraid that Mary Beth was in for a disappointment if she was expecting much from that old property, but he didn't want to be the one who let her down. He'd leave that up to Dwight Murdock.

His own strawberry sundae melted as he watched her eat, watched the dimple at the bottom corner of her mouth appear and disappear as she spooned ice cream between her lips. God, he'd spent many a night thinking about that dimple. She seemed to savor every bite, closing her eyes and sighing every once in a while in a way that was downright sexy.

Even though she looked tired, she was more attractive than any woman within a hundred miles. No, make that a thousand miles—or maybe farther. There was still something about her that made him want to cuddle her close and bury his nose in her thick blond hair—a thought he shouldn't be thinking if there was a Mr. Parker still around. He'd noticed right away that she wasn't wearing a wedding ring, but these days lots of women didn't. He tried to think of subtle ways to ask about her husband and couldn't think of any. He'd never been much of one to pussyfoot around.

"You still married?"

She shook her head. "Divorced. Almost two years ago."

He tried not to smile. Oh, hell, what was he thinking? A man would have to be crazy to get involved with Mary Beth again and get his heart broken twice. No, he wasn't going down that road again.

But, damn, she sure stirred up something potent inside him.

"So how did you break your foot?" he asked.

"It would sound a lot more exciting if I said I hurt myself skiing in Vail, but the truth is, I fell down the steps of my apartment. A silly accident. I was carrying groceries. A bag started slipping, and I tried to save it. I lost the bag anyhow and broke two bones in my foot. That was the end of my career, too."

"And what career was that?"

"I taught aerobics at the local health club. It wasn't much of a career, but I was good at it, and I could leave Katy at the nursery there while I taught my classes. Child care is expensive these days. Everything is expensive these days. News of my inheritance couldn't have come at a better time. Things were getting pretty tight for us." Mary Beth paused for a moment, taking a deep breath.

So things had been hard lately for Mary Beth...

Her voice broke into his thoughts. "What about you? Do you have a family?"

"Just my folks, my brothers and my sister. I never got married. Guess I'm not the marrying kind."

"Never even came close?"

"Only once." He grinned. "Then I sobered up."

She laughed and wiped her lips with a napkin. "There has to be a story in that."

"Not really. I had too much champagne at Frank's wedding and proposed to a bridesmaid from Texarkana. Luckily, she didn't take me seriously." Actually, there was more to the story than that, but he didn't want to go into it.

"Oh, is Frank married?"

"He was. His wife was killed in a car wreck last year. He has twins, a boy and a girl, about Katy's age."

"I'm so sorry to hear that. Is Frank okay?"

J.J. shrugged. "Well as can be expected." He glanced at his watch. "Let me go over to the courthouse and see how much longer Dwight will be. Stay here and visit with Mama till I get back."

J.J. rose and hurried from the shop. Damn! He could hardly wait to get hold of Dwight Murdock. He might skewer that knuckleheaded lawyer for dragging him into this mess. He didn't want to see the look on Mary Beth's face when she found out about her inheritance.

MARY BETH PICKED UP their ice cream dishes and carried them to the counter. Katy, a paper napkin tucked under her chin, knelt on a stool watching Miss Nonie spooning sprinkles on an ice cream cone.

Katy beamed as Miss Nonie handed her the cone. "Thank you very much."

"You're welcome, precious."

Mary Beth raised her eyebrow. "A second one?"

"Well, you see, I had sort of an *ac-ci-dent* with the first one. Miss Nonie said I shouldn't worry. It happens to Janey and Jimmy all the time. We cleaned it up slick as a whistle. Isn't that right, Miss Nonie?"

"It is indeed. Slick as a whistle." The gray-haired woman gave Mary Beth a wink.

"Are Janey and Jimmy your grandchildren?" Mary Beth asked.

"Frank's twins. A pair of imps."

Mary Beth could tell by the twinkle in her eyes that she adored those imps. "Do you have any other grandchildren?"

"Not a one," Nonie said. "There's not a single in-law among the whole bunch of Outlaws. Frank married, but his wife was killed in a car wreck, and he doesn't seem much interested in looking for another."

"J.J. told me. A real tragedy. What about Cole?"

"Divorced. No children. He's a homicide detective in Houston."

"A homicide detective? And J.J.'s the sheriff. I love it. Did all the Outlaws end up in law enforcement?"

"Every single one of them," Nonie told her.

Cole Younger Outlaw was the oldest son. Each of the Outlaw clan was named after an infamous character of the old West. J.J. was Jesse James, his older bother was Frank James; then came Sam Bass Outlaw and Belle Starr Outlaw.

J.J.'s grandfather, old Judge John Outlaw, had said that having a memorable name was an asset in business and politics. He named his sons John Wesley "Wes" Hardin Outlaw, Jr. and Butch Cassidy Outlaw and aimed them toward lives of public service. His idea must have worked. Wes had served as sheriff of Naconiche for as long as Mary Beth could remember and his brother Butch was a state senator.

Now, Nonie had told her, Frank was a judge, Sam was a Texas Ranger and Belle was an FBI agent. Holy!

Mary Beth glanced over her shoulder and was happy to see J.J. returning from the courthouse with a tall, slightly stooped man with a fringe of white hair and a red bow tie. She had enjoyed visiting with Miss Nonie, and Katy had been enthralled with everything in the ice-cream parlor and gift shop, but she was physically and emotionally exhausted. She wanted to get settled and have that bath she'd been fantasizing about.

Mr. Murdock, a courtly gentleman of the old school, apologized profusely for not being able to meet the bus. "The case simply couldn't be rescheduled."

"I understand, sir. J.J. took good care of us."

J.J. grinned. "We aim to please. Now, if you'll excuse me, I have to get going. Just got a call that Cletus Medford's cows broke the fence and several head are blocking the highway. Duty calls." He winked at Mary Beth. "I'll check on you later." He touched the brim of his hat, turned and trotted for his car.

Mary Beth dragged her gaze from his retreating form, telling herself that she should be grateful for the duty that took him away. Try as she might, she couldn't think kindly of those cows.

"I have some papers for you to sign in my office," Mr. Murdock said, "and I expect you'll be wanting to inspect the property. Shall we do that tomorrow morning?"

"Well, I suppose that the papers can wait until then, but I'd like to go on to the motel now. I'm without transportation. Could you drive us?"

"Certainly. I would be delighted. I see you've injured

your foot. Let me retrieve my automobile, and I'll pick you up out front.''

''Great. Our bags are over at the feed store.''

The lawyer hurried out, and Mary Beth said her goodbyes to Miss Nonie. ''I'd love to see Sheriff Wes. What is he doing now that he's retired?''

Nonie laughed. ''Trying to keep from sticking his nose into J.J.'s affairs. He has a clock-repair business in the back of the store. He's usually around since we live upstairs now, but he drove over to Cherokee an hour or so ago.''

''You don't live on the ranch anymore?''

She shook her head. ''With all our brood grown, the two of us just rattled around in that big house, so we divided up the ranch and gave it to the kids. We have a nice apartment upstairs that suits us fine. Oh, there's Dwight.'' Nonie gave Mary Beth and Katy another hug and waved to them as they went outside to the aging red Cadillac parked at the curb.

After they retrieved their luggage from the feed store, Mr. Murdock drove out toward the edge of town—which was really only a quarter of a mile or so from the square.

''I took it upon myself to make reservations for you at Ouida's Bed-and-Breakfast,'' the lawyer said. ''I think you'll find the place quite cozy. After you've had a chance to look over the property, I'm sure you'll be anxious to rest and refresh yourself from your long trip.''

Mary Beth frowned. Why were they pushing the B and B? ''That's very kind of you, but we were planning to stay at the motel.'' She didn't add that they couldn't afford to stay at Ouida's place.

''The *motel?* But—but you can't do that!''

"Why not? I own it, don't I?"

"Yes, of course, but it simply isn't *suitable*."

"Why not?"

He pulled to a stop in front of a row of ramshackle buildings. "See for yourself."

Stunned by the sight, she couldn't speak. What had once been a neat strip of rooms separated by individual carports, with flowers overflowing from window boxes, was now an uninhabitable mess. Most of the paint had peeled away and the little that was left was a grimy, unrecognizable color covered by layers of graffiti. Windows were broken out and boarded up. Weeds grew waist-high around the place. Even the For Sale sign in front looked dilapidated and forlorn.

A sick feeling coiled in the pit of her stomach. She wanted to weep, but she wouldn't—not yet, not here. She ground her teeth and tried to control the panic threatening to erupt.

Katy hung over the back seat, gawking. "What's that place, Mommy? Is it haunted?"

"No, sugarplum, it's not haunted. Mr. Murdock, is the restaurant this bad?"

"Actually, no. It was in use until last week. A Mexican place. Quite good food, in fact. Unfortunately, the tenants skipped town owing two months rent and with six months left on their lease."

"Let's look at it," she said, her shoulders sagging. She didn't hold out much hope that it would have a bathtub.

Chapter Two

It didn't have a bathtub.

The restaurant *did* have electricity and a roof. There were bathrooms, labeled Señors and Señoritas, one of which was reasonably sanitary, Mary Beth decided after she'd checked them out. There was even a pay phone on the wall by the door. She picked up the receiver. It still had a dial tone. If she was lucky, maybe the previous tenants had left behind some food in their haste to skip out on their bills.

In any case the Tico Taco was now home.

"We won't be going to Ouida's," she'd told Mr. Murdock. "We'll be staying here. Could you help bring in our bags, please?"

"*Here?* But—but—but—" he'd sputtered like a rusty motor boat. "You can't stay *here!*"

"Don't I own it?"

"Well, of course."

She smiled brightly. "Then I can stay here if I choose."

"But it's a *restaurant*. There are no *beds*."

"I noticed that, too. But we can improvise, can't we, Katy?"

"What's improvise, Mommy?"

"It's making do with what we have. We'll pretend we're camping and have lots of fun," she said with a forced gaiety. "Those red booths look like they might do for beds. Pick out a soft one that you like," she told her daughter.

"Okay." Katy skipped away with her flop-eared dog.

Mary Beth turned to the elderly lawyer, who looked alarmed. "We'll be just fine here, Mr. Murdock."

"But, Mrs. Parker, it simply isn't *suitable* for a woman and a child alone, especially with your injury. You'll be much more comfortable at Ouida's."

"Perhaps so, but the plain truth is, sir, that I can't afford to stay at the bed-and-breakfast. This will have to do."

"Perhaps you could stay with friends, or I could advance you a small sum—"

She lifted her chin and stiffened her spine. "Thank you, Mr. Murdock, but no. The Tico Taco is perfectly adequate for the time being." She pasted a big grin on her face. "Why, it's the next best thing to a vacation in Mexico. We'll have a grand time here. And it's free."

He hadn't wanted to leave them alone, but she finally convinced him to go. After their bags were unloaded— Mr. Murdock muttering something about the modern generation of young ladies all the while—the man left. Mary Beth gripped the handles of her crutches tightly and resisted the urge to hobble after him, yelling for him to wait.

While Katy was still exploring, Mary Beth stood alone in the middle of the dining room and looked around at her new home.

Smells of corn tortillas, spices and old grease hung in the air. A coating of dust covered everything from the faded paper piñatas hanging from the ceiling to the scarred wood floor. It was a far cry from the lovely two-story home with the pillars that she'd lived in when Brad was embezzling money from the savings-and-loan company where he was vice president.

She ached to sit down in one of those old chairs, lay her head on the table and bawl like a baby.

But she didn't. She'd learned early on that crying didn't help her situation. It only made her face blotchy and alarmed Katy.

She was sick of playing the victim role. It was time for her to take charge of her life. A dozen times a day she told herself that. But that wasn't as simple as it sounded, and she often overreacted in one extreme or the other. She was new to this business of being independent; it wasn't her nature. There had always been a strong man around to handle things and it had been easy to acquiesce. Her father had been authoritarian and overly protective, and Brad had been mega-domineering. Come to think of it, J.J. had been that type as well—not as bad as Brad perhaps, but inclined in that direction. He was definitely a take-charge kind of guy. Was he still?

In a way, she supposed, this whole experience with Brad's arrest and the mess she found herself in might be a good thing. ''Things happen for a reason,'' her mother had always said. Maybe one day she'd look back on this time and think of it as character-building, but it was hard for her to be philosophical when she was tired and scared and broke. She was beginning to think that character-building was vastly overrated. Maybe being an independent woman was overrated, too. She felt like a tangle of contradictions: determined to stand on her own two feet on one hand while wanting to yell for someone to save her on the other.

Sometimes life was a bitch.

Mary Beth knew that she couldn't depend on a white knight riding in to save her—although it had been tempting to simply melt into J.J.'s arms and never let go. When he'd hugged her at the bus station, it had seemed so right. He'd seemed like a knight in a cowboy hat, and Naconiche had seemed like Camelot.

"Things always work out for the best" had been another of her mother's sayings. That had become Mary Beth's mantra. Somehow, some way, things were going to work out. She was determined to believe that.

And, dammit, she was going to become an independent woman or die trying.

Mary Beth turned on the ceiling fans and opened a couple of windows to air out the place, then she made her way to the kitchen. First things first. She and Katy had to eat.

Luck was with her. The pantry yielded a treasure trove, including several restaurant-sized cans of tomatoes, salsa, jalapeño peppers and beans. And more chili powder, cumin and other spices than she could use in fifty years. There was even part of a bag of rice and a ten-pound sack of onions that looked okay. The former tenants must have been in a powerful hurry not to have taken all the food along with them.

She found several blocks of cheese in the walk-in refrigerator, along with a few items past their prime, such as smelly milk, some rusty-looking lettuce and a couple of mushy bags of food she couldn't identify. A shame about the milk. But she did find a box of individual cream cups, the kind used for coffee, two cartons of butter pats and five eggs that seemed okay.

In the big freezer, she discovered several packages of tortillas, an unopened box of chicken breasts that would feed Katy and her for weeks and another big box of ground beef.

She heaved a huge sigh and sent a prayer heavenward. At least they wouldn't starve.

Making a quick tour of the rest of the kitchen, she found that the grill and the large stainless-steel gas stove were reasonably clean and in working order. She was grateful for her volunteer stint in the Junior League kitchens, since the stove was similar to one she'd learned to operate there. The grease in the deep fryer needed to be tossed and the fryer could stand a good scrubbing—but not now. Several big pots hung from an overhead rack, and there were enough smaller ones to do for Katy and her. There were two huge dishwashers and a triple stainless-steel sink.

"Mommy!"

"I'm here, honey." She hobbled from the kitchen.

"Penelope and I have to go to the bathroom."

"It's right there," Mary Beth said, pointing to the Señoritas door.

Katy frowned and glanced from the door to Mary Beth. "Would you go with us? Penelope is kind of…" The girl glanced at the door again.

Mary Beth smiled. "Uncomfortable in a new place?"

"Yes. I told her it was okay, but she's uncomfortable."

"No problem, sweetie." She took Katy and her dog to the bathroom. And while she was there, she scoured the sink and other fixtures with an industrial-style cleanser she found in a cabinet.

The whole place needed cleaning, but she was too tired to tackle it all. She gave Katy a dust rag and instructions to wipe down the tables and booths while she tackled the kitchen and came up with dinner.

Other than a surface layer of greasy dust, the kitchen wasn't too bad—apart from some things that looked suspiciously like mouse droppings. Rodents of all shapes and sizes gave her the willies. She convinced herself that the evidence was very old and that any self-respecting mouse would be long gone in search of better provisions.

Using a little ingenuity, including her defrosting skills, she put together a rather tasty meal of grilled chicken breasts along with rice topped with onion and tomatoes. She even managed to fix Katy some chocolate milk by mixing half a dozen coffee creamers with water and some chocolate syrup she'd located in the pantry.

"Mmm," Katy said. "This is good, Mommy." She wiped her mouth with a paper napkin from the table dispenser. "My tummy's full." She rubbed her belly and yawned.

"Tired, sweetie?"

"Just a little. Does this place have a TV?"

"Sorry, no. But let's have our baths and I'll read a story to you."

"Is there a bathtub?"

"Not a regular one, but there's a deep sink in the kitchen that's just about your size."

Katy was a little wary about taking a bath in the kitchen sink, but she was a trouper and the two of them were soon giggling as Mary Beth helped her bathe and shampoo her hair. She wrapped Katy in a tablecloth from a stack of clean ones she'd located in a cupboard and nuzzled her daughter's soft, sweet-scented neck. "All clean and smelling like honeysuckle."

"All clean," Katy echoed. "Are you going to take a bath in the sink?"

Mary Beth laughed. "I don't think my cast and I would fit. I'll make do with a basin bath in the Señoritas."

"Mommy, what's a señorita?"

"That's the word written on one of the bathroom doors. It's Spanish for young lady or for an unmarried woman." She began brushing Katy's fine blond hair.

"But you're married."

"Well, technically, I'm not. Daddy and I are divorced, remember?"

"Oh, yeah. He's in the pokey."

"Where did you hear that word?"

"From Aunt Isabel. I heard you and her talking. Aunt Isabel said my daddy was a con and in the pokey."

Isabel was Mary Beth's best friend in Natchez. She had offered them her garage apartment to live in and the two of them had lived there comfortably, although Mary Beth had hated imposing on her friend. "Isabel shouldn't have said that. That was very rude."

"He isn't in the pokey?"

"Pokey is a rude word. Daddy is in a correctional institution. He's being punished for doing a bad thing."

"Like when I get a time-out for spitting on Eric."

"Yes, except that grown-up punishment is more serious. I think it might be best if we not mention where Daddy is to anybody. Okay?"

"Okay. What's written on the other door?"

"Which door?"

"The other bathroom."

"Oh. That one says Señors."

"Is it for married ladies?"

Mary Beth chuckled. "No. That one is for men."

"Then where do the married ladies go?"

"All the ladies and girls, unmarried or not, use Señoritas. You're a pill, know that?" She kissed Katy's forehead, then tickled her tummy until she giggled.

By the time Katy's hair was dried and she was dressed in her pink-checked nightgown, Mary Beth was exhausted and her foot was aching. She would have loved to soak in a warm bubble bath, but if wishes were dollars, she'd be rich. Instead, she cleaned up as best she could in the ladies' room and pulled on an old nightshirt.

She spread tablecloths over the benches of the booth Katy had selected. Thankfully, she'd brought along Katy's favorite little quilt and pillow, so her daughter was snuggled securely with Penelope in her makeshift bed. On the table she had placed a small lamp that she'd found in a back closet.

Mary Beth shook the dust from a serape she took from the wall and rolled it into a pillow for herself. She wrapped it with a clean tablecloth and set aside a couple of the other cloths for her covers. After turning off the overhead lights, she picked up the book Katy had chosen and began to read by the glow of the table lamp.

Her daughter was so droopy-eyed that she fell asleep before Mary Beth got to page three of the storybook. Exhausted from the trip, she thought that she would fall asleep quickly, too, and twisted and turned until she was reasonably comfortable, given that the bench was a foot shorter than she was.

Sleep didn't come.

Her foot throbbed like crazy. It needed some support.

Carefully she scooted from the booth, trying not to disturb her bedding. Naturally, the tablecloth and the serape followed her and fell on the floor. She shook them out and repositioned them.

Using only one crutch, she limped to a chair at a nearby table and quietly dragged it toward the booth.

It screeched.

She froze and glanced toward Katy. Her daughter was still.

Trying again, she wrestled the chair into position with minimal racket. Using another serape from the wall for padding, she covered the seat and climbed back into her makeshift bed. By that time, she'd broken into a clammy sweat and lay back exhausted.

The extension made things better. Not great, but better.

Events of the day replayed in her brain—especially her time with J.J. His masculine scent haunted her, the smell of his fresh-starched collar and the faint citrus of his shaving lotion. It stirred old memories of playing in his truck, of his warm embraces, of his kisses, of the feel of his hand on her skin. A shiver ran over her. Funny how evocative smells were, as if they were attached to memories with strong threads. There had always been a special magic between them that made her knees go weak and her brain shut down. One look from him, one simple touch, and she knew that the magic was still there.

She thought of him over the years, wondering how his life had gone. Strange that he'd never married—not that she planned to get involved with him again. He was the type who would march in and take over, and that was the very worst kind of man for her. Magic or not, this wasn't the time to get involved with another man. She'd be smart to avoid him. Yet his eyes…

Stop thinking about him! She had to get some rest.

She was tired, so tired.

But her body buzzed like a high-wire and her brain felt as if hummingbirds were having a convention inside her head. She tried every relaxation technique she'd ever heard of. Nothing worked.

In the middle of her second set of deep-breathing exercises, she heard it. Little scurrying noises.

Her eyes popped wide-open. She would never get to sleep now.

J.J. COULDN'T SLEEP. Every time he closed his eyes, he could see Mary Beth's face. By thinking about her and not paying attention to his business, he'd damn near been run over by a semi when he was herding Cletus's cows off the highway. Even a couple of beers at the Rusty Bucket and a little flirting with Tami who'd served them hadn't taken the edge off his preoccupation with Mary Beth—with remembering old times.

He turned over, punched his pillow and tried again.

It was no use.

Finally he gave it up, pulled on a pair of jeans and strolled out onto the second-floor balcony of his four-plex. He leaned against the railing and stared down at the full moon reflected in the swimming pool.

The image reminded him of Mary Beth's shimmering hair. Even after all these years, he could remember the way her hair smelled. Like honeysuckle. And he could remember the taste of her lips and the softness of her skin.

He thought he'd gotten over her long ago. Obviously he hadn't. One glance at her and all the fires sprang to life again. Guess people always remembered their first loves with tenderness. He certainly remembered his—he'd thought of Mary Beth often over the year. But seeing her get off that bus, he remembered why they weren't together. She'd broken his heart.

He'd dated more women than he could keep up with after she'd dumped him and moved away. None of them could hold a candle to her. He rarely saw anyone for long. Just didn't seem to find that spark with anybody. His mother had worried about him, and his brothers had called him a lovesick fool. Then a few years ago, he'd met somebody when he was visiting friends in Dallas. Tess had looked a little like Mary Beth, only taller. Smelled like her, too. They'd carried on hot and heavy for two years—even talked about getting married, but things hadn't worked out. Tess wasn't about to move to Naconiche and he hated the notion of living in Dallas. Tess found someone who loved city life, and she'd given him his walking papers.

He hadn't been as broken up about it as he should have been.

Figuring that he ought to set his sights closer to home, J.J. had tried keeping company with a first-grade teacher at the local elementary school. Pretty young woman. Sweet natured. Crazy about Naconiche. His mama had loved Carol Ann. He'd dated her for over a year.

But the chemistry just wasn't there. Maybe it was because she didn't smell right. Anyhow, as gently as he could, he ended their relationship. She married the associate pastor of the Baptist church the following year, and they had moved to the Valley when he got a church of his own there a few months ago. Carol Ann was better off with the preacher.

Now Mary Beth was back. The spark was still there. And she still smelled like honeysuckle.

Damn.

One whiff, and he was like a bull after a cow at mating time.

Fool.

He wasn't about to get mixed up with her again. He planned to give her a wide berth. She'd waltzed back into town, thinking she'd inherited a tidy sum. No way would she hang around when she discovered the truth. She'd be on the next bus out of town.

That little Katy was cute as a button. She should have been his.

But she wasn't.

Hell, he had to get some sleep. He strode back inside, shucking his jeans on the way to bed. He had to get his mind off Mary Beth. Anything between them was over and done with a long time ago. His plan was to totally steer clear of her and do no more than tip his hat if they met on the street. No need to go asking for trouble.

THE NEXT MORNING, J.J. was on his third cup of coffee at the City Grill when Dwight Murdock took the stool beside him.

"Good morning," the lawyer said.

J.J. merely grunted. He didn't see a damned thing good about it. He hadn't slept more than a couple of hours and he'd cut himself twice while he was shaving.

"I was hoping to find you here," Dwight said. "I'm concerned about Mary Beth Parker and her little girl."

"How so?"

"Well, their sleeping accommodations for one thing."

"Coffee, Dwight?" Vera Whitehouse said, pouring a cup for him even as she asked.

Vera, who wouldn't weigh ninety pounds dripping wet, had been the morning waitress at the Grill for as long as J.J. could remember. He'd heard once that she'd arrived on the bus forty-some odd years ago, saw a sign in the window advertising for help and stayed on. She knew everybody in town by their first name—and most of their business.

She warmed up J.J.'s cup. "You ready to order yet, J.J.?"

"In a minute. What do you mean about their sleeping accommodations, Dwight? Ouida's is a nice place, isn't it?"

"From what I understand," the lawyer said.

"Top-notch," Vera chimed in. "Why, you could eat your dinner off Ouida Tankard's floors."

"Problem is, they're not staying at Ouida's."

"Then where are they staying?"

"At the restaurant."

Puzzled by the answer, J.J. asked, "What restaurant?"

"The Tico Taco. The people who were leasing it moved out last week, left in the middle of the night owing two months rent. I tried to talk her out of staying there, but she was determined."

J.J.'s boots hit the floor, and he swung around on his stool. "Do you mean to tell me that you went off and left them at that Mexican joint on the old highway?"

"She insisted. Reminded me that she owned it."

Vera rolled her eyes and muttered, "Men! Leaving Mary Beth on crutches and with that baby to tend to. Why, I'd bet my bottom dollar the sorry bunch that ran the place didn't even leave a scrap of food in the place."

"Hell's bells, Dwight!" J.J. slapped a couple of bills on the counter and stalked off, grabbing his hat from the rack on his way out the door.

"Wait! Wait, J.J.," Vera yelled. She came running after him with three small cartons of milk cradled in one arm and a bag in the other. "Here's some milk and doughnuts. You bring them to town for a decent meal. I'll bet that poor lamb is starving."

J.J. cursed Dwight Murdock all the way to the Tico Taco. For a smart lawyer, sometimes that old man didn't have the brains God gave a billy goat.

Chapter Three

"Mommy, Mommy, are you awake?" Katy asked as she shook her.

Mary Beth opened one eye. "I am now."

"I have to go to the Señoritas, and somebody is knocking on the front door."

Groaning, Mary Beth struggled from the position she'd slept in. Her knee was stiff and her neck had a terrible crick in it. The banging on the door would wake the dead. How could she have slept through it? "I'm coming! I'm coming!"

Katy began dancing from one foot to the other. "Mommy, I've gotta *go*. Now."

Since Katy's need seemed more critical, she took her to the washroom, splashing cold water on her own face while they were there. The racket was still going on when they came out.

Not taking time to locate a robe, she grabbed one of the tablecloths and wrapped it around her, sarong style. But the blasted thing fell off before she got to the door, tangling around one of her crutches as she darned near went sprawling.

"Hold your horses!" she yelled. "I'm coming as fast

as I can." She unlocked the shaded front door and opened it a crack. There stood J. J. Outlaw breathing fire.

"Dammit, have you lost your cotton-pickin' mind?" he shouted.

She felt as if he'd smacked her in the face with a bucket of slop. "I don't think so," she said in a tone that would have frozen a rump roast. "I've lost just about everything else, but my mind seems intact, thank you very much." She slammed the door and turned the dead bolt.

He started knocking again. "Mary Beth, let me in."

"Eat dirt."

"Mommy, who's that outside?"

"That's Sheriff J.J., sweetie."

"Aren't you going to let him in?"

"No. He said a rude word. Besides, I'm still in my nightshirt. How about we get dressed and I'll fix breakfast."

"He's making an awful lot of noise."

"I know. Just ignore him, and he'll go away. Would you like an omelette?"

"With cheese?"

"Absolutely."

"And orange juice?"

"We don't have any orange juice, honey, but I can make you some more chocolate milk. Will that be okay?"

Katy nodded, then glanced anxiously at the front door. "I think we should let Sheriff J.J. in. He sounds mad. He might put us in the pokey."

"Not likely. And don't say pokey. Tell you what, let me get my clothes and go to the washroom, then you can let him in. Okay?"

Katy looked relieved. "Okay."

Mary Beth grabbed a few things and hobbled away. She hurriedly brushed her hair and her teeth and dressed in a blue T-shirt dress and one sneaker. She even took time to dab on a bit of blush and some lipstick—though she couldn't imagine why. It wasn't as if she cared how J.J. saw her.

She glared at her reflection. *You are the worst liar in seven states.* Her heart was practically doing a tap dance at the notion of seeing J.J.

When Mary Beth came out, Katy was sitting on the bar that ran along the wall separating the dining area from the kitchen. J.J. stood beside her, one boot heel hooked over the bar rail. Katy was eating a doughnut, and J.J. was grinning at the little scamp.

"Hi, Mommy. Sheriff J.J. brought us some doughnuts. They're good. Want one?"

"I thought we were going to have a cheese omelette."

Katy looked sheepish. "I forgot."

"Just one doughnut, young lady. No more. You shouldn't have too many sweets."

"Sorry about that," J.J. said. "Vera from down at the City Grill sent them. And some milk. She was afraid you didn't have anything to eat. Tell the truth, so was I."

"The former tenants must have decided that they didn't have room to take both booze and food when they hit the road. Luckily, they cleaned out the bar, except for a few liqueurs, and left the food. The menu might be a bit limited, but we have plenty to eat."

"What's booze?" Katy asked.

"Grown-up drinks," Mary Beth said.

"Like coffee?"

"No, stronger than coffee. Speaking of coffee, J.J.,

do you know how to work that coffee machine? I'd love a cup. I was too tired to figure it out last night. Have you had breakfast?''

"No. I thought I'd take you to the City Grill for a bite."

"Thanks, but I'll fix that omelette I was planning." She turned and headed for the kitchen.

"Still think your mommy is upset with me?" J.J. asked.

Mary Beth heard Katy whisper, "I don't know, but you should 'pologize for saying a rude word. I always have to 'pologize."

In the kitchen, she fired up the monster of a stove and laid out eggs, cream and cheese. In no time, she cooked a perfect large cheese omelette and divided it among three plates, giving a small portion to Katy.

"Need some help?" J.J. asked behind her.

"Yes, thanks. Carrying things is a problem with crutches." She put the plates and forks on a tray, along with mugs for coffee, and he carried it to a table.

He glanced at the remnants of their bedding. "That where you slept last night?"

"Yes. It was quite comfortable."

He raised an eyebrow. "I'll bet." He got a booster seat for Katy from a spot near the cash register and lifted her into her place at the table. He brought over a steaming pot of coffee and poured mugs for Mary Beth and himself. He also brought a small carton of milk and a straw for Katy.

"Thanks," she told him.

"No problem. And I'd like to apologize for saying a rude word earlier."

"Apology accepted."

J.J. glanced at Katy and winked. She giggled.

After he'd taken a couple of bites, he said, "This is really good."

"Thanks. Sorry I can't offer toast or croissants, we're fresh out."

"We don't have any orange juice either," Katy said. When Mary Beth frowned slightly at her, she added, "But this milk is very good, Sheriff J.J. And Mommy made chocolate milk for me last night."

J.J. didn't say much until Katy finished eating and left to find a puzzle in her bag of toys. Then he said, "Mary Beth, I hope you're not planning to spend another night in this place."

"Actually, I'm planning on spending several. For the time being, this is our home."

"Hell's bells, Mary Beth, you can't—"

"J.J., don't tell me I *can't.* I own this property and I don't have any other options but to stay here. My family is all gone, I'm just about broke, and until I get my foot out of this cast, I can't work. We're staying *here,*" she said firmly. "It's mine and it's free."

"But you have friends in town, and I'll bet that my brother—"

"No, J.J. Until I can stand on my own two feet again, we're staying here, and that's final. There's plenty of food in the freezer, and we have utilities for another couple of weeks."

"Mary Beth, that doesn't make a lick of sense."

"It does to me. The matter isn't open for discussion."

"Dwight said you were hidebound and determined."

"He's right."

"How long before your cast comes off?"

"About another week."

He sighed and shook his head. "Well, I guess staying

here for a week won't hurt. Do you need any groceries or anything?''

"There's quite a bit of food here, but I would appreciate it if you could pick up some milk and bread and eggs for me. And a jar of peanut butter. Katy adores peanut butter.''

"Anything else?''

"No, those are the essentials. Except for a mousetrap.''

"Got mice?''

"I don't know, but I heard some suspicious sounds last night.''

J.J. reared back in his chair. "Might be rats instead of mice. Big ones. You might want to rethink staying here." His expression was just short of smug.

She fought a shudder. "Uh-uh. Won't work. I'm not going to be chased away by rats—either the two-legged or four-legged variety. Just get a bigger trap. Let me get my purse.''

"I'll spring for the stuff," he said gruffly.

"I'm not ready to accept charity.''

"Don't go getting your nose all out of joint. I'm just being neighborly. That's the way we do things around here in case you've forgotten.''

A sudden lump formed in her throat and she swallowed hard. "I haven't forgotten," she said, her voice barely a whisper.

Their eyes met for a moment, then he glanced away and rose quickly, clearing his throat. "Thanks for the omelette. I'd better get a move on. Got work to do.''

He grabbed his hat and was gone before she could get to her purse. J.J. was a truly nice man. And still sexier than buttered sin. If all those years ago, he hadn't—

She sighed.

But he had and that was that. She called Katy to help her take the dishes to the kitchen.

"I like Sheriff J.J.," Katy said as Mary Beth loaded the dishwasher. "He's nice."

"Yes, he's very nice."

"He said he had a niece and a few about my age that I could play with sometime. What's a niece and a few, Mommy?"

Mary Beth smiled. "I think he meant a niece and a nephew. The children of a person's brothers and sisters are called nieces for girls and nephews for boys. They must be his brother Frank's children."

"Can we play today?"

"Maybe not today, but soon."

"We don't have any nieces and nephews of our own, do we?"

"Nope, sweetie, sorry. I don't have any brothers and sisters, so I don't have any nieces or nephews, and you don't have any aunts or uncles on my side of the family."

"I have an aunt. Aunt Isabel."

"Aunt Isabel is just a very good friend in Natchez. She's like an honorary aunt."

"Oh. Is Aunt Katherine my ornery aunt, too?"

Mary Beth was tempted to say that Katherine was as ornery as they came, but instead she simply said, "No, Aunt Katherine is your daddy's sister, so she's a real aunt and you're her niece."

"I don't think Aunt Katherine likes me."

"Do you remember Aunt Katherine? You've only seen her once, and that was a long time ago."

"She had a red mouth and looked mean at me."

Yep, that was Katherine, the witch. Brad's only sister

had breezed into town, hired a lawyer for him, then breezed back to the social scene in Philadelphia. She had made it abundantly clear that she didn't want to see or hear of any of them again. The whole sordid affair— embezzlement, jail, scandal—was dreadfully embarrassing to her. It had been embarrassing for Mary Beth, as well, but she hadn't had the luxury of breezing off anywhere.

"Mommy, can I have another doughnut?"

"Not right now. Maybe later."

There was another rapping at the front door followed by a feminine "Yoo-hoo. Anybody home?"

Now who could that be? Mary Beth wondered as she dried her hands and made her way to the dining area.

Two older women stood there with foil-covered dishes. They looked familiar, but— She suddenly remembered one of them. "Mrs. Carlton?"

Mrs. Carlton, her next-door neighbor from childhood, beamed. "Yes. And it's so good to see you again, Mary Beth. You've grown into a lovely woman." She hugged Mary Beth with her free hand. "Your mother would be so proud of you. This is my sister Opal McMullen. She moved here six years ago when her husband died. We've brought you a little something—homemade rolls and a squash casserole. I know how you used to love my homemade rolls, and I had some in the freezer. Found a squash casserole in there, too. Made just last week, and Opal brought a pint of her strawberry preserves. Nobody makes strawberry preserves like Opal."

The women set the food on the bar and chatted a few minutes after oohing and aahing over Katy. Soon another car pulled up with another of her family's former neighbors, bearing a ham and two quilts. Then came the minister's wife with potato salad and a pillow with a lace-edged pillowcase. Mary Beth was excited to see her old friends and was warmed by their hometown hospitality. She hugged them all and gushed her thanks and reminisced with those who called.

When a very pregnant Dixie Anderson, an old and dear friend from high school, showed up at the door, Mary Beth let out a whoop. Dixie's dark hair was cropped short instead of being long and lush, and her face was rounder, but Mary Beth would have known her anywhere.

"Dixie Anderson!" she squealed as they hugged. "How wonderful to see you!"

"It's not Anderson anymore. Russo now. I married Jack Russo the year after we graduated. Golly, it's good to see you, too. When I heard you were in town, I parked my two-year-old in mother's day out, and here I am. I brought you some chocolate-chip cookies. My brood eats them by the bushel." She set the box on the bar. "Looks like you've already made a haul. I expect you'll be up to your a-double-s in cakes and casseroles before nightfall. Everybody was tickled to death to hear you were back in town. Ellen has an appointment, but she'll be over as soon as she can shake free."

Dixie hugged her again. "Golly, it's good to see you. Nobody had heard a thing from you after we read that your mother and daddy had died in that plane crash a few years back. We were sorry to hear about that. And this must be your daughter," she said, smiling at Katy who was hiding behind Mary Beth. "She's the image of you when you were that age."

Mary Beth laughed. "I can't even remember that far back. Yes, this is Katy. She's not usually shy. I think she's overwhelmed with all the folks who have dropped by." She coaxed Katy from her hiding place. "Katy, this lady is Dixie Russo. She was one of my very good friends when I used to live here. We were cheerleaders together.''

''Hello, Katy. I brought a present for you.'' She reached into her tote bag and brought out a coloring book, crayons and a package of stickers.

Katy's eyes lit up. ''Thank you very much.''

Dixie laughed in the wonderful rich way that Mary Beth remembered. ''You're very welcome. You're much more polite than my herd.''

''How many children do you have?'' Mary Beth asked.

Dixie rubbed her stomach. ''This one makes six.''

''*Six?* Good heavens, how do you manage?''

''Some days I wonder that myself.''

Mary Beth settled Katy at a table and offered Dixie a cup of coffee. No sooner had they gotten settled and started to catch up on news of the town than a pickup truck drove up. Wes Outlaw, the former sheriff, got out carrying two grocery bags. A gray-haired version of J.J., he'd gained a thickness around his belt that showed his enjoyment of Nonie's cooking. His deeply lined face was that of a man who had spent too many days in the Texas sun.

''Morning, ladies.'' He smiled broadly. ''Mary Beth, you're a sight for sore eyes. Welcome home. I've come with milk and bread and eggs and peanut butter. Plus a few other items that Nonie added to the list. Keep your seat. I'll put the stuff in the kitchen and set the traps.''

''What traps?'' Dixie asked.

''Don't ask,'' Mary Beth said. ''Sheriff Wes, it's so wonderful to see you. Do I get a hug?''

''You betcha. Let me take care of this first.''

When he left for the kitchen, Mary Beth turned to Dixie. "Tell me about your family."

Dixie didn't need much coaxing. She obviously loved her husband and kids. Jack Russo owned an insurance company and was on the school board, and the Russo brood, except for the two-year-old, were all in elementary school. "Two of mine are the same age as Ellen's children. She's divorced, you know. And selling real estate. Doing right well."

"No, I didn't know. I've lost touch with everyone."

"Well, you're back home now, and that's all that matters. I gather that you're divorced, too."

"Yes," she said simply. Even though Mary Beth and Dixie and Ellen had been very close friends who told each other everything, she didn't want to relate all the grisly details of her life with Brad.

When Sheriff Wes—Mary Beth couldn't bring herself to call him anything else—rejoined them, he collected his hug and took a cup of the coffee she offered, along with a cookie, and reminisced for half an hour or so. After another cookie, he stood. "If you ladies will excuse me, I have another couple of pickups and deliveries to make. I'll see you later."

Ellen rushed in as he was on the way out. "Mary Beth!" she squealed, her arms open wide. "Puddin', I can't believe it's you!"

When Ellen grabbed her, Mary Beth's tears began to flow. She'd kept herself together until now, but she couldn't keep it up any longer. She was blubbering like a baby and laughing at the same time. Maybe it was hearing that old nickname or seeing Ellen and Dixie again, or maybe she was crying because she'd held back her tears as long as she could, but she couldn't stop.

She and Ellen held each other for a long time.

"God, it's good to see you, Mary Beth. You look fabulous! I bet you haven't gained a pound since high school, and I've put on at least ten."

Dixie snorted.

"Oh, all right," Ellen said. "Twenty. And if I don't stop squalling, I'll look like a raccoon." She began fishing in her purse.

"Too late, Tammy Faye," Dixie said, plucking several paper napkins from the dispenser on the table and passing them around. "The mascara has run amok."

"You don't look like a raccoon," Mary Beth said, dabbing her eyes and blowing her nose. "You look gorgeous, as always."

Ellen had always been a beauty. She had put on a bit of weight and her hair was blonder and her makeup thicker, but she was still a stunning woman in her smart red suit and high heels.

It was like old-home week. They fell into conversation as if they'd talked only yesterday. How good it felt to see her old friends, to feel as if she belonged again.

They both stayed for lunch, put together from her new stores of food, then Dixie had to leave. "I'll drop by tomorrow," she promised.

Ellen lingered. "I hate to see you staying here, Mary Beth. You're welcome to stay with me. My couch makes into a bed, and you and Katy—"

"No, but thanks. We'll be okay here until I can figure out something. I was hoping that the property would be income-producing, but as you can see…" She fluttered her hand.

"I know. The old motel is a mess. It's been listed with my company for ages, and there hasn't been a nibble. And the people who were leasing the Tico Taco just couldn't make a go of it. Too much competition.

Another Mexican restaurant on the new highway just opened last month, and there was already one next to Bullock's Supermarket on Second Street.''

Mary Beth sighed. "That's a shame. Well, maybe some other sort of restaurant might consider leasing the place. It seems to be in pretty good shape.''

Ellen took her hand. "Don't count on it, Puddin'. The market is pretty well saturated and the location isn't the best. I've gotta run. I have an appointment to show a house, but we'll think of something.'' She hugged her again and wiggled her fingers as she hurried out the door.

Mary Beth didn't have much time to think about anything for the steady parade of old friends who stopped by. None of them came empty-handed. She had enough homemade pickles and pies and casseroles to last for months. And her former Sunday-school teacher, bless her heart, showed up with two roll-away beds.

"Mommy,'' Katy had asked, "is it Christmas already?''

"No, sweetie. Christmas isn't for a long time. Why do you ask?''

"'Cause so many nice people brought presents to us.''

"It *is* like Christmas, isn't it?'' Mary Beth smiled and hugged her daughter. "And these very nice people are old friends from when I was growing up here. It's a custom to bring food and gifts if someone is sick or if there's a funeral or if someone is new to town. This is their way of being neighborly, of welcoming us to Naconiche.'' And she had felt welcomed. These were old friends, caring people holding open their arms to her. Their offerings hadn't felt like charity at all. It was simply small-town neighborliness, and she'd love being able to spend a bit of time with every one of them and renew old ties. She kissed the top of Katy's head. "I feel very welcome, don't you?"

Katy nodded. "I like it here. Are we going to stay?"

"I think so. At least for a while. Would you like that? You don't mind living in a restaurant?"

"It's kind of funny, but remember what you always say?"

"What's that?"

"We can think of it as a 'venture."

Mary Beth laughed and hugged her again. "Yes, it's really an adventure. Dixie tells me that there's a pre-school at the church. How about we get you enrolled so you can have some children to play with."

Katy's eyes lit up. "When? Now?"

"I'll call tomorrow."

Her daughter threw her arms around Mary Beth. "I love you, Mommy."

"I love you, too, Katy."

THAT EVENING after a sumptuous dinner, Mary Beth sat on a bench out front of the restaurant and watched Katy chase lightning bugs.

"I got another one, Mommy!"

"Wonderful! Bring it here and put it in the jar." She opened the top, and Katy dropped the glowing insect inside.

"I'll get some more," Katy said, bounding off. "This is fun."

"Catch one more, then it's time to get ready for bed."

Mary Beth smiled, love welling up as she watched her daughter run off with endless energy. For the first time since she'd learned about Brad's awful crime, she began to feel at peace. And hopeful. Coming here had been good. Getting back to her roots and being among people who cared for her was renewing her strength. This old place might not be much, but it was hers, and somehow she would make something of it—and of herself. For so long it seemed that things had gone from bad to worse, onc catastrophe after another. Now, deep inside, she sensed that she'd turned a corner and her life was going to turn around.

That was before the first clap of thunder.

And before the rain.

Chapter Four

The first drop hit her on the forehead, the second on the nose. Mary Beth shot up and bolted from her bed.

She immediately stumbled and went sprawling.

She'd forgotten the blasted cast. Muttering a few choice words, she shook herself awake. A storm rattled the windows, and a steady drip of water plopped on her pillow.

After pulling her bed to a safe spot, she checked on Katy, who was fast asleep and dry. Grabbing her crutches, she hurried to the kitchen and grabbed a stock-pot. There was a steady leak over the stove. She shoved another pot under that drip, left one crutch behind and hobbled back to the leak as quickly as she could. Quietly she set the pot on the floor of the nook she'd made into their bedroom. The tinny *ping-ping-ping* of the drops against the aluminum seemed awfully loud, but Katy didn't stir.

Not wanting to disturb Katy with a bright light, she made her way around the place using only the illumination from their small lamp, the neon sign behind the bar and the light that spilled from the kitchen. She located another three leaks in the restaurant: one in the men's room and two others in the dining area. When she had placed containers under all the places that dripped, she tossed her soaked pillow on a table and fell back into bed sweating from the effort.

Rain came down in torrents, beating against the windows, the wind howling as if in rage. Lightning flashed and thunder cracked, boomed and rolled. The storm sounded very close. She counted between the lightning flashes and the thunderclaps, trying to judge how far away the center of the storm was. It was close.

Another deafening crack and boom shook the walls.

The lights went out. She slapped her hand against her chest, trying to contain her runaway heart.

Water dripping into the pots sounded like a discordant steel-drum band. Windows rattled with the wind and rain pelted the panes.

Except for an occasional flash from outside, everything was dark as a tomb. The air grew heavy and she had a hard time breathing.

She hated storms.

And the dark.

Then, between the steady *plop-plop-plop*, she heard a rustling, scurrying sound.

Her heart almost stopped.

She wanted to scream bloody murder and run somewhere, anywhere. Instead she pulled the quilt over her head and prayed, filling the time until morning.

"MOMMY, MOMMY, WAKE UP."

Mary Beth opened a bleary eye as Katy shook her. She must have dropped off to sleep sometime after the storm passed.

"Are you awake? Sheriff J.J. is here."

"Where?" she asked, throwing an arm over her eyes to avoid the morning light.

"Here," J.J.'s deep voice answered from the foot of her bed.

She grabbed for the quilt and raised herself up on her elbows. There he stood, hat shoved back and thumbs hooked over the front of his gun belt.

"How did you get in?" she asked.

"The usual way. I knocked. Katy opened the door. Here I am. We had a heck of a storm last night. Trees down everywhere. I was just checking to see if you were okay, and if your power was on. Some areas lost electricity for a few hours."

She glanced at the neon sign behind the bar. It hummed and glowed its usual red. "It was off for a while, but the power seems to be back on now."

He stared pointedly at the huge pot on the floor. It was nearly full of water. "Looks like you had a leak."

"I had several. Would you like a cup of coffee?"

"I've had coffee, thank you. I need to see about some other folks in the county. Want me to empty those pots for you?"

"I can manage, thank you."

He snorted. "Like hell you can. That one alone must weigh thirty pounds."

"Sheriff J.J. said an ugly word," Katy whispered loudly.

"I noticed."

"Sorry about that. I can see I need to clean up my language. Please accept my most profound apologies, ladies." He took off his hat and swept a low bow.

Mary Beth rolled her eyes while Katy giggled.

He hefted the big stockpot near Mary Beth's bed and strode toward the kitchen. In a minute, he returned to take the other containers to the kitchen. She merely sat in bed with the quilt wrapped around her and watched.

His task finished, he came to the foot of her bed. "Need anything else?"

"No, I can manage, but thank you very much," she said stiffly.

"You've got a rat in one of your traps."

Her stomach turned over.

He tipped his hat. "Ladies, I'll be going now."

Darn his hide if he didn't turn and sashay toward the door with that loose-hipped walk of his. "J.J.!"

He turned and gave her an innocent "Yes?"

"Would, uh—would you mind disposing of the—uh—uh—"

"Rat?"

"Yes, please."

He grinned. "Pretty please with sugar on it?"

She ground her teeth. "Yes."

"Sure."

He started to the kitchen, and Katy danced after him. "Could I see the rat? Is it dead?"

"Gruesome child," Mary Beth mumbled, shuddering.

She listened to Katy's childish chatter interspersed with J.J.'s deeper voice and heard the back door open and close. In a few minutes she heard them return.

Katy, still in her nightie and now with muddy feet, galloped in, grinning from ear to ear. "Mommy, we buried that scalawag. And we said some words over him, didn't we, Sheriff J.J.?"

A hint of a smile played at the corners of his mouth. "That we did, Katy. Gave him a right nice send-off." He tipped his hat again. "I'll be moving along."

Mary Beth watched J.J. go, torn between wanting to throw her sneaker at him and wanting to throw herself at him. Every time she was around him, she became more and more aware of his blatant masculinity. It radiated from him. She sighed. Despite her efforts to ignore the obvious, she had to admit that J. J. Outlaw was one sexy guy. Maybe it was because she'd been celibate for so long, but hadn't she found herself thinking positively naughty thoughts about him since she'd been back in town? He'd always been good-looking, but the years had added a layer of confidence and experience that made him even more appealing. If only—

She pushed the thought aside and rose from her bed. "If only" never changed anything. The past was past. She had to start thinking about today. And tomorrow. Soon utility bills would come due on this place, and bills had to be paid. She needed to come up with a plan. But first she needed to get dressed and fix breakfast.

Shoving thoughts of J.J. to the back of her brain, she dressed herself and Katy and made a scrumptious meal from the bounty her neighbors had graciously provided.

Mary Beth and Katy had barely finished eating when there was a knock on the front door.

"The casserole parade must be beginning," she said to Katy.

"What's a casserole parade? Is it like when you were queen?"

"No. I was just teasing, sweetie." She kissed the top of Katy's head and went to the front door.

A young man in a T-shirt and jeans stood there. He didn't look to be more than eighteen or so. Blond with big brown eyes, he had a killer smile that must have set six counties of teenage girls' hearts aflutter.

"Mornin', ma'am," he said, tugging at the bill of his red ball cap. "I'm Dean Gaskamp. Wally Gaskamp from Wally's Feeds is my daddy."

"Yes?"

"I've come to fix your roof."

"My roof? But I can't afford—"

"Oh, there's no charge, ma'am. I mean, I'm a roofer by trade, so I know what I'm doing, but working on yours is part of my community-service hours. If you don't mind, I'll just get to work."

"Community service?" Her eyes narrowed. "Did J.J. think up this community-service business and send you out here?"

"Oh, no, ma'am. It was his brother Frank—Judge Outlaw, I mean—who thought it up. J.J.—I mean Sheriff Outlaw—called and told me to add you to my list. I'll get on with it. With the storm and all, a bunch of folks are needing some help. I'll get in a lot of my hours this weekend." He tipped his cap, turned around and started unloading a ladder from the back of his truck.

In no time, Dean was hammering on the roof.

Mary Beth had barely cleaned up the kitchen when the casserole parade did indeed begin again. It seemed as if everybody in Naconiche dropped by—many, she suspected, out of simple curiosity, but nobody arrived empty-handed. One kind soul—an old classmate—even brought a small television set and a VCR, insisting that they were extras "just sitting around and gathering dust." Another brought a stack of children's videos with the explanation that her children had outgrown them. Katy was delighted. She insisted on watching *Snow White* immediately. Mary Beth fixed her a peanut-butter-and-jelly sandwich to eat while she watched the movie.

Dixie dropped by for lunch, bearing a box of toys and games for Katy. "My girls don't play with these anymore," she said, "and I need the room if you don't mind hand-me-downs."

"I don't mind at all. We had to leave many of our things behind with a friend in Natchez. Katy's a trouper, but things have been difficult for her. At least where I worked, she had children to play with."

"Where did you work?"

"At a health club. I was an aerobics instructor, and Katy stayed in the nursery there while I taught my classes."

"An aerobics instructor! God knows I need one—or will when Robert here is born." She patted her belly.

"What will you need?" Ellen said as she came in the front door.

"An aerobics instructor," Dixie said. "Did you know that Mary Beth taught aerobics in Natchez?"

"If she mentioned it, I conveniently ignored it," Ellen said, grabbing a plate and filling it from among the goodies lining the bar. "I see Mabel Fortney has been here. Tomato aspic with lima beans. She brings it to every event and it's ghastly." She joined her friends at the table. "You do have some tasty items here, though. I swear, I wish there were a decent place for a woman to have lunch around here. I think I gained all my weight just eating hamburgers at the Burger Barn and chicken-fried steak at the Grill. Even their blue-plate specials are loaded with stuff better suited to loggers. But it's either that or Mexican food, and I can handle just so many taco salads or enchilada dinners."

"Lord, I hear that," Dixie said. "Wouldn't it be nice if this town had a tearoom like the one in Travis Lake?" Travis Lake was a larger town twenty-five miles away in the next county.

"Mmm-hmm," Ellen said. Then she stopped and glanced from Dixie to Mary Beth.

"Are you thinking what I'm thinking?" Dixie asked.

Ellen nodded. "Mary Beth, what kind of a cook are you?"

"As a matter of fact, I'm not bad. But I don't know if I could run a tearoom if that's what you have in mind."

"Now, don't dismiss the notion until we've had a chance to talk about it some," Ellen said. "I never thought that I could sell real estate either, but I'm kicking butt these days." She grinned. "Let's do some brainstorming."

For the next hour or so, they came up with every conceivable crackpot scheme they could think of, laughing wildly as they considered every option from turning the Tico Taco into a cathouse with Mary Beth as madam to refurbishing The Twilight Inn as a home for aging aerobics instructors or renting it out as a haunted house on Halloween.

Actually, some of their ideas weren't half-bad.

"You know," Dixie said, "Naconiche really does need a health club—or at least a place where people could take some exercise classes."

"I don't think the town could support a health club," Ellen said. "Remember when JoNell Davis tried it several years ago? All that equipment—and she lost her shirt. But really, I'll bet there would be some interest in a few classes. Maybe aerobics for some of us and stretching classes for seniors. Dr. Kelly is always trying to get my mom to do some stretching for her arthritis."

"Who's Dr. Kelly?" Mary Beth asked, reaching for another chocolate-chip cookie. "I don't remember him."

"Her. Dr. Kelly Martin. She came here a couple of years ago to take over Dr. Bridges's practice when he retired. She's about our age. I really like her."

They batted around several other plans, trying to think of ways to use Mary Beth's talents and the facilities available.

That was how the germ of an idea for The Twilight Tearoom was born. Ellen and Dixie were thrilled to hear that Mary Beth had been a member of the Junior League and had worked in its tearoom before she and Brad had split.

"I had to drop out after the divorce," Mary Beth told them. "I couldn't afford to keep up with my more affluent friends." She didn't mention that she was too humiliated to show her face, nor did she mention that Brad was a criminal, locked up in prison. "But I did learn how to pour tea and which fork goes where and how to make chicken crepes to die for. I learned to make the crepes and several other fancy dishes when a group of us took lessons from a French chef. And we used to serve as hostesses when some of the local charity events sponsored luncheons at the league building."

"I can't believe it," Ellen said. "This is perfect. The garden club is looking for a place to have their big luncheon, and I heard Annie Schultz say that the hospital auxiliary needs somewhere, too. The VFW hall just doesn't have much ambience. Why couldn't they meet here?"

Mary Beth glanced around at the garish walls, the scarred tables and the tattered piñatas. "Here? You've got to be kidding. This place is a far cry from the Junior League Tearoom. I'll bet it doesn't have as much ambience as the VFW hall."

"A coat of paint would do wonders," Dixie said.

"True," Ellen agreed. "Take all the Mexican stuff down and add some pretty tablecloths and flowers. The place has some possibilities. And if you opened it just for lunch or for special parties, you'd still have time to spend with Katy. Why, she'll be in kindergarten in the fall, and you could teach some aerobics here in the mornings. Just move the tables aside. How about it, Puddin'?''

Mary Beth shrugged. ''I'll have to give it some thought, but it has some possibilities. I might even be able to earn enough to slowly restore the motel. I could either run it or sell it.''

''Good idea,'' Ellen said. ''For sure nobody's going to buy it as it is.'' She glanced at her watch and stood. ''Gotta run. I have a closing in a few minutes. We'll chew all this around more later.''

''I have to go, too,'' Dixie said. ''My mother-in-law is sitting with Eddie, and I imagine he's about ready to wake up from his nap. We'll talk some more tomorrow.''

Mary Beth said goodbye to her friends, then checked on Katy. She was sound asleep in one of the booths, and the TV screen's snow testified that the movie was over.

A lump formed in her throat as she watched her precious baby's innocent nap. It cut her to the core to see Katy having to sleep on an old cot in the middle of a run-down restaurant. She deserved better. Much better.

And, by damn, she was going to see that her daughter had a proper place to sleep. Mary Beth was bright and she was strong. She could provide a decent life for Katy.

She looked around the Tico Taco with new eyes. A little paint—no, a lot of paint—would make a world of difference. She squinted her eyes a little and imagined butter-yellow on the walls and crisp tablecloths and napkins and flowers on every table.

It was true that she was a pretty good cook. And

hadn't she spent hours with her foot propped up watching Emeril and Bobby and Martha on TV? She learned a few tricks from them. Shoot, she'd even learned a bit about painting and remodeling from watching Bob Vila and his sidekick.

Yes, the tearoom idea just might work.

But was she willing to gamble her last few dollars on it?

J.J. WAS HOT AND MUDDY after tending to his cows and mending the pasture fence. It was getting late, and he wanted nothing more than to go home, shower and relax with a beer. But as he approached the Tico Taco, he knew he couldn't go home until he checked on Mary Beth. There was a fifty-percent chance of rain tomorrow, and he wanted to make sure that Dean had fixed the roof. Or at least that's what he told himself as he stopped his pickup in the parking lot.

The lights were on, the shades up, and he could see Mary Beth and Katy sitting at one of the tables. He started to drive on but, hell, he was already stopped, so he knocked on the door, then opened it a crack and stuck his head in.

"Hi, Sheriff J.J.," Katy said, waving. "I have a new TV and a Barbie doll with a horse."

"That's great, Katy. Just wanted to check on you two before I headed home," he said.

"Thanks. Come on in," Mary Beth told him, "and join us for dinner. Have you eaten? We have plenty."

"I'm muddy, and I don't want to interrupt your meal. I just wanted to see if Dean came by to fix the roof."

"You're not interrupting. Leave your boots at the door, and you can wash up in the men's room. I cleaned it today, so it's presentable. Come on, at least I owe you a hot meal. Lots of this food is going to waste if somebody doesn't eat it.''

"Please, Sheriff J.J.,'' Katy said. "Why are you all muddy? Have you been chasing bank robbers?''

"Nope. No banks robbed today. The storm blew down a tree in my pasture and damaged a fence. I didn't want the cows to get out.''

"You have cows?'' Katy's eyes were big.

"Let Sheriff J.J. wash up, honey,'' Mary Beth told her. "Then you can hear about his cows.''

J.J. hesitated, then thought, *What the hell?* He was tired and hungry and that fried chicken they were eating looked awful good. He hung his hat on the rack, left his boots at the door and headed for the men's room to get rid of a layer of mud. After he'd washed up as well as he could, he slicked back his damp hair with his fingers and joined them at the table.

"You like light meat or dark?'' Mary Beth asked while spooning beans and potato salad on his plate.

"I'm not choosy.''

"I like drumsticks best,'' Katy said.

"I like drumsticks, too. And thighs. But, I guess I'd have to say that I'm really a breast man.'' He grinned at Mary Beth, and damned if she didn't blush.

She quickly forked two pieces of chicken onto his plate and set it down with a clatter. "Would you like some iced tea?'' She started to reach for her crutches.

"Keep your seat. I'll get it. Where is it?''

She motioned to the pitcher on the bar. He poured a glass and rejoined them.

After a few bites, he said, "I didn't realize how hungry I was. This chicken is good. It tastes like my mother's.''

"That's because it is your mother's. Nonie brought it a few minutes ago."

"She didn't happen to bring one of her blackberry cobblers, did she?"

Mary Beth laughed. He liked to hear her laugh. He liked the way her eyes crinkled and her dimples appeared. "Sorry, no. But I have tomato aspic with lima beans if you'd like some of that."

"Mabel's been here, has she? Think I'll pass."

She laughed again.

He dug into his food, enjoying the company of Mary Beth and Katy. Too often he ate by himself in front of the TV—burgers, frozen dinners, simple stuff.

"Do you live on a ranch?" Katy asked. "With cows?"

"Not exactly. I live in a fourplex."

"What's that?"

"It's kind of like an apartment house."

"My Mommy and I lived in a garage apartment at Aunt Isabel's house. Like that?"

"Not exactly. I built a big house with two stories and divided it into four apartments. I live in one of them, and I rent the other spaces to different people."

"And you have cows there?"

He grinned at the little imp. "No, I live in town. I keep the cows in the country, but I'm building a house there. It's where I grew up."

"Nonie told me that she and Wes had turned everything over to the family when they moved to town," Mary Beth said.

He nodded. "Frank and his kids live in the old house. I'm building a place down the road, and I keep a few head of cattle on my part of the land."

"Do you have horses, too?" Katy asked.

"Only one. I don't have much time to ride."

"'Cause you have to chase bank robbers."

"Among other things."

"Mrs. Akin's chocolate pie or Dottie Grant's lemon pound cake?" Mary Beth asked.

"Mrs. Akin's pie."

After she sliced and handed him a piece, he said, "You didn't say if Dean fixed the roof."

"He came early this morning. What a nice young man he is to be donating his time for community projects."

J.J. frowned. "Is that what he told you?"

"Well, not exactly."

He finished his pie, then said, "Dean's not donating his time. He's doing time."

"I don't understand."

"He got in some trouble and, since it was his first offense, Frank gave him probation so Dean's required to serve time in community service. Since we don't have a formal program here, usually Frank and I come up with the projects. There are lots of things around the county that an able-bodied man can do to help out."

Mary Beth had turned pale as he explained. "You mean that boy is a—a *criminal?* And he was here and unsupervised?"

"Did he escape from the pokey?" Katy asked, fascinated by the conversation. Then she clamped her little hand over her mouth, hunched her shoulders and sneaked a peek at her mother. "I'm not supposed to say pokey," she whispered loudly.

"No, no, sweetheart. He didn't escape from jail. Nothing like that. I've known Dean and his family all my life. Why, you know Wally at the feed store, Mary Beth. They're good people. I wouldn't have sent anybody out here who was dangerous. He and a couple of his buddies just got into a little trouble a while back.''

"Did they rob a bank?" Katy asked.

He grinned. "I think you've got bank robbing on the mind, squirt. No, he and two of Will Frazier's boys got to feeling a little too frisky one Saturday night and put a pig in the mayor's new Cadillac."

A fist shoved against her mouth, Mary Beth looked as if she was about to choke trying not to laugh. He was pretty close to laughing himself—and would have if Katy hadn't been following the conversation solemnly. He winked at Mary Beth and managed to keep a straight face.

"That was a very naughty thing," Katy said. "Was the pig hurt?"

J.J. did laugh then. He couldn't help himself. "No, honey. He was just scared, but he made a big mess in the mayor's car and tore up the seats pretty good. The mayor was madder than a swarm of hornets, so the boys had to be punished. They're really good kids. I think they've learned their lesson." He stood. "Thank you for the dinner, but I have to go, ladies."

"Thank you for sending Dean," Mary Beth said. "And for the other things you've done." She started to rise.

"Keep your seat," he said, resting his hand on her shoulder to stop her from getting up.

Touching her was a mistake.

His hand stayed longer than was necessary for a casual gesture. His fingers stroked the edge of her collarbone ever so slightly while his thumb strayed over the cap of her shoulder. Her hair brushed the back of his hand and he wanted to—

Whoa, buddy! He jerked his hand away. He remembered his promise to himself not to start up anything with Mary Beth. First thing you know, she'd be off again and he'd be left behind cut to ribbons.

Chapter Five

J.J. hadn't seen or heard of Mary Beth in a week. Well, that wasn't exactly true. He'd heard a lot about her. Everybody in town was talking about Katy and her living in the restaurant. It was as if Naconiche had adopted her. Vera Whitehouse, the waitress at the City Grill, recounted all the latest doings from the Tico Taco every morning while he ate his eggs. He even heard about Katy from his niece and nephew. His mother had invited Katy on a Sunday-afternoon outing with the twins, and now Katy was Janey and Jimmy's new best friend. And to tell the truth, Mary Beth and Katy had been on his mind a lot.

Maybe that's why he turned his patrol car into the restaurant's parking lot that morning despite his resolve to stay out of her business and keep his distance. He couldn't get Mary Beth and that cute little carbon copy of her out of his thoughts. What if they needed something?

J. J. Outlaw, you haven't got the sense God gave a goose, he told himself. He knew he was asking for trouble, but he got out of the car anyhow.

When he knocked on the door, he heard Mary Beth call, "Come in!"

He found her sitting at one of the tables, her hair pulled back into a ponytail that made her look a dozen years younger. She wore shorts, and the leg with the cast on it was propped on a chair. In her hand was a pair of garden shears, and she was whacking at the top of the cast.

"What in the *hell* are you doing?"

She must have jumped a foot, then she turned and glared at him. "I'm trying to take off this blankity-blank cast, but I swear it must be concrete."

"Mary Beth, are you crazy? You can't get it off with those shears. It has to be sawed off."

"I don't have a saw, and even if I did, I'd probably cut my leg off trying to saw it. This is the day that the orthopedist said the cast could be removed. I'm removing it." She began wielding the shears with both hands, bearing down to cut the cast, but she didn't do much more than break off a few small chunks of plaster.

"Give me those," he said, jerking the shears from her.

"Thanks, it looks like I need a little more muscle to get the thing cut off."

"I'm not going to cut it off. I'm going to take you to the doctor."

"No," she said, setting her jaw, "you're not."

"Yes, I am. Your foot needs to be x-rayed first, then the cast needs to be sawed off by a professional."

"How do you know what my foot needs?"

"Because I broke my arm a few years ago." He crammed the shears in his back pocket, then called Kelly Martin's office on his cell phone. After walking away and talking to the nurse quietly for a few minutes, he hung up and strode back to the table. Mary Beth was giving him a look that would have melted the war monument on the courthouse lawn.

"We're going to the hospital. Let's go."

"No," she said, jacking her chin up another notch, "we're not."

"Yes, we are."

She crossed her arms. "I don't have insurance. I can't afford it, so I'm not going."

"That's what you think. Where's Katy?"

"At preschool. The church bus just picked her up."

"When will she be home?"

"One o'clock."

"Good, we'll have plenty of time."

"J.J., read my lips," she said, repeatedly stabbing her finger toward her mouth. "I'm not going to the hospital or to the doctor. Can't you get it through your thick head?"

He watched her lips, but he didn't pay much attention to reading them. A sudden urge, powerful and unexpected, struck him, and he leaned down and planted a kiss on them instead.

While she sat stunned, he scooped her up in his arms and headed for the door. She tried to protest again on the way to the car, so he kissed her again. When he pulled back, her eyes were big as saucers.

Kissing her felt damned good. Better than he remembered. He'd have kissed her again if Mabel Fortney hadn't driven up just then.

"Good morning, J.J. Good morning, Mary Beth. I just dropped by to pick up my Pyrex dish." Mabel, eyes wide with surprise, looked back and forth between the two of them.

Mary Beth looked as if she wanted to disappear. J.J. merely gave Mabel a wide grin and said, "How about getting that another time? I'm on my way to take Mary Beth to the doctor.''

"Oh, dear. Is something wrong?''

"No, it's just time for her to get her foot checked. Mabel, would you mind getting the door for me?''

"Not at all.'' Mabel scurried around to open the door of the patrol car. "Want me to get a pillow to prop up your foot?''

"I'll be fine, thanks.'' Mary Beth gave Mabel a weak smile. "And your aspic was delicious.''

Mabel beamed. "The lima beans are the secret. I'll drop by tomorrow for the dish.''

J.J. strapped Mary Beth in, then got into the driver's seat and took off before she could get the belt undone. "Liar,'' he said to her.

"Liar?''

He laughed. "Babe, I've tasted Mabel's aspic.''

She laughed, too, and he relaxed. Their years apart seemed to disappear. How easily he could slip back into the role of taking care of Mary Beth. Tending to her and watching out for her felt as natural as breathing.

MARY BETH WIGGLED HER TOES. "Golly, that feels good.''

"I'm sure it does.'' Dr. Kelly Martin smiled. "And you can scratch where it itches now.''

Dr. Kelly was a sweetheart. Not much older than Mary Beth, she was a tall, stunning redhead with green eyes, porcelain skin and a smattering of freckles across her nose that she didn't try to hide. Her long, curly hair was twisted into a knot held by a banana clip, and her lab coat was covered with smiley faces.

"These are the exercises that you need to do every day.'' Dr. Kelly handed Mary Beth several photocopied pages, instructions for strengthening her foot and leg, and cautioned her about exercising too strenuously.

"What about teaching aerobics?"

"I'd like for you to hold off a couple of months on that. Were you planning to teach some classes here?"

"I was hoping to start in the fall."

"I think that would be fine," Dr. Kelly said. "That will give you the rest of May and all summer to get in shape. Let me know about the classes. I'd like to join, and I have several patients that I would encourage to join, too."

"Great. I'll keep you posted. Now, about your fee—"

"Don't worry about it. J.J. said—"

"I pay my own way," Mary Beth said firmly. "It may be a while, but I'll take care of the bill."

"Tell you what," Dr. Kelly said. "How about we barter? Aerobics classes for doctor's fees. If you or your daughter need any other services, we'll simply trade."

She felt a huge weight drop from her shoulders. "You're on. Katy is due for a checkup and some shots soon."

"Then we have a deal."

Mary Beth was grinning when she walked out of the office.

J.J. rose from a chair in the waiting room. "Feel better?"

"Enormously." She looked down at her feet. "Except that I seem to be missing a shoe."

"Want me to carry you again?"

"I'll pass."

On the way home, she said, "I really like Dr. Kelly, and we made a deal to barter for her fee. I'll repay you for the X rays as soon as I can."

"That's not necessary, Mary Beth. I can afford it. Don't be so bullheaded."

Irritated by his comment, she glared at him and shot back, "*Me* bullheaded? J. J. Outlaw, you're like a runaway steamroller. I had forgotten exactly how domineering you can be. I can't breathe when you get like that. I couldn't stand it when we were younger. I can't now. I'm a grown woman, and I can make my own decisions. Back off."

He didn't say anything until they drove up in front of the Tico Taco. When he'd killed the engine, he turned to her, frowning. "What's this about me being domineering? Is that why you ran out on me?"

"I didn't—" She sighed and dropped her head back against the seat. "I don't want to go into old stuff. There's too much water under the bridge. We're both very different people now—or at least I'm very different. Those days and the girl that existed then are long gone. Could we simply say that we were both young and foolish and forget the past? I'd like for us to be friends."

He hesitated for a moment, then smiled. "Sure."

She returned the smile. "Good. Thanks for the ride." She got out of the car and went inside, an ache in her throat.

It was true she had forgotten how domineering J.J. could be. He'd been more than take-charge. He'd been overly possessive and jealous as hell. As a high-school kid, she'd gone along with him managing her life. It was the path of least resistance, and she'd been flattered that J. J. Outlaw was so crazy about her that he was jealous of her other friends, especially the male ones. His behavior had made her uncomfortable, but she'd been too chicken to confront him with her feelings. Too chicken and too young and too sheltered. But she had big dreams that she'd never shared with anyone—except maybe Ellen. She'd wanted to major in archaeology and go on digs in exotic places—the dream of a romantic teenager.

She'd been secretly relieved when her dad had announced that they were moving from Naconiche that summer after she graduated. Down deep, she knew that she needed to get away from J.J., from Naconiche, and experience more of the world before she settled down. Still, if she hadn't spotted J.J. that following night, she might have relented and made a different choice. But she *had* seen him and it had almost broken her heart.

She'd always been eager to please, always ready to go along to get along. Her personality had won her popularity contests in high school and in college, but it also made her easy prey. Wasn't that the reason Brad Parker had married her? And Brad was a thousand times more domineering than J.J., though he'd been slick in concealing his true colors during the year when they were dating, plying her with gifts and treating her like a princess.

They had met when he was in graduate school and she was a sophomore. They married when he got his M.B.A., and she dropped out of school when they moved to Natchez. *He* would take care of her, he said. She'd been little Miss Sunshine, dancing to his tune and never questioning his behavior. What a dope she'd been to have married him; what a mistake to stay married to him. But by the time she'd figured out what an ogre he was, she was pregnant with Katy, her parents had just died and she felt totally vulnerable. After Brad had been sent to prison, it had taken her months of counseling to get up the courage to divorce him and reclaim her life.

J.J. was a nice man, an honest man, but Mary Beth wasn't going to let any man, even one as sexy and appealing as the sheriff, dominate her again. Learning self-reliance and assertiveness had been a hard-fought battle. She wasn't about to slip back into her old style.

They could be friends. Good friends, she hoped. And if his kisses had taken her breath away…well, she just couldn't let herself dwell on that.

WHEN ELLEN CAME BREEZING in around noon, she said, "Hi, what's for lunch?" Mary Beth and Ellen had made a deal—a month of lunches for Ellen in exchange for her providing paint to brighten up the place.

Except for a couple of cakes stashed in the freezer and some jars of pickles and jelly, the food that townspeople had brought to welcome them home was long gone. Thankfully there was still plenty of frozen chicken and ground meat left, and she'd bought a few inexpensive items at the grocery store to manage meals for a while.

"We're having chicken spaghetti, green salad, rolls and my special raspberry tea."

"Sounds scrumptious. I hope you don't mind, but a couple of people from the tax office heard me bragging about my lunches here, and they want to drop in. Do you have enough to feed them?"

"Sure, but do they know that we're not officially open for business? We haven't painted the walls."

"I told them that the place wasn't fixed up yet, but they didn't seem to mind." Ellen grinned. "I think that today's special at the City Grill being liver and onions had something to do with it. They should be here in a few minutes. I'll help you set up another table."

"I can handle it," Mary Beth said. "Hey, look, no cast." She held up her foot.

"That's fantastic. When did it come off?"

"This morning." She related the story of J.J. and her trip to the doctor as she spread fresh tablecloths on three of the tables and set out knives and forks. "I also found out this morning that these tablecloths don't belong to me or to the former tenants. They're owned by the linen service. Thank goodness, there's still a deposit that will cover linens for a couple of weeks anyhow. They left a brochure." She sighed. "Just one more unexpected expense."

"Always happens, but we'll handle it. Who's the extra table for?"

"Dixie is treating her mother-in-law to lunch."

Ellen laughed. "We'd better get this joint painted before you have so many customers that you can't afford to stop and spruce it up."

"I don't think there's any danger of that."

"Oh, I don't know," Ellen said, giving her a sly look. "What if I told you that I've booked a luncheon for twenty-five in three weeks?"

"You're kidding!"

"I kid you not. The garden club wants to hold their annual luncheon here. I told them that your chicken crepes were to die for."

"This is fabulous! I can't believe it." Mary Beth hugged her friend. "You're a sweetheart, but you've never tasted my crepes."

Ellen shrugged. "So I fudged a little. And the hospital auxiliary is booked for the week after that. Eighteen ladies for that one."

Mary Beth's initial elation flagged, and panic set in. "Lord, I hope Isabel sends my cookbooks soon. All my

Junior League stuff is packed away with my other things in her garage. I phoned her a couple of days ago and told her the plan.''

She looked around at the restaurant, at the dingy walls and the scarred tables. At least all the tattered, dusty Mexican decorations were gone, but the alcove where the roll-away beds were stored was hidden only by a hand-me-down quilt strung across the opening, and the neon sign still sizzled behind the bar. The Tico Taco was a long way from resembling a tearoom.

''Oh, Ellen, I don't know if I can have things ready by then.''

''Sure you can. You have lots of friends who can help. Look, here come your first paying customers. I'll play hostess while you get the iced tea.''

That day, Mary Beth's raspberry tea became the talk of the town and her trademark drink. The two women gushed over the chicken spaghetti, as did Dixie and her mother-in-law, Florence, who came a few minutes later.

Florence Russo was a tall, slender woman with beautifully cropped white hair and a bright smile. Although she wore dark slacks and a simple coral blouse, she wore them with a dash that showed her innate sense of style. Her jewelry was understated but of excellent quality, and Mary Beth knew from their cut that the simple slacks and blouse weren't from a local discount store. She was profuse in her praise of the food.

After thanking everyone, Mary Ellen even managed to whip up a dessert by using a pound cake she'd stuck in the freezer and a star-shaped cookie cutter she'd found in the back of a drawer. She put a half jar of strawberry preserves in a pot to warm with a little bit of cream and butter while she cut stars from cake slices and zapped them in the microwave.

When everything was warm, she drizzled a bit of Katy's chocolate sauce on each plate, topped it with three cake stars, then added a spoon of strawberry cream in the middle along with a dusting of sugar. A bit of mint would have made a nice garnish, but she didn't have any mint, so she served them sans greenery.

The praise for the simple dessert was lavish.

"This was so wonderful, Mary Beth," gushed one of her new customers. "I hope you're going to be open tomorrow."

"Nope," Ellen answered for her. "Tomorrow's Saturday, and we'll be closed for renovations. We're hoping to be open by Monday."

"We'll be here," the other woman said. "Could we have our check, please?"

Mary Beth went blank. So far she'd been winging it, but she had no idea what to charge. She glanced to Ellen for help.

Ellen smiled brightly, seeming to enjoy this little game of hers. "Want me to handle the cash register for you?"

"That would be great," Mary Beth said, putting the onus on Ellen. "We don't have guest checks yet. Or a menu."

Ellen named a price to the women, who seemed to think the charge reasonable, took their money and returned with their change. "Come again next week," she said brightly.

"We will. And we'll be telling our friends about it."

The minute the door closed, Ellen turned to Mary Beth and grinned from ear to ear. "Puddin', you're a success."

"You certainly are," Dixie added. "This food is sensational. I loved the cake stars."

"It was all excellent," said Dixie's mother-in-law, Florence. "I think you can do well with this place after a bit of painting and decorating."

Mary Beth looked around. "I think it's going to take more than a bit. The job seems so overwhelming that I don't even know where to begin. I wish I could afford a decorator."

Dixie glanced at Florence and winked. "You can."

"Trust me," Mary Beth said, "I can't. I can barely afford spackling paste to cover all the nail holes in the walls. This project is going to be on a shoestring budget."

"Ah," Florence said. "I love a challenge."

Puzzled, Mary Beth frowned.

Dixie laughed. "Florence was an interior designer in Dallas until she retired and moved here. I've told her about your plans, and she's just itching to get her hands on this place."

"Yes, indeed. I'm weary of spending my days watercoloring and pulling weeds in the garden."

"Hey, this is wonderful, Florence," Ellen said. "What color do you think we ought to paint the place? I'm going to pick up the paint and supplies this afternoon."

"I would like to hear Mary Beth's ideas before we decide," Florence said.

"That's very sweet of you to offer, Florence," Mary Beth said, "but I can't allow you to—"

"Oh, nonsense, my dear. I need something to do with my time. I tried opening a decorating shop in Naconiche, but it didn't work out. I'm positively dying of boredom. Please let me help. I even have a storeroom full of stuff that I need to get rid of that would look great in here, and I have several ideas for brightening the room without spending a dime. In fact, you can earn money with some of the projects I have in mind.''

''Do you carry a wand, Florence?''

''A wand?''

Mary Beth laughed. ''You sound like a fairy god-mother. Tell me, are you interested in trading your talents for exercise classes?''

J.J. STARED DOWN at the unappetizing glop on his plate. ''I hate liver and onions,'' he said to his brother.

''Then why did you order the special?'' Frank asked.

''Because Vera talked me into it. Said it was good for me. Nothing with that much grease could be good for me.''

''I always stick with the chicken-fried steak. It may be just as greasy, but at least it's tasty.''

J.J. shoved his plate back. To tell the truth, he wasn't all that hungry anyhow. ''Frank, would you say that I'm domineering?''

Frank snorted. ''God bless a moose. What brought that on?''

''No, I'm serious. Am I domineering?''

''Not any more that any of the rest of the Outlaw bunch, I don't suppose. Now if I had to pick the worst one of us, I'd say Cole is the one who likes to rule the roost. I guess that comes with being the oldest. He's got the hardest head and was the biggest bully when we were kids. You got pretty good at going toe-to-toe with him.''

''You were always the quiet one who tended to your own business, but I always tried to be tough big brother and watch out for Sam and Belle, though I don't think they ever appreciated it.''

Frank shook his head and grinned. ''Nope. I think

they thought you were as bossy as Cole. Sam let it roll off his back, but it made Belle hopping mad. It was bad enough being the only girl in the family. Being youngest only made it worst. As I recall, it wasn't too long ago that baby sister told you where you could stick your advice.''

J.J. laughed. "Nobody ever accused Belle of being shy.''

"That's the truth. I reckon that sometimes you take being big brother too seriously.'' Frank motioned for Vera to bring them pie and coffee. "You've always been protective of other people, J.J. It seems to be your nature. That's what makes you a good sheriff.''

"But some people don't appreciate being protected.''

Frank waited until Vera served their pie and coffee. When she left, he said, "I think some people don't appreciate being *overprotected*. They need to learn to stand on their own two feet. They need breathing room, too.''

"That's what she said. She said she couldn't breathe. What the hell does that mean?''

"Who are we talking about here?''

"Mary Beth Beams. Parker. Mary Beth Parker.''

Frank took a sip of his coffee. "Hmm.''

"*Hmm?* Is that all you can say?''

His brother chuckled. "Judges get good at saying *hmm*. We take seminars on it. Whose turn is it to get lunch?''

"Yours,'' J.J. said. "I'm certainly not paying for this stuff. I wouldn't feed it to my pigs.''

"You don't have any pigs. You should have ordered the chicken-fried steak.''

"Next time I will.''

"Next time they'll probably have meat loaf on the

special. You like meat loaf.'' Frank tossed a couple of bills on the table. ''I've got to get back to court. Recess is almost over.''

After his brother left, J.J. realized that Frank hadn't told him a darned thing of much use. He left the Grill, got in the patrol car and drove out to the lake. He parked where he and Mary Beth had parked the last night they were together. He wasn't there long before the pain of that night hit him, smacked him in the gut like a baseball bat.

He had loved Mary Beth with all his heart. Hell, he'd worshiped the ground she walked on. She had been his whole life. When he went off to college, he'd leave the campus as soon as he could on Friday and drive like hell to make it to the high school by the time she got out. He stayed in town until her curfew on Sunday night and drove back to school. He'd lived for her. He would have carried her around on a silk pillow if he could have.

Losing her had damned near killed him. It took him forever to get over her. Hell, he still wasn't over her. The scars were still there. Nobody really knew how bad it had been for him.

Had he somehow driven her away?

Chapter Six

The smell of paint was intoxicating. Mary Beth felt giddy as she watched the metamorphosis of the Tico Taco. Blue-gray, the shade of an evening sky, covered the water-stained ceiling, and soft butter-colored walls transformed the room from dark and drab to light and cheery. A darker glaze accented cracks and crevices in the plaster—some of which were fashioned with a compound applied the night before—giving the walls the shabby-chic, old-world look that Florence had suggested.

By noon, the neon sign was gone, the ceiling was dry and the walls were almost done. The Señors and Señoritas had been refurbished and were absolutely pristine. Only the washroom doors remained to be painted and rechristened. Many helping hands had made the work go quickly. Florence was there, looking ten years younger in her paint-streaked jeans and positively glowing as she worked and supervised the project. Ellen had brought along her younger brother and one of his friends to help. And all the Outlaws in town were there, except Nonie, who was running the ice cream shop. J.J. and Frank had been wielding paint rollers while Wes and one of his cronies had been assigned to screen-making outside.

Maybe Mary Beth should have felt conflicted about accepting help from everyone, but she didn't. To her, being independent had never meant trying to go it alone; it simply meant not having someone else control her life. These people were helping her get on her feet and she appreciated it. Things felt more like a party or an old-fashioned barn raising with neighbors pitching in rather than charity or interference in her private business.

Now sometimes J.J. was another story. It must all be in the attitude. Nobody here seemed nearly as bossy as he was. Everyone was having fun, and so was she. She hadn't felt so great in years.

The afternoon before, Florence and Mary Beth had poked around a bit in the old motel rooms. They were a disaster and didn't yield much to work with except a few odds and ends and some interior doors that Florence had gone ape over.

"Oh, these are perfect!" Florence had exclaimed.

Mary Beth didn't see their perfection. She saw only dingy old doors coated with grime and scaly paint. "I suppose that after a bit of sanding and a coat of—"

"Bite your tongue. All they need is cleaning. We'll hinge them together in twos and threes, put a big potted fern or ficus in front of them, and they'll be wonderful as room dividers."

"But those big potted plants are expensive," Mary Beth had said.

"Don't worry about it. I have a couple of silk ones in my storeroom, and I'm friends with the owner of the Hilltop Nursery. I'll bet that I can make a deal with Sandy to supply all the plants you need in exchange for your selling them at a small commission. It's a win/win situation. Merchants do it all the time.''

Mary Beth was extremely grateful for Florence. And for Dixie. Forbidding Dixie to paint because of her pregnancy, Florence had assigned her the task of sewing simple window draperies from a bolt of muslin she unearthed from her storeroom.

Dean Gaskamp and his two errant friends had come by early Saturday morning, mowing the long grass and weeds out front and trimming the overgrown bushes. Having the outside tidied up really helped. It still looked a bit forlorn, but anything was an improvement.

Katy and Frank's twins had spent the morning outside with Wes Outlaw and his buddy helping scrub the old doors and having a grand time with the water hose. Their shrieks of laughter made Mary Beth smile, and she went to the door and watched them for a while.

"They'll be okay," J.J. said. "Dad is a great babysitter."

"I wasn't worried," she told him. "It's just great hearing Katy laugh like that and seeing her run." She went back to her painting but stopped from time to time to watch them play.

Her daughter was the one who'd had to suffer because of the circumstances Brad had left them in. Mary Beth had felt terribly guilty about not being able to provide her with a stable home and friends. But Katy was blossoming in Naconiche. She loved the preschool she attended with the twins, and had made friends easily. Mary Beth was glad that she'd swallowed her pride and accepted the church's offer of a scholarship for Katy. She could see positive changes in her already.

Mary Beth smiled and went back to painting woodwork.

The next time she peeked out the window, Katy saw her and came running. "Mommy, Mommy, come out and see what Mr. Pawpaw Wes did. Look! Look!"

Mary Beth went outside to see the new attraction.

While the doors dried, Wes had built a swing for the kids using a rope from his pickup and an old tire that he found behind the motel. He hung it from the limb of a huge oak tree between the restaurant and the ram-shackle inn.

"Look! It's a swing."

"That's wonderful, Katy. Sheriff Wes, you're a dear to do this."

He gave an "aw shucks" grin. "I've made many a tire swing in my day. I get a kick out of it. Well, looks like the doors are about dry. Willard and I better get on with putting the hinges on or Florence will have my hide."

Mary Beth laughed and went back inside.

Several people had dropped by throughout the morning to help or just to see what was going on. Even Mabel Fortney stopped in, bringing another aspic with lima beans. "You'll be wanting a bite to eat after a while," she'd said, leaving her dish on the tarp-draped bar.

About twelve-thirty, Mary Beth called a lunch break and served a huge pot of spaghetti with meat sauce to the working crew. Thank goodness pasta was cheap. The night before, she'd made two gallons of meat sauce from the restaurant's stores. Ellen had brought several loaves of garlic bread and Nonie had sent a large carton of butter-pecan ice cream for dessert.

Drop cloths came off tables and everybody, including the children, grabbed plates of food and glasses of iced raspberry tea and settled into chairs. The children shared

a booth, and Mary Beth ended up at the table with J.J.
and Frank, who were halfway through their spaghetti
before she sat down.

"Say, this is good," J.J. said.

"Better than liver and onions for sure," Frank added,
grinning.

"Thanks, I think," Mary Beth said.

"Inside joke," Frank said. "It really is very good."

"I think you're going to give the City Grill a run for
their money," J.J. added.

"We'll be offering very different kinds of menus, so
I don't imagine I'll be cutting into their trade very
much. Also, I'll only be open from eleven o'clock to
one o'clock for lunch so that I can spend time with
Katy. And in the fall, when she's in kindergarten, I'll
be teaching classes in the mornings."

"What kind of classes?" J.J. asked.

"Aerobics, stretching, that sort of thing. I'm anxious
to get started. I need the exercise myself. I'm getting
out of shape."

"Not that I noticed," J.J. said.

His comment seemed innocent enough, but Mary
Beth felt herself blush.

Frank cleared his throat and said, "Believe I'll have
another helping. How about you, J.J.?"

Mary Beth jumped to her feet. "I'll get it."

"You eat," J.J. said. "We can fill our own plates."

Several of the men went back for seconds. A couple
of them had thirds. In the end, the pot was licked clean
and all the bread and ice cream had been devoured.

Nobody had touched Mabel's aspic.

"Poor Mabel," Mary Beth said to Florence. "She
needs to find a better recipe."

"That's for sure," Florence said, picking up the dish

to take to the kitchen. "This stuff is ghastly. But truth be told, she's not much of a cook—I've tasted some of her other creations. She's simply lonely and really wants to help in the community. She's been at loose ends since she retired from the chicken-processing plant—you know, Mabel was bookkeeper there for years. I can certainly understand her feelings. I didn't realize how very bored I was until I joined in this project. I'm having a blast."

"And I'm thanking my lucky stars that you volunteered."

"Speaking of stars, since you've decided to name the place The Twilight Tearoom, I think hanging a few stars from the ceiling would be fun. What do you think?"

"What kind of stars?"

"I have some lovely brass and mica ones in my storeroom that would be charming. I once used them in a very posh Christmas setting, and I'm sure they're in a box somewhere."

Mary Beth laughed. "Is there anything that you don't have in that storeroom of yours?"

"Not much. I'm a pack rat. I have at least two of everything."

They took a load of dishes to the kitchen, and Florence discreetly disposed of the aspic.

Mary Beth and Ellen had barely loaded the big dishwasher when J.J., Frank and Ellen's brother shooed them out of the kitchen.

"We need to paint in here," J.J. said.

"But there isn't enough paint to do the kitchen," Mary Beth said.

"Turns out there is," Frank said.

"Enough for two coats," J.J. added.

Mary Beth frowned at Ellen, who shrugged.

"We must have overestimated," Ellen said, affecting a suspiciously innocent expression. "This area could use a little freshening up, don't you think? Come on, Puddin', we need to finish the glazing." She hooked her arm through Mary Beth's and guided her into the big room. "Doesn't it look great already?"

"It really does. I can't believe the difference." She looked down at the scarred wooden floors. "I just wish I could do something about the floor."

"Relax. The Twilight Tearoom is coming together. Florence said that with a good scrubbing and a coat of wax or oil, the floors will be perfect."

Mary Beth snorted. "Florence is an optimist."

TURNED OUT Florence was right. By five-thirty, everything was painted, the floors looked great, and Mary Beth was exhausted. Frank had taken the twins home an hour before, and Katy had been invited to spend the night with them. Since she really hadn't wanted Katy to breathe paint fumes and Frank had a live-in housekeeper to help with the kids, Mary Beth agreed.

J.J. had been called away on an emergency about five o'clock and, except for Ellen, the others had packed it in and gone home, as well.

"I'm pooped," Ellen said, flopping down in a chair with a glass of raspberry tea.

"Me, too," Mary Beth said, joining her. "It's unbelievable that we got so much accomplished in one day. I can't tell you how much I appreciate all you've done."

"You've told me and everyone else a dozen times, Puddin'. We're happy to help. How about we lock up this place and you come home with me? The kids are spending the weekend with their dad, and we can put on our jammies, fix a big bowl of popcorn and watch a sappy movie. We might even have a glass or two of wine and reminisce. Want to?''

"You're on. But I might not last through the whole movie."

"THIS FEELS SO GREAT," Mary Beth said. "Like old times."

They were both in nightshirts, sprawled on Ellen's couch and chowing down on pizza.

"I'm stuffed," Ellen said. "Another glass of wine?"

"Sure." Mary Beth held out her glass. "But this is my last one. I'm getting a buzz on."

"I'm so glad our lives have brought us back together. I've missed you all these years."

"And I've missed you. Funny, though, I never thought in a million years that I would come back to Naconiche."

"And I never really considered leaving. I always assumed that Bobby and I would get married, have a house with a picket fence, a couple of kids, and live happily ever after."

"Well, you have the house and the kids."

"Yes, but Bobby flew the nest with Sara Nell Esterbrook."

"That dog! I don't understand it."

"I suppose that I loved Bobby more than he loved me. And he always had a wandering eye. Sara Nell wasn't the first. He wasn't a one-woman man—not like J.J."

Mary Beth frowned. "What do you mean?"

Ellen shrugged. "He was crazy in love with you, and he was never the same after you left. What happened between the two of you anyhow? I always figured that you would get married. Didn't you love him?''

Mary Beth sipped her wine. ''Sure I did. But we were young, and I felt…oh, I don't know, stifled by J.J. and by Naconiche. I wanted to see a bigger part of the world. And J.J. was very possessive and jealous as the dickens.''

''Lord, I'd forgotten about that. I remember that he used to go ballistic if you even danced with anyone else.''

''It was a little scary sometimes—to have somebody that totally focused on you. My parents, while they liked J.J., thought that I needed some time apart from him. Even before my dad's transfer came up, they had encouraged me to go to a different college than him. He, of course, assumed that I would go to Sam Houston University where he was enrolled.''

''And what did you want to do?''

''I was torn,'' Mary Beth said. ''My head said that I needed to listen to my parents and give myself time before settling down. My heart said something else—or at least part of it did. I wanted to be with J.J., but I also longed to experience more of the world than the little corner of it where I'd grown up. My dad's sudden transfer sort of took the decision out of my hands. I had to go with them, or at least I told myself that I did. J.J. and I had a terrible fight the night I told him I was leaving. It broke my heart. I went home in tears.''

''His heart was broken, too, Mary Beth.''

''Oh, I don't know about that. He didn't seem that broken up when I saw him the next night with that slut.''

Ellen frowned. ''What are you talking about?''

''After I'd about cried my eyes out, the next evening

I decided that I couldn't leave J.J., so I tried calling him, but he wasn't home. My folks had gone to bed early, so I sneaked out and drove around town looking for him. I finally spotted his pickup. To make a long story short, I discovered that he spent the night with Holly Winchell, the trashiest girl in town. Everybody knew she was hot for J.J. Why, we had dinner at the Inn Restaurant one night and she was our waitress, and I'll swear she did everything but sit in his lap and stick her tongue down his throat. And with me sitting right there! To think he went running to her so quick—well, I was devastated. Just talking about it makes me angry all over again."

"Oh, Mary Beth, how awful. But are you sure it was J.J.? Maybe one of his brothers—"

"It was J.J. I parked across the street from her apartment and waited most of the night. He came out about four o'clock in the morning, tucking his shirttails in his pants and with her hanging on him. He was so interested in her that he didn't even notice me there."

"I'm so sorry, Mary Beth. You never told me about it."

"I was too mortified to tell anybody. I wanted to crawl in a hole and die. For sure I wanted to leave Naconiche then."

"And you didn't talk to him again after that?"

She shook her head. "He phoned a couple of times and came by my house once, but I wouldn't talk to him. I couldn't bear it."

"I swear, men can do the dumbest things," Ellen said. "I think all that testosterone makes them goofy."

"It was worse than dumb. It was a terrible betrayal of all we had meant to each other if he didn't have any more respect for me than to go panting after Holly so quickly. One-woman man, ha! It made me wonder if he'd had her on his mind all along. It was a terrible blow to my ego.

"Anyhow, I didn't see J.J. again until he picked up Katy and me at the bus station. Now, enough of this old maudlin stuff! We were all only kids, and it's best forgotten. Let's watch that movie."

WHEN ELLEN DROPPED her off on Sunday morning, Mary Beth found a surprise waiting at The Twilight Tearoom. Two big pots filled with red geraniums flanked the front door. Nearby, a cedar post had been newly planted in concrete, and from its arm hung a beautifully painted wooden sign. Big letters proclaimed THE TWILIGHT TEAROOM. Smaller letters at the bottom read Mary Beth Parker, prop.

Mary Beth burst into tears. "Who did this?"

"Don't you like it?" Ellen asked.

"I love it, but who did it?" Mary Beth swiped at her eyes with the backs of her hands.

"Some of our old classmates wanted to give you a gift celebrating your opening, so they chipped in for the sign. Lester Hawkins—remember, he was class president—anyhow, Lester and some of the guys were supposed to put it up first thing this morning. They must have been here early. I don't know who the flowers are from."

"They're from Mama." J.J.'s voice came out of nowhere.

Startled, Mary Beth whirled around to find him standing at the corner of the building, grinning. Her heart did a little flip-flop. Why was it that the mere sight of him could push all her buttons? A conglomeration of emotions swirled inside her—some old, some new, many she was sure, stirred up by the painful memories she'd shared with Ellen the night before. "I didn't see your car. What are *you* doing here?"

"Fixing that rear door. I noticed that it didn't seem too sturdy yesterday. My pickup is around back."

"Your pickup is often places where it shouldn't be, isn't it?" she said in a tone that was cooler than a frosted frog. She unlocked the door, then marched inside and slammed it so hard that the panes rattled.

Puzzled, J.J. looked at Ellen. "What was that all about?"

"If I had to guess, I'd say it was about that waitress who used to work here."

"What waitress?"

Ellen had merely rolled her eyes at him before she got in her car and drove off.

Chapter Seven

For the life of him, J.J. couldn't figure out what was going on. What was Mary Beth in such a lather about? She acted as if she was mad at him, and he hadn't done a damned thing except deliver those flowers from his mother and fix the back door lock.

What waitress was Ellen talking about? The waitress from the Tico Taco had been the wife of the guy who ran the place, middle-aged and with a tattoo of a dragon on her arm. God, he couldn't even remember her name. Rita? Nita?

Nita, that was it. Why was Mary Beth upset about Nita?

One way to find out.

He knocked on the door and waited.

And waited.

He knocked again. "Mary Beth!"

She flung open the door. "Yes?" she said in a tone that would freeze the balls off a Brahma bull.

"Is something wrong?"

"Not a thing. Please thank your mother for the geraniums, and thank you for fixing the back door."

"You're welcome. Now what's this about Nita?"

"Nita? Who's Nita?"

"The waitress."

"I don't know any waitress named Nita," she said. "Have you been drinking?"

"Hell, no, I haven't been drinking. Have you? You're acting squirrelly, Mary Beth. Ellen said it was something about the waitress who used to work here."

"Ellen has a big mouth."

"I'll grant you that, but I still don't know what's going on with you. Have I done something to piss you off?"

"Not lately, but I'm getting there. Now if you'll excuse me, I have to finish dressing. The church bus will be by at any minute."

"It's already been by—not a minute before you and Ellen got here."

"Oh, rats!"

"Get dressed. I'll take you to church."

She looked as if she wanted to hit him with that hairbrush she held in her hand. "Thank you, but I think I'll pass," she said in a sugar-sweet tone. "I do have tons of things I need to do around here before the gang arrives this afternoon to finish up."

"What sorts of things? I'll lend a hand." Why was he pushing to stay when it was obvious she didn't want him to? Damned if he knew. He bulled his way in anyhow. "And I sure could use a cup of coffee."

Her sigh would have discouraged a lesser man. He ignored it and gave her his sappiest smile while he waited for her answer.

Finally she stepped back. "Come on in, and I'll make a pot. Have you had breakfast?"

"Now that you mention it, my stomach is a little empty." Truth was, it *had* been a couple of hours since he'd had that big plate of sausage and eggs at his mother's table.

She sighed again—and he ignored it again as he followed her inside.

"This place looks a hundred and ten percent better than it did," he said as she made coffee behind the bar.

"Doesn't it? I don't know how to thank all my friends for pitching in. I couldn't have done any of this by myself."

"That's what friends are for, Mary Beth. You're one of ours."

She looked a little teary, then she blinked hard several times. "You like Belgian waffles with strawberry preserves?"

"I don't know, but I'm game to try."

"Ellen loaned me her waffle maker. I think it was a wedding present she never used. And she loaned me her bread machine. I need to try out both of them."

"I'm a willing guinea pig."

"As I recall, you always had a cast-iron stomach. You could eat anything."

He chuckled. "I'm a little more choosy these days."

"I *certainly* hope so." She strode off to the kitchen as if she had a burr under her saddle again.

J.J. followed her and cornered her by the sink. "Okay, that's it. I want to know what your problem is. Obviously I've done something, but I don't have any notion of what it is. And if I don't know, I can't fix it. Spill it."

She tried to turn away, but he held her upper arms to prevent it. Her eyes shot daggers clear through him. "Take your hands off me!"

Immediately he let go and held up his hands. "Mary

Beth, I would never hurt you. Never in a million years. Surely you know that.''

She took a deep breath, then let it out slowly. "I know that, J.J. I'm sorry that I overreacted. It's just that Ellen and I were talking over old times last night, and…well, I suppose I opened some old wounds. Sorry, you and I agreed to let bygones be bygones and be friends. Have you ever made bread in a bread machine?''

"Babe, I've never made bread in anything.''

"It's easy. Here are the directions, a book of recipes and enough stuff to make a few batches.''

"Wouldn't it be easier to buy some bread at the store?''

"Maybe, but wouldn't you rather eat a sandwich made with onion-dill bread than with plain old white bread?''

"Can't say. I don't recall ever eating any onion-dill bread.''

"Trust me. It's delicious. Let me dump the ingredients in the bread machine, and I'll fix our waffles. I wish I had some fresh berries instead of the preserves.''

"There's a big patch of wild dewberries across the road.''

"There is? I *love* those things. Let me put the bread on, and we'll go pick some.''

"Okay by me. Got a bucket?''

She had him look in the cabinets while she put a bunch of stuff in the contraption on the counter. He found a couple of plastic pails and rinsed them out. By the time he was done, she was ready to go, her eyes as bright as a kid's.

"I haven't been berry-picking in ages,'' she said,

swinging her bucket as they crossed the road. "How do you know that there are any here?"

"I saw them blooming a while back. There should be lots of them."

And there were. Dark, fat berries. Probably a couple of bushels of the things. Mary Beth picked a handful and popped them into her mouth.

"Aah," she said. "These are delicious."

He tried a few himself. "They are good. When we used to go berry-picking, my brothers and I always used to eat more and chuck more at each other than went into our buckets."

He playfully lobbed one at Mary Beth. It hit her on the shoulder.

"You dog!" She threw one back at him and nailed him mid-chest.

J.J. dodged the next one and threw another at her. Laughing like kids, they started hurling and feinting and ducking in a full-fledged berry fight. Blobs of purplish juice stains dotted their clothes.

"Stop! Stop!" Mary Beth yelled, still laughing. "We're wasting all these dewberries, and I need them to make desserts."

"Sorry," he said, grinning and standing up from his crouched position. "Something just came over me."

"Me, too," she said, her eyes shining. Lord, he loved to see that light in her eyes.

She hurled another berry, hit him square on the chin, then shrieked with laughter.

"That tears it, sugar!" He grabbed a handful of ammunition and began pelting her unmercifully.

"Stop! Stop!" she shrieked, hunching over and covering her head.

He didn't stop. He closed in, picking and throwing as he went. "You give up?"

She straightened and turned to him, her eyes still bright with laughter. "Never," she said, then smushed a handful of berries in his face.

Kissing her then seemed as natural as breathing.

Her mouth was sweet, berry sweet, nectar sweet. Sweeter than all the honey in Texas.

At first she seemed stiff, then he felt her relax in his arms, and he was in heaven tasting her, touching her, aching for her. He might have kissed her forever if some kids hadn't started honking as they drove by.

She pulled away, acting flustered. "I—I— That shouldn't have happened."

"Why not? Didn't it feel good?"

"That's not the point. I thought we agreed to be friends," she said.

"Can't friends kiss each other?"

"Not like *that*."

"Like how?"

"J. J. Outlaw, don't you play games with me. You know very well what I'm talking about."

"Friends don't breathe hard and use a lot of tongue?" The devil made him say it. He tried hard not to laugh as he watched a variety of animated emotions play across her face.

"Just shut up and pick berries."

He tipped his hat. "Yes, ma'am."

They picked silently until both buckets were full. When they started across the road, Mary Beth stopped by the mailbox. "I forgot to check the mail yesterday. I'm hoping I get something from my friend in Natchez." When she opened the box, she said, "Yep, there it is,'' and retrieved a package. ''My cookbooks. I'm saved.''

She tucked the package under her free arm and didn't even glance at him until they started back to the tearoom. When he held open the door for her, she glanced up, then laughed.

He lifted his brows, questioning the joke.

''Your face is purple. You look like you've been in a pie-eating contest.''

He worked his mouth. ''I do feel a little sticky. Let me put these berries in the kitchen and I'll wash up. What's that I smell?''

''Bread. Isn't it divine?''

''Makes me hungry.''

''That's the idea. I plan to keep some baking all the time. Not only is it delicious, but also it's better than any perfumed spray.''

By the time he'd scrubbed the worst of the berry stains off his face and hands and walked out of the men's room, Mary Beth was setting a table.

''The waffles are almost ready. Pour us a cup of coffee and I'll finish them.''

He filled two mugs and placed them on the table, and in a couple of minutes, she brought out two plates filled with big-holed waffles and a heap of berries on top.

''Those look good.''

''I hope they taste good. I'm experimenting. Take a bite and give me the verdict.''

She watched him so anxiously as he cut into the waffle that he'd have pulled his tongue out with pliers before he'd have said that they weren't the best thing he'd ever tasted. Turned out he didn't have to lie. ''These are great. What did you do to them?''

Beaming, she said, ''I simply cooked them with some

sugar and a touch of amaretto. Lucky for me, when the last tenants cleaned out the bar, they left behind a few dusty bottles of liqueur. They're great flavorings.''

Mary Beth tasted her waffle. ''Not bad. I think a dusting of powdered sugar or maybe a dollop of whipped cream would make it even better. I'll add those to my list. I'll have to get a few things at the grocery store before we can open tomorrow. I need to check my cookbooks and see if there's anything else that's critical. I'll have to shop carefully until I have some cash flow going.''

''Mary Beth, I'll—''

She eyed him sharply. ''Don't say it.''

''But I—''

Her eyes narrowed. ''J.J.''

He threw up his arms. ''God, you're hardheaded.''

''I believe we've had this conversation before.''

''Sounds familiar.'' He finished off his waffle and scraped his plate.

''Want some more?''

''No, thanks,'' he said, patting his belly. ''It was really good, but I think I ate too many berries while we were picking. Why don't you get your list together, and I'll take you to the grocery store.''

''It doesn't open until after lunch.''

''The superstore over in Travis Lake is open twenty-four hours a day, seven days a week. We can go over there. It's got a better selection anyhow. Where is Katy?''

''She spent the night with Frank and the twins, and they invited her to stay until this afternoon to let me get some stuff done.'' She glanced at her watch. ''Think we can be back before two o'clock? The others are coming then.''

He grinned. "I'll turn on the siren."

"I don't think we're in that much of a hurry. Let me check those recipes real quick." She tore open the package she'd received in the mail and dumped out two books, a smaller package and an envelope. She opened the envelope, then broke into a smile as she read the letter. "Praise be, Isabel sold my TV, and here's the check." She waved it. "It couldn't have come at a better time. Think the superstore will take a cashier's check?"

"I'm sure they will. Make your list, and I'll clean up these dishes."

THE SUPERSTORE IN Travis Lake was fabulous. Mary Beth felt as excited as a kid in a candy store when she saw all the terrific produce. And the prices were sensational. They were running specials on corn, avocados, apples, lemons and limes. She loaded her basket, altering her menu as she shopped for deals, keeping track of her purchases with the calculator on the basket handle. The cashier's check was a godsend, but she still had to be cautious with her money. Oranges, yes; cantaloupes, no. Parsley? Yes, she needed lots of parsley.

Because there was still plenty of ground beef and chicken in the freezer, as well as several other staples, she'd decided to serve shepherd's pie and corn on the cob on Monday and creole chicken and rice on Tuesday. She would also offer two sandwich selections, a soup and a salad every day. She tossed several heads of various kinds of lettuce into the basket, as well as cucumbers, tomatoes, red and green bell peppers, celery, mushrooms and radicchio.

The leeks looked very nice. "What do you think about leek and potato soup for Monday?"

"I've never had leek and potato soup, but it sounds good to me."

"No, I think I'll have Italian tomato on Monday, and leek and potato on Tuesday."

"Okay," J.J. said. "What's a leek?"

She picked up several bunches. "These are leeks. Now I need some white potatoes and some sweet potatoes for making chips."

He ripped off some plastic bags and held them while she added potatoes. "I've never heard of sweet-potato chips."

"Trust me, they're fantastic. Speaking of potatoes, I need to get some boxed ones. I'm going to fudge and use the instant kind for the shepherd's pie."

The first basket and most of a second one was full by the time they had gotten everything on her list, but she'd stayed within her budget and even received change from the cashier's check.

They barely made it back to Naconiche by two o'clock. In fact, Florence was pulling up as they arrived.

"Hi!" Mary Beth called as she got out of the car. "We've got groceries. Let me unlock the door."

"I'll help unload," Florence said.

With the three of them, plus Wes and Nonie who arrived just then, they soon had all the bags of food stowed in the kitchen.

"These avocados look wonderful," Nonie said. "Want to leave them out?"

Mary Beth nodded. "I'll use the ripest ones for sandwiches tomorrow and the others the following day."

"*Avocado* sandwiches?" J.J. asked.

"Of course," Mary Beth said. "With apples and walnuts."

"Sounds divine," Florence said.

"Sounds peculiar," J.J. said. "I like roast beef—"

"Son, uh, I believe I'll go finish putting those hinges on the doors," Wes said. "Want to help?"

"Sure." J.J. left with his dad.

Nonie chuckled. "Saved by the bell. Men don't understand anything except meat and potatoes and maybe purple-hull peas or pinto beans."

"I know. J.J. thought sweet-potato chips sounded very strange, but they're delicious. One of the restaurants in Natchez used to serve them and always got raves."

"I'm excited about your having something a bit different," Florence said. "That reminds me, I was thinking about menus. Are you going to have some printed?"

"Oh, dear," Mary Beth said, her heart sinking. "I hadn't even thought of menus."

"I have an idea," Nonie said. "Why don't you post a blackboard somewhere and simply write the day's menu on it. It would save time and money."

"An excellent idea! I have one in my storeroom."

"What else do you have in your storeroom?" Dixie asked as she came in to the kitchen.

"A blackboard for the menu," Florence said. "Oh, look, you have the curtains. Let's get the men to put up the hardware."

"We don't need the men," Mary Beth said. "I'm handy with a screwdriver."

"I'm sure you are, dear," Florence said, "but men like to feel needed." She went bustling off to find help.

BY FIVE-THIRTY, The Twilight Tearoom was finished and looked absolutely charming. The curtains were up and pulled back, softening the walls, half-a-dozen brass and mica stars hung from the ceiling and light blue cloths adorned every table. The screens made from the doors turned out to be quite striking, their crystal doorknobs gleaming.

The owner of the Hilltop Nursery had dropped by with plants, large ones to put in front of screens, hanging baskets to brighten the nooks and small pots of blossoms or herbs for each table along with a small cardboard stand with a price list. All were on consignment with a twenty-five-percent commission for Mary Beth— as were the various paintings hung on the walls, courtesy of Florence's watercolor class.

Silverware was rolled into blue napkins and artfully arranged in a large basket on the bar; the chalkboard was up and Monday's menu printed on it. Florence and Ellen had even volunteered to act as hostess/waitress/cashier until Mary Beth could afford to hire somebody to help. Everything was ready except the food, though the third batch of bread, sourdough this time, was baking in the bread machine and infusing every inch of the place with its aroma.

Katy was outside on her new swing, and everyone had gone home except J.J.

"Who would have believed it?" he said, looking around.

"I know. Everything is done, and it's just beautiful." She smoothed a tablecloth, then straightened a salt shaker.

"Now all you need are customers."

A sudden panic rolled over her. "Oh, Lord, J.J., what if nobody comes?"

"Relax." He threw his arm around her neck. "They'll come. Count on it."

Chapter Eight

Mary Beth couldn't sleep. Oh, she'd dozed fitfully for a couple of hours, checking the clock every few minutes. Finally she gave up and got out of bed, careful not to rouse Katy. Still in her nightshirt, she left the alcove and tied a bandanna around her head as she slipped through the dining area to the kitchen. If she couldn't sleep, she might as well do something productive.

The evening before, she'd prepared the greens she would need, chopped vegetables and made chicken salad, so in the wee hours she put seasonings and soup stock on to boil while she made a big container of avocado and apple filling.

By the time she went to awaken Katy for school, she'd made two more batches of bread, a huge pot of soup and umpteen Belgian waffles. Several pans of shepherd's pie were in the fridge and ready for baking. She'd even made her own mayonnaise for the sandwiches and come up with a special house dressing for the salads.

Really, there wasn't much else to do except slice bread and make potato chips. She only hoped she could make it through the day. If nobody came, a lot of food would be wasted. And she was counting on receipts to pay the utilities on the place and keep a roof over her head.

Fortunately for Mary Beth, one of her old high school friends, who had been the drum major of the band, now owned the *Naconiche Daily News*. On Sunday, there was a great article on the front page of the business section about the opening of The Twilight Tearoom. At least she had some publicity beyond word of mouth.

Mary Beth said a prayer, then went in to dress and wake Katy.

She had done all she could.

DIXIE CAME AT NINE-THIRTY bearing a sack full of fresh mint. "This stuff has practically taken over my back flower bed, and Florence told me that you wanted some."

"Bless you," Mary Beth said, hugging her. "Garnish does wonders for presentation—and presentation is everything. Or so my cooking instructor said."

"At my house, garnish is gravy on the potatoes," Dixie said, "but if you want to grow some mint here, I'll dig up a bunch of it and plant it for you."

"I'd love it. Wouldn't an herb garden be neat? But I'll do the digging. You're pregnant, remember."

Dixie rubbed her belly. "It's not something I forget. But actually, I planned to have Jack handle the shovel. My neighbor is keeping Eddie for a few hours. What can I do to help?"

"How are you at slicing bread?"

"How straight does it have to be?"

"It's a no-brainer. I found a commercial bread slicer in the back of one of the cabinets. All you have to do is set the dial and watch your fingers."

"I can handle that." She sniffed the air. "Are you baking more bread?"

"I'm baking it continually. I have a horror of running out." Mary Beth grinned. "I think I have enough to last until next month, but it will freeze if I don't use it. I have to get the sweet potatoes sliced and fried. I've decided not to have two kinds of potato chips. That complicates things. What do you think?"

"I think simplicity is smart. I've never eaten sweet-potato chips. Are they good?"

"Very. You can sample the first batch. Let me heat the oil in the deep fryer and get out the mandolin," Mary Beth said as they walked back to the kitchen.

"I didn't know that you played."

"Played what?"

"The mandolin."

Mary Beth laughed as she put on her new yellow chef's apron with The Twilight Tearoom embroidered in blue across the bib. "Not the kind with strings that makes music. I was talking about this little gizmo." She pointed to the slicer. "This is a mandolin for slicing veggies and stuff. Don't you ever watch Martha Stewart on TV?"

"Are you kidding? Our TV is permanently glued to the cartoon network with grape jelly. That's a cute apron. Where'd you get it?"

"From Mrs. Carlton, you know, our neighbor from the old days. She brought by five of them a few minutes ago as an opening gift. She can't come to lunch today, but she said she would be here tomorrow. Would you believe that she sewed this in just a few minutes on her machine? I'm going to put one on display and take special orders for her."

"On commission, I hope?"

"Yep. Same deal as with the paintings and plants."

Mary Beth showed Dixie how to work the bread slicer, then tackled the big pan of sweet potatoes she'd washed. She put the first batch on to fry and immersed the rest of the raw chips in water.

When the sweet potato chips were done, she dumped them on the draining rack, shook some of her secret seasoning on them and handed one to Dixie. "What do you think?"

She waited anxiously while Dixie took one bite, then two. "Well?"

"Mary Beth, these are scrumptious! Be sure to make plenty. People are going to love them. I predict that the tearoom is going to be a success on these alone. You ought to come up with a catchy name for them." She reached for another.

In a few minutes, the bread was all sliced and bagged, the corn was shucked, halved and ready to be dropped into boiling water, all the sandwich and salad ingredients were assembled, and the first pans of shepherd's pie were in the oven.

"Oh, Dixie, what if nobody comes?"

"Hush your mouth. Don't even consider it."

"Yoo-hoo! Anybody home?" Florence called.

"We're in the kitchen," Mary Beth called back.

Florence and Ellen popped in. "This is the big day," Ellen said. "Are you ready?"

"As ready as I'll ever be, I suppose. I'm terrified that nobody will show up."

"Hush up about that, I said." Dixie plucked a couple of chips from the draining rack and handed one each to Florence and Ellen. "Try these. Aren't they scrumptious? Mary Beth says the secret is in the seasoning."

"Oh, this is fabulous," Ellen said, polishing off hers and reaching for another. "What is the seasoning?"

Mary Beth grinned. "It's a secret."

"Ah, I love a mystery," Florence said. "And I love these chips. I've never tasted anything like them."

"How about we call them 'mystery chips'?" Dixie said. "I'll put it on the chalkboard."

Mary Beth shrugged. "Fine by me." She dumped the chips from the draining rack into the warming oven and checked her watch. Her stomach was in a thousand knots. "Fifteen minutes until opening. Want to take a last minute check?"

"Good idea," Florence said. "And by the way, I hope you don't mind, but I asked Mabel Fortney to come by and help with the cash register. She's a whiz with that sort of thing, and I promised her a free lunch for her help."

"I can use all the help I can get. Let me put the corn on."

After the corn was cooking and another basket of mystery chips was sizzling, the four of them checked the dining room. It was charming. The tables were set, the raspberry tea was made, coffee was brewing, the aroma of baking bread permeated the place. Everything was ready.

Florence and Ellen donned the yellow aprons with the tearoom name embroidered on the bib, stuck a pen and a new order book in the front pocket and waited.

At eleven o'clock, Mary Beth turned the Closed sign around to Open, and they waited.

And waited.

Five after eleven.

Ten after eleven. Nobody.

Florence straightened the salt-and-pepper shakers. Ellen added ice to the tea pitchers.

Mary Beth's stomach knots increased tenfold. "Nobody's coming."

"Of course they're coming," Florence said. "But who eats lunch at eleven o'clock?"

At twelve minutes after eleven, the bell over the door tinkled, and Mary Beth's heart leaped.

"Oh, I'm sorry that I'm late," Mabel Fortney said, bustling in. "But my blasted car wouldn't start. The battery again. I had to bang it with a hammer to get it to turn over. The cables corrode, you know." She glanced around. "No customers?"

"No." Mary Beth sighed. "'Fraid not."

"Oh, don't worry about it yet," Mabel said. "Nobody much eats lunch at eleven o'clock. Except me. And I'm starved. Is that the menu?" She pointed to the chalkboard over the bar.

"That's it," Ellen said. "Have a seat here, Mabel, and I'll get your raspberry tea while you decide on your order." She seated their first customer, although a nonpaying one, at a table for two.

Florence said, "I think I'll join you, Mabel. Things are going to be so busy in a few minutes that we won't have time to eat. Ellen, I think I'll have the avocado and apple sandwich and the mystery chips."

"I'll take the chicken salad," Mabel told Ellen. "What are mystery chips?"

"Oh, my dear, they're fabulous!" Florence said. "Wait until you taste them."

Mary Beth hurriedly assembled the two sandwiches. Dixie added mystery chips and a sprig of parsley to the plates, and Mary Beth finished the creations with a thin orange slice curled over the parsley. Ellen served the food.

Eleven-twenty.

The bell over the door was silent.

At eleven twenty-five, two old high school friends showed up. Mary Beth was overjoyed to see them. After greeting them, she went off to fix their orders.

At eleven-thirty, six more people came.

By eleven forty-five, the tearoom was half-full.

At twelve o'clock, every seat was filled, and people were waiting. Mary Beth barely had time to stick her head out of the kitchen. The food was going fast. Dixie made a quick trip to the local market for more sweet potatoes and sliced turkey for sandwiches. By twelve-thirty, most of the food was gone. The shepherd's pie ran out first, and Mary Beth had thrown some diced chicken breasts into a pan with onion, peppers and to-matoes and filled the rice steamer. The chicken creole she'd planned for tomorrow couldn't wait.

Dixie stayed busy helping in the kitchen and erasing the menu to delete and add. Ellen and Florence were frazzled from their waitress duties but valiantly keeping up with orders and serving with a smile and small talk. And wonder of wonders, the old cash register was ring-ing.

"These are the last of the berries," Dixie said, scrap-ing the pot.

"Oh, Lord, what can I serve for dessert?" Mary Beth asked. "Look in the fridge. What's there?"

"Let's see. Milk, butter, cheese, a couple of heads of lettuce, a few ribs of celery, jelly and several packages of tortillas."

Mary Beth, stirring the creole dish, glanced around

the kitchen and tried to think of something quick for dessert.

"What kind of cheese?"

"Cream and cheddar."

"Those tortillas, are they flour or corn?"

"You've got both."

"Grab a package of the flour ones and some cream cheese, then come stir this for a minute, would you?"

Dixie took over the creole. "What on earth are you going to do with tortillas and cream cheese?"

"Improvise with these bananas." She grabbed two, halved them, then quartered and peeled them. Dealing a stack of tortillas onto the counter, she placed a piece of banana and a strip of cream cheese on each. Next, she quickly spooned on sugar, gave each a dusting of cinnamon and rolled them burrito-style. After securing the rolls with a toothpick, she placed several in the deep fryer and hurried to the freezer for the gallon of vanilla ice cream Nonie had brought for Katy. "Dixie, mix about a half cup of sugar and two teaspoons of cinnamon in a shaker for me, please."

By the time the first of the rolls were golden and on the draining rack, Dixie had the sugar mixed. Mary Beth put a small scoop of ice cream on each of six plates, cut the rolls diagonally and placed the halves against the ice cream, then dusted the top with cinnamon sugar.

"Voilà!"

Dixie grinned. "Darlin', you're a genius. Here, let's stick a little bit of mint on the side for color."

"Perfect. How many more orders for dessert?"

"Looks like that's it."

"Thank God." She slumped against the counter.

By one o'clock, the crowd had thinned and by one-fifteen, only one customer lingered—J. J. Outlaw. Mary

Beth spotted him as she and Dixie came out from the kitchen. He sat having a cup of coffee, with Katy across from him eating her favorite—a peanut-butter-and-jelly sandwich.

"The opening was a total success!" Dixie said, hugging Mary Beth. "Everybody raved about the food and the new look of the place. I'd love to stay and gab, but I have to run. It's past time for Eddie's nap."

"Oh, Puddin'," Ellen said, "you should have heard the compliments. It was a total smash. Listen, sweetie, I've got to go. I have to show a house in ten minutes. Talk to you later." She gave Mary Beth a big hug as well, stripped off her apron and hurried out.

Florence said, "Mary Beth, you go sit down before you fall down. You look exhausted. Mabel and I will get everything tallied, but it looks as if we did very well."

"We did super-duper," Mabel said. "Even sold six plants and a painting. And I got four orders for Mrs. Carlton's aprons to boot."

"You both did a great job," Mary Beth told them. "I wish I could afford to hire you to do this every day."

"Honey," Mabel said, "I'd just about do this for nothing. I've been having more fun than I've had in ages. It sure beats staring at four walls or watching soap operas all day. I expect we can work out something. We'll talk about it later. You go take a load off and visit with your young'un."

"And I'll stay for a few days until you can hire someone," Florence said. "Let's not worry about it. Here, have a glass of tea. Want some lunch?"

"There's not much left."

"I'll go rustle up something," Florence said. "You sit."

Mary Beth was tired. And lack of sleep was beginning to get to her. She took her tea and joined J.J. and Katy, kissing her daughter's head and greeting J.J. before she sat down.

"Did you have a good day at school, sugarplum?"

Katy nodded. "We rode on a fire truck, and I petted Spots."

"Spots?"

"The fire dog."

"Ah, must be the proverbial dalmatian."

J.J. grinned. "Nope. Spots is Harlon Pruitt's prize bird dog, but he's the station mascot just the same."

"Who is Harlon Pruitt?" Mary Beth asked.

"Mr. Harlon is the fire chief," Katy said. "He wore a funny hat and big boots. Can I go swing, Mommy?"

"*May* I go swing? And, yes, you may. Don't go beyond the swing though, okay?"

"Okay." Katy ran out the door.

"Sorry I missed lunch," J.J. said. "I had an emergency down at the jail."

"I can probably rustle you up something to eat," Mary Beth said, starting to rise.

"You sit back down, young lady," Mabel said as she joined them. "Florence will dish up something for J.J. to keep him from starving. I just wanted to show you the totals before I left." She opened a spiral notebook on the table and pointed to a page with neat rows of figures and printing. "I made a mark for the dishes that sold out first so that you can have an idea of what was the most popular. And this is the take for the day, excluding the commissioned items, which I've noted on the next page."

Mary Beth's jaw dropped. "We actually made that much?"

"Yep, and that doesn't include the tips that Ellen and Florence took in. They're in a jar over by the register. I didn't know what you wanted me to do with them."

"Tips?"

"Yes," Florence said as she served a plate of food to J.J. and Mary Beth. "We'd forgotten about tips. We thought you could use the money to hire some help, though honestly, I had a ball today. I wouldn't mind working a couple of days a week just for tips and fun. I'll bet that there are some other women who feel the same."

"Absolutely," Mabel said. "It's only a couple of hours, and the lunch alone is worth the little dab of work. Count me in to help out—except for Thursdays. I bowl on Thursdays."

"I can't thank the two of you enough."

"Oh, it's nothing," Mabel said with a dismissing wave. "Now, eat. I'm going to get along."

"Me, too," Florence said. "I have a bridge game."

When both women left, she and J.J. turned their attention to the food. J.J. dug in. Mary Beth was too exhausted to eat.

"Say, this is good. I thought you were going to have shepherd's pie today."

"I did. We ran out. We ran out of almost everything. I don't know what I'll cook tomorrow."

"I'll take you to the store in Travis Lake this evening."

"Thanks. I'll make a list."

"Wouldn't it be easier to buy from a wholesaler and have stuff delivered?" J.J. asked.

"Probably. At least the staples. Now that I have some cash, I'll look into it. And I have to order more linens. I didn't anticipate so much business. Ellen said it will probably die down to a manageable amount once the novelty wears off.''

"I wouldn't count on it slacking off too much. This chicken stuff is really good."

"Creole. Chicken creole over rice. Except we ran out of rice. The shepherd's pie special was our most popular item. And would you believe that the avocado and apple sandwich was the second most popular?'' With a great effort she managed to bring her fork to her mouth and eat a bite or two.

"How's your foot?" J.J. asked.

"My foot?"

"The one that was broken."

"It hurts. Both my feet hurt."

J.J. scooted his chair around and patted his lap. "Put your feet up here."

She was too tired to ask why. She just did it.

He unlaced her sneakers and took them off, then stripped off her socks and began gently massaging her feet. His hands worked magic. She must have purred because he chuckled. "Feel good?"

"Heavenly." She closed her eyes and drifted while he massaged her feet. "My shoulders ache, too."

"I'll get to those in a minute."

She sighed and purred again. "I really need to go clean the kitchen. It's a wreck."

"Later. Just relax for now."

MARY BETH OPENED HER EYES and, disoriented for a moment, panicked. Then she realized she was in her bed. But why was she still wearing her clothes? And her apron?

She sat up and held her forehead, trying to shake off the muzziness that clouded her brain.

The last thing she remembered was J.J. massaging her shoulders.

Katy! Where was Katy?

Bounding from bed, Mary Beth began calling her daughter's name as, still groggy, she staggered through the dining room.

"We're in here, Mommy!" Katy called. "In the kitchen."

She stopped at the door to the kitchen and held on to the jamb. There, at the sink, stood J.J. and Katy. Both were wearing yellow chef's aprons. J.J. was up to his elbows in soap suds, and Katy, her apron hitched up in an awkward wad and hanging below her toes, stood on a box beside him holding a dish towel.

"What are you *doing?*" Mary Beth asked.

J.J. looked up and smiled. "Well, hello, sleepyhead."

"We're cleaning up as a surprise, Mommy. Are you surprised?"

"I surely am. J.J., you didn't have to do that."

"I know, but I figured you could use some rest. You were so exhausted that you went out like a light."

"Out like a light," Katy echoed. "I showed Sheriff J.J. how to make down your bed, and he carried you. I carried your shoes and socks. And he said, 'Wouldn't it be a nice surprise for Mommy if we cleaned the kitchen?' and I said, 'Oh, yes.' So we did. We put all the dishes in the dishwasher except these big pots. They wouldn't fit, so we scrubbed these suckers by hand."

"Katy!"

"Well, we did. And Sheriff J.J. said I was a good helper. He said when you woke up that we were going to Travis Lake and get a hamburger and fries and go to the grocery store and get provisioned up for the thunder—" Katy looked to J.J. for help.

"Thundering herd."

"For the thundering herd tomorrow." She beamed.

Mary Beth didn't quite know why, but the tears began to flow. Or maybe she did know why. Nothing had ever touched her quite as much as seeing J. J. Outlaw, a gun on his hip and wearing an apron, washing dishes for her.

"Mary Beth, are you okay?"

"Mommy, did we do something wrong?"

"No, sweetheart," she said, hugging her child. "You did a very nice thing." She glanced over Katy's head at J.J. and smiled. "Thank you very much."

"You're welcome. Why don't you make your list while Katy and I finish up in here?" He nudged Katy. "How 'bout it, pardner?"

She held up her little hand, and they slapped a high five.

Chapter Nine

By Friday, Mary Beth had hired help and had settled into a routine, so the pace wasn't as hectic at the tearoom. They still had plenty of business; in fact, she swore that everyone she knew had shown up for lunch at least once. Having Mabel to handle the cash register and the books was a godsend, and Dixie filled in on Thursday when Mabel went bowling. Bless Ellen, who insisted on working an hour or so a day for the first week.

As for other help, Mary Beth hit a gold mine when she called the junior college in Travis Lake. They had a hospitality-and-food-service program there, and she connected with several students who wanted to work part-time. Two of them had already started—one working Monday, Wednesday and Friday, the other, Buck Morgan, was her kitchen assistant every day. Florence would work Tuesdays and Thursdays for lunch and tips. If Mary Beth would act as his work-practice supervisor, Buck agreed to hire on for a tad above minimum wage. She was delighted. He was worth ten times that amount.

Buck was a jewel. Easygoing and hardworking, he was all grin and muscle. At six-three and with a shaved head and several fierce-looking tattoos, he could have been scary to meet in a dark alley, but he was a gentle giant. J.J. had vouched for him, and he'd started work on Wednesday. With Buck helping in the kitchen, Mary Beth's life had become considerably easier.

On Friday, when the last order was served, Buck fixed a plate and handed it to Mary Beth. "You go sit down and eat. I'll get this kitchen shipshape in no time."

"Shipshape?"

His grin widened. "I was in the navy."

She didn't argue. Her feet hurt.

J.J. and a couple of other latecomers were in the dining room when she entered. The other customers sat in a booth having dessert. J.J. sat at his usual table. He'd been by almost every day for lunch—and had lingered afterward to talk a few minutes or lend a hand with some chore or other before he left in his patrol car.

J.J. stood as she approached and held out her chair. "Well, you've made it through your first week. How does it feel?"

"Fantastic. I'm glad I decided to close on weekends. I need the recovery time. And you'll be happy to know that the wholesaler will be delivering this afternoon, and I'll have to only pick up some fresh vegetables on Sunday."

"I'll take you to Travis Lake."

"J.J., I hate for you to spend your Sunday afternoon in the grocery store. Ellen will take me."

"*I'll* take you. I don't mind a bit."

"Having to rely on friends to tootle me around is an awful imposition. If things keep going well here, I'm hoping to save up enough to get some sort of transportation of my own. It doesn't have to be anything fancy, but I'd like to have something reasonably dependable to drive. An old pickup truck might be good.''

''You can borrow mine for a while if you want to.''

''Then what will you drive?''

''The patrol car. I'm on call most of the time anyhow.''

''Thanks for the offer, but I'd rather not. I'll be able to get something soon, especially if business stays good.''

''I don't see much sign of it slacking up.''

Katy came running in, waving a paper. ''See what I colored, Mommy! I got a star.''

''Wonderful,'' Mary Beth said, taking the paper and looking at the colored scribbles. ''Tell me about it.''

''This is our house and this is my room, and it has three beds in it so Janey and Jimmy can spend the night with me. And this is your room, and this is a fireplace where you can burn real wood in the wintertime—like the one we used to have in Natchez.''

''Do you remember having a fireplace in Natchez? You were very little.''

''I think so. I had a stocking over it, and Santa came. Sheriff J.J., do you want to see my picture?''

''I sure do.'' He took the paper and looked at it carefully. ''This is a very fine picture. Is that a tree I see by the front door?''

Katy nodded.

''Excellent tree. Better than any Picasso I've ever seen.''

Katy beamed.

Mary Beth hugged her daughter close and kissed her soft hair. J.J. had given Katy more attention than her own father ever did. ''Why don't you go in the kitchen and ask Buck for a snack and show him your picture?''

Katy grabbed her paper and was off like a whirlwind.

"I wish I could afford to give her a room of her own so that she could have friends over," Mary Beth said.

"I've still got an empty apartment in my fourplex that you're welcome to have."

She shook her head. "Thanks, but no. Actually, I've been thinking about trying to restore the old motel. I could do it a little at a time as I can afford the materials, starting with a small apartment for Katy and me. Maybe when you have some time you could look over it with me and tell me what you think. Wes told me that you're quite an accomplished builder."

"Oh, I wouldn't go so far as to say that. I built my fourplex and I'm building a house on my part of the ranch when I have the time."

"And you've been spending most of your time helping me instead of working on your own place."

"No problem. I've been working on it hit and miss. I'm in no hurry. How about I drop by tomorrow, and we'll take a look at the old motel and see if it can be salvaged?"

"That would be great."

"Well, I'd better get moving. I have to transport a prisoner to Houston this afternoon."

Mary Beth watched him go. She was getting entirely too used to having J.J. around. Her mind wandered back to the first day the tearoom was open and the wonderful touch of his hands as he massaged away the tiredness of her feet and shoulders. He hadn't touched her since. Once or twice, she'd thought he wanted to, but he hadn't.

She sighed. It was just as well. Leaning on J.J. too much could become a habit, and she was determined to make it on her own, without depending on a man. She didn't want to fall into that trap of becoming dependent and letting him take over her life again. Also, it wouldn't do the sheriff's reputation any good if folks knew he was consorting with the ex-wife of a convict.

MARY BETH SEEMED to be on J.J.'s mind all the time. On the long trip to Houston and back, there didn't seem to be much else to do except think about her or talk to the armed robber he had cuffed in the back of the patrol car. Thinking about Mary Beth was blamed sight more palatable.

While he was in Houston, he did have a chance to see Cole, his oldest brother and a homicide detective with HPD. They'd grabbed a quick dinner and had a few minutes to talk. His mom and dad had been worried about Cole—maybe with good reason. It was hard to tell. He never had been much of a talker. But it seemed to J.J. that his brother seemed even surlier than usual and had knocked back too many drinks in the short time they were together. He'd lost weight, too, and had a hollow look in his eyes. He was talking about quitting the police department.

Cole's wife had left him a couple of years before, and despite his shrugging it off, J.J. knew that it had hit him hard. He'd turned into a cynical bastard, swearing that sappy crap like love and family was for suckers.

What was it about the Outlaw brothers and women? Even though all of them loved their women and loved them fiercely, their luck seemed lousy. Cole's wife had divorced him, Frank's had died, and…well, J.J. hadn't had a wife, but his batting average was pretty sorry. His youngest brother Sam hadn't married either, and showed no signs of wanting to. Maybe Sam was smarter than the rest of them.

Might be that Nonie and Wes Outlaw's long and happy marriage had given their kids an impossible example to follow. J.J. had heard his father say a thousand times that he was a one-woman man, and that Nonie was his first and only love. Maybe all the Outlaws were one-woman men. Cole sure didn't seem to be interested in getting married again. Neither did Frank. He couldn't talk about anybody but Susan, and she'd been dead for well over a year.

And as for him, J.J. had felt as if somebody had pulled the rug out from under him when Mary Beth left. He'd hoped for the longest time that maybe, when she got a little older, she'd come back. Now that he recalled the situation, it seemed like a stupid notion, but it was the truth. When he heard she'd gotten married, it had nearly killed him. He'd gone on a week-long toot and ended up in a cathouse somewhere in Louisiana. The days and months after that were pure hell. He'd lost twenty-five pounds and was a bear to be around—not too different from Cole now.

He could feel himself slipping back under her spell again, and that voice inside kept telling him to run like the devil. If they got involved again, he didn't know if he could stand it if she left him.

But damnation, she needed somebody to look out for her. She didn't have any family left and she was hanging on by her fingernails. Who would take care of Katy and her if he didn't?

J. J. Outlaw, you'd better cut a wide path around Mary Beth Parker. She's gonna break your heart again if you let her.

He didn't listen. No matter how many times he warned himself, he didn't listen. She needed him. So on Saturday afternoon, just like a homing pigeon, his truck headed straight for The Twilight Tearoom. And when he saw Mary Beth and Katy crossing the road with buckets and purple-stained fingers, his heart swelled up like a balloon and a broad grin spread across his face despite himself.

Little Katy was the image of her mother, smiling brightly as she ran toward him. It burned a hole in J.J.'s gut to think that another man was her father. No other man should have had Mary Beth. Katy should have been his. Damn that sorry son of a bitch!

"Look, Sheriff J.J.," Katy said, thrusting her bucket toward him. "We've been picking berries."

He chuckled. "Looks like you've been eating a few, too. Your lips are purple."

"Mmm, they're good. Want some?"

"Sure." He took a couple from her small plastic pail.

"They're almost gone," Mary Beth said. "We didn't find nearly as many as you and I did."

"I think there's another patch or two on my place if you want some more."

"I may take you up on that," she said, smiling so damned sweetly that he wanted to grab her and kiss her right there in the middle of the road. "I'd love to make another dessert for the tearoom before this year's crop is gone."

"We'll go berry-picking later then. Still want to look over the old motel?"

"Sure. Let me wash up and get Katy settled. I promised that she could watch *The Little Mermaid* video again this afternoon. She must have seen it a hundred times."

"But I *love* Ariel, Mommy. Don't you, Sheriff J.J.?"

"I don't rightly know. I don't believe we've met."

Katy giggled. "Ariel is the mermaid, silly. Want to watch it with me?"

"Maybe some other time. Your mom and I have to do some reconnoitering."

"What's recon—" She furrowed her little brow.

"Reconnoitering. Exploring and investigating. We'll go berry-picking over at my place later. Okay?"

"Do you have any horses there?"

"Just one. Want to go for a ride with me?"

Her eyes lit up. "Oh, yes! I love horses."

"Come along, Katy, and let's wash up," Mary Beth said. "J.J., want a cup of coffee?"

"Is it made?" he asked, holding open the tearoom door for them to enter.

"No, but I can make some easily enough."

"Maybe later. Want me to put the berries in the refrigerator for you?"

"Thanks."

J.J. took their buckets and stashed them away while Mary Beth and Katy cleaned up.

While he waited for Mary Beth to get Katy settled, he started thinking about some sort of vehicle for her. He certainly didn't mind taking her places, but she was far enough from town for transportation to be a problem if she had an emergency. What if Katy got sick in the middle of the night?

Ephraim Hobbs had a nice little SUV on his used-car lot that had belonged to Hollis Firbank. Hollis had died a few months back, and his daughter had sold the vehicle to Ephraim last week. If J.J. knew Hollis, the vehicle was in good shape. The old codger had rarely driven over thirty miles an hour and had been as persnickety as an old maid. J.J. would drop by Ephraim's lot later in the afternoon and see if he could make a deal with him. The SUV would be perfect for Mary Beth and Katy—clean, dependable, and cheap—especially if J.J. kicked in part of the cost. Mary Beth didn't have to know that part.

In fact…

J.J. punched the car lot's number into his cell phone. "Ephraim, J.J.," he said quietly. "Hang on to Hollis's SUV until I can talk to you later. I may have a buyer."

When Mary Beth came in the kitchen, he disconnected quickly. Damn, it wouldn't do for her to catch him dealing for that SUV. She'd be madder than a scalded cat. "Ready to check out the motel?"

"If you have time and don't mind," she said, glancing at his cell phone.

He stuck the phone in his pocket and grinned. "Looks like I'm free as a bird unless somebody decides to hold up Cooter Graves's bait shop. Let's go."

They left Katy watching her video and walked the short distance to the old motel.

"It looks pretty pitiful," Mary Beth said. "Do you think it can be fixed?"

"I'm sure it can. The question is, how expensive is it going to be? There comes a point in renovations when it's cheaper to bulldoze the structure and start over. The whole building needs a new roof, that's for sure."

"How much will that cost?"

She looked worried already. Damn, he hated to see that anxious expression on her face. She shouldn't have to be scrabbling to keep afloat. Mary Beth was the sort of woman who ought to be playing cards with her friends and volunteering at the school or the hospital instead of slinging hash and trying to make something out of this old pile of boards.

"Depends on the condition of the substructures and

the kind of material you want to use. Also, using a contractor would be more expensive. If we do the work ourselves, we could save a lot.''

''J.J., I can't expect you to work on this. It would take too much time, and you have an important job.''

''I have weekends free most of the time, and I could come by a couple of hours in the afternoons after five. No problem. And Dad would love to help. He needs something to keep him busy and he has a lot of cronies that would pitch in. I can get Dean Gaskamp to come by and take a look at the roof for a more professional estimate.''

''Is he still doing community service?''

J.J. chuckled. ''No, he's served his time. I don't think he'll be putting another pig in the mayor's car anytime soon.'' He tried the door to the first unit, the one with a faded Office sign and a boarded-up window. ''Locked. Do you have the key?''

Mary Beth dug in her pocket, then handed him a ring of numbered keys. ''I think this one is the master.'' She pointed to a tarnished gold-toned key with a red plastic collar. ''The place is pretty junky. I think the manager's apartment is behind the office. Florence and I rummaged through most of the units last week but we didn't check this part out very well because it was so dark. I know that all the furniture will have to go. It's gross.''

And it was, he discovered as he swung open the door. Dust an inch thick covered the dilapidated desk in the small reception room. With only the open door providing light, it was hard to see much. ''Let me get a flashlight and a crowbar from the truck.''

''A *crowbar?* What are you going to do?''

''I'm just going to pry the boards off the windows so that we can see better.''

It didn't take long to remove the rotting plywood from the windows along the side, then from the front window. Thankfully, the big plate glass panel was intact.

"Not a crack," Mary Beth said, touching it. "But lots of dirt. There must be a thousand spiderwebs in these rooms."

"More than that, I imagine. And a few other critters, too, I suspect," he said, pointing to some droppings on the floor.

Mary Beth shuddered, and he could have kicked himself for mentioning it. He forgot that she was terrified of rats and mice. He flicked on his heavy-duty flashlight and they moved from the office area through a door in the rear.

"Oh, look!" she said. "It *is* an apartment."

It was an apartment of sorts, with two rooms and a bath. One of the rooms held a rotted and sagging couch with holes in the cushions and God knows what inside. Moldy shag carpet that had probably once been dark green covered the floor. There was a rickety table and a couple of chairs past their prime. The beds and other furniture were in worse shape, the bathroom was filthy, the fixtures unusable and tile had fallen from the wall in spots. All the plaster in the apartment was in bad shape, and the ceiling sagged. From leaks, he suspected.

Mary Beth looked dejected. "It's too terrible, isn't it? I don't see how this can be fixed. I—I was hoping that maybe we could fix up this unit at least so that Katy and I could—" Tears welled up in her eyes.

Hell, she was about to cry. He couldn't stand it if she cried. "Shh," he said, taking her into his arms. She melted against him as he patted her back. "Don't get upset yet. It's only the surface stuff that's bad. Let's see if the structure is sound.''

He eased her away from him before he did something really dumb—like kiss those sweet lips.

When he glanced down at her, she had that look on her face—the one that said she was waiting for him to kiss her. He knew that look well. Hadn't he dreamed about it a thousand times and more? Didn't he ache like a son of a gun to do more than just kiss her?

He didn't give in. Instead he turned away and said, ''I'm going to rip down a section of this wallboard and see what's behind it.'' He plied the crowbar with a little more muscle than was necessary and tore off the old rock. After it was down, he rapped on the frame and inspected the two-by-fours that had probably been put up not long after World War II.

''What do you think?'' she asked anxiously.

''This part looks sound. Whoever built this used good lumber. And the floor seems solid, though we can't tell until we rip up the old floor coverings and carpet.''

''So there's a chance that we can remodel it without too much expense?''

''I'd say so. Of course we'll have to get a professional to check out the electrical wiring as well as the plumbing and gas lines.''

Her face fell. ''That sounds expensive.''

''Maybe not. A couple of Dad's domino buddies might help. One is a retired plumber and the other used to be an electrician. You might work a deal with them and trade lunches for their help.''

She perked up. ''You think?''

''Sure. I'll check with Dad this afternoon.''

''That would be great. And J.J., you'll never have to buy your lunch at The Twilight Tearoom again.''

He laughed. "Don't be giving away all your profits. Besides, as sheriff, I can't be accepting free lunches." Truth was, there wasn't any rule against it as far as he knew, but she didn't have to know that.

"Oh. Sorry. Shall we look at the other units? I hadn't planned to do the entire motel at once—just a little at a time, but maybe we can get some idea about what needs to be done first."

"Good idea."

They locked up and moved on to the next unit, which was separated from the office by a carport.

As they stepped inside, there was a rustling noise, a series of squeaks and a flurry of movement along the floor. Something must have run across Mary Beth's foot because she let out a scream that would wake the dead, grabbed hold of him and tried to climb him.

He wrapped both arms around her. "Shh, darlin'. I've got you. I've got you."

She laid her head against his shoulder and hung on to him for dear life. He could feel her heart beating ninety to nothing, and she was trembling.

"Was that a rat, J.J.? Was that a rat?"

"I don't know, darlin', but you scared the pants off of whatever it was. I'll bet it's halfway to Shreveport by now."

"Are you sure it's gone?"

"I'm sure. Seems to me we ought to get you a cat."

"Or two. Or three. Or maybe a dozen." She still clung to him.

"A dozen might be overdoing it a tad. But seriously, a cat might not be a bad idea. Frank's cat had a litter about two months ago and he's been looking for good homes for them." He rubbed her back and held her close. Damn, but she felt good. She fit up against him perfectly, as if her body had been molded precisely for him.

He felt her relax and sigh. He didn't relax. Nothing about him relaxed. In fact, he was growing more un-relaxed by the minute.

"J.J.?"

"Hmm?"

"I think you can let me go now."

"In a little bit."

Her hands began to move over his back, and he was a goner. He kissed her then. He couldn't help it.

Her lips were warm and moist and soft. So soft. And her tongue was like velvet.

His hands stroked the curve of her back and slid downward to stroke the curve of her butt. She arched against him, and he could feel her breasts against his chest. He yanked her shirt from her jeans to get to her bare skin, and she groaned against his mouth.

"Mommy!" Katy said. "Did you call me?"

Mary Beth jumped back. They both looked at Katy, who stood in the doorway.

"Uh—uh, no, sweetie, I didn't call you. There was a mouse or something in here and it startled me. I screamed."

Katy looked from one of them to the other.

"I was protecting your mom," J.J. said quickly.

"You were kissing her."

"I was thanking him for protecting me," Mary Beth said.

"Oh," Katy said, as if she didn't believe a word of it. "Can we go ride the horse now?"

Chapter Ten

J.J. arrived on Sunday afternoon in a shiny blue SUV. "Is this new?" Mary Beth asked as she touched the hood. She'd give her eyeteeth to have one like it.

"Nope. It's a few years old, but it's a cream puff, so Ephraim Hobbs said."

"Who's Ephraim Hobbs?"

"He owns a used-car lot on Third Street. Where's Katy?"

"She went home with Janey and Jimmy after church. I thought you loved your pickup truck."

"I do. This isn't for me. It's for you, if you like it."

"What's not to like? But J.J., I can't afford something like this."

"Sure you can. Ephraim picked it up cheap in an estate sale, and he said you could pay it out, nothing down and a hundred dollars a month for three years. It's a honey of a deal and I know that it's in great shape. Somebody's bound to snap it up in a hurry if you don't take it. Why don't you drive it to Travis Lake and see how it handles?"

It handled like a dream. The leather seats were like new, and there wasn't a scratch on it. She couldn't believe the price. It cost less than the little used car she'd bought when she'd had to sell her Lexus in Natchez. Still, as she mentally calculated the cost, she wondered if she could afford it. A lot of her profits would go into renovating the apartment unit of the motel. Plus, she had to consider the cost of shipping what was left of her furniture and things from Mississippi.

What if business at the tearoom fell off? She had employee wages to consider now, along with utilities and bills from the suppliers. Taking on another financial burden, even a small one by most people's standards, was scary.

"How does it drive?" J.J. asked.

"Beautifully. It's a fantastic vehicle, and it would be perfect for us, but I was thinking more along the lines of buying an old clunker for five or six hundred dollars."

"Mary Beth, you'd end up spending more on an old clunker than you would on this. First thing you know, you'd need a new battery and a new set of tires, then the transmission would go out or the fuel pump or the alternator. It would stay in Tick's Garage half the time—unless you know how to repair an old car."

"I don't even know where the transmission is. What's an alternator?"

"Exactly. And any old clunker you'd buy wouldn't have an air conditioner. Imagine August in Texas without an air conditioner."

"It would be miserable."

"Worse than miserable. Think about it, for twenty-five dollars a week, you could have a nice, dependable, air-conditioned vehicle with an almost new set of tires and an engine that looks like it just rolled off the assembly line."

"Maybe I could get a bicycle. I could probably pick up one at a garage sale for twenty bucks."

He didn't even smile; he merely scowled at her as if she'd lost her mind. "Mary Beth, get serious. You're not going to find a better buy than this. Trust me."

"It seems almost too good to be true." Still she had her doubts, but by the time they'd loaded the sacks of fresh vegetables in the roomy rear cargo space and driven home, J.J. had convinced her that she'd be sorry if she passed up a deal like the one Ephraim Hobbs was offering her on the SUV.

Truthfully, he didn't have to twist her arm too much. She loved driving it, loved sitting up high where she could see everything. It wasn't one of those big things that rivaled a motor home, but a smaller, sturdy vehicle that was perfect for the business and hauling stuff. She could get one of those magnetic signs for the door. Thinking about tooling around with a Twilight Tearoom advertisement made her chuckle.

"What's the joke?" J.J. asked as he helped carry bags to the kitchen.

"I was just thinking about putting a magnetic sign on the door advertising the tearoom."

"Sounds like a good idea to me. You've decided to buy it?"

She nodded. "I'll go down tomorrow and sign the papers."

He grinned. "There ya go. I'll go with you."

"I can handle it by myself, but thank you."

"No problem. I'll be here for lunch anyhow. We'll drive down to the lot after you close up."

His insistence made her uneasy. No, it made her angry. "J.J., back off. I appreciate your help. I really do. But there are things I need to do for myself," she told him firmly. "This is one of them. I'll take care of the transaction tomorrow. Alone."

He held up his hands in surrender and backed up a step. "Yes, ma'am. I hear you loud and clear."

"J.J., I don't mean to seem ungrateful, it's just that depending on other people to take care of me is why I landed in the mess I'm in. I've had to learn the hard way how to look after Katy and me."

"Mary Beth, you're among friends now. We all care about you and want to help."

"I know, and I appreciate all the help everybody has been. But it would be very easy to slip back into the old role and let others take over. I'm determined that that won't happen to me again. You're a take-charge kind of person, J.J., and I don't want you taking charge of me."

He raised his eyebrows a tad, then said quietly, "I get the message."

Oh, blast, she'd hurt his feelings and she hadn't meant to. She searched for words to make amends, then decided against it. If it took some straight talk to make him understand, so be it. She didn't know if any sort of relationship other than a platonic one was in the cards—Lord knows, his kisses had about singed her eyebrows—but if there was going to be anything between them, things would have to be very different from their younger days. He'd have to get it into his head that she wasn't the same malleable girl she'd been at seventeen.

Their conversation was strained after that. When all the vegetables were put away, he said, "Would you mind giving me a lift to pick up my truck?"

"Your truck? Where is it?"

"At Ephraim's car lot."

"Can't you get it when you take the SUV back?"

"You can keep the SUV here overnight."

She shook her head. "I'd rather not. I'll pick it up when I sign the papers tomorrow."

"How will you get there?"

"I have two perfectly good feet—or I can get Florence or Buck to drop me off on their way home."

"Florence or Buck, but not me."

When she realized that her answer had stung him again, "I'm sorry" was on the tip of her tongue. She bit back the words. Saying "I'm sorry" and acquiescing to keep everybody happy was part of her old pattern. She refused to play nice at the price of her self-respect.

Instead, she laughed and said, "J. J. Outlaw, are you sulking because your feelings are hurt?"

After a couple of seconds, he laughed, too. "Sounded like it, didn't it?"

"It did, indeed. How about a cup of coffee? I'll even throw in a piece of chocolate pie for all your help this afternoon."

"Sounds like a good trade to me."

Dixie and Jack Russo dropped by before the coffee was made. Jack, a burly guy with a shock of sandy-colored hair, had dug up a big clump of mint and brought along some other herbs they had picked up at the nursery. He and J.J. planted them in a bed near the door while the coffee brewed. Dixie and Mary Beth set out cups for everyone and cut the pie.

"This is fabulous," Mary Beth said after she surveyed the men's work. "Not only will I have my own herb garden, but it will look and smell fantastic. Thanks, guys. Jack, let me pay you for the plants from the nursery."

"Nope," Jack said. "Consider it a gift for your opening. Sorry I wasn't able to help with the painting. Maybe this will make up for it.''

"This more than makes up for it." She gave him a hug. "Let's have some pie."

Halfway through his pie, J.J.'s cell phone rang.

"Outlaw," he said, answering. After a few seconds, he said, "I'm on my way." He took another sip of coffee, then stood. "Excuse me, y'all, but there's been a bad wreck out on the highway. I've gotta go."

Mary Beth walked him to the door. "Thanks for everything, J.J. I really appreciate it."

He gave a curt nod and was gone.

When she rejoined Dixie and Jack, Jack said, "J.J. tells me that you're going to buy Hollis Firbank's SUV."

"Who is Hollis Firbank?"

"You must remember Mr. Firbank," Dixie said. "He was the old fellow who used to be the postmaster. Tall, skinny, had a face like pelican. He died a few months back."

"Oh, yes. I do remember him. He was always slow as Christmas. I'm sorry to hear that he died. J.J. said that Ephraim Hobbs bought the car at an estate sale. That's why I can get it as such a good price."

"And I'm sure it's in excellent shape," Jack said. "Looks like you might be needing some insurance." He grinned and handed her a card from his pocket.

"Jack!" Dixie said, giving him a playful slap. "Stop trying to hustle my friends."

"Oh, dear," Mary Beth said, her heart sinking. "I'd forgotten about insurance. I'm not sure that I can afford to buy the car and insurance, too."

"You can wait on comprehensive, but the law requires that you have liability coverage. If you want me to handle it for you, we can work out a plan so that you can pay monthly until you get on your feet.''

''I would appreciate it, Jack. And Ellen was reminding me the other day that I need to have insurance on the tearoom, not only for fire and such, but in case somebody falls and decides to sue me—not that I have anything to sue for.''

''She's right,'' Jack told her. ''Want me to work up a proposal for you?''

Mary Beth sighed. ''I suppose so. Being a business-woman can get expensive, can't it?''

''Just wait till tax time.''

She groaned. ''Lord, I hadn't even thought about taxes. Now I'll need an accountant. Maybe I'd better forget about getting a car and go back to the idea of a bicycle. Even paying a hundred dollars a month might strain my paltry budget.''

Dixie gave Jack an odd look. ''A *hundred* dollars a month?''

''I don't think you can pass up the deal on the SUV,'' Jack said. ''Look at it this way. If you can't meet the payments, you can always sell it— and for a profit, I'll bet. At the very least, somebody would be happy to take up the payments. I don't see how you can lose.''

''I suppose you're right. How about another piece of pie?''

''Don't mind if I do.'' Jack offered his empty plate.

Dixie patted his paunch. ''You can have another piece of pie, or dinner tonight. Your choice.''

Jack laughed. ''Looks like I just got outvoted, Mary Beth. Guess I'll pass on the pie. But that piece was delicious. We'd better go and pick up the kids. The movie should be over by now.''

''And Florence should be exhausted from chasing

Eddie,'' Dixie added. She stood and started gathering dishes.

"Leave those,'' Mary Beth told her. "I'll have them cleaned up in a jiffy. Thanks so much for my mint and herbs.''

After Dixie and Jack left, Mary Beth put on bread to bake and checked the menu for the next day's lunch. She made all the advance preparations possible and still had part of the afternoon left. Why not start on clearing out the apartment unit.

Remembering the little furry creature gave her a queasy feeling, but she pushed it aside. She put on her painting clothes, tied her hair in a bandanna, and grabbed her work gloves along with a pot and a wooden spoon.

She unlocked the peeling door and eased it open. Banging on the pot like crazy, she yelled, "Get out! Get out, all you critters!'' She stomped through all the rooms, banging and yelling.

Finally convinced that she had scared the pants off any four-legged creatures, she looked around, trying to decide what to tackle first.

Most of the furniture was unsalvageable. She started with the awful couch and the nasty mattresses, dragging them outside and then around to the back to what looked like a dump at one time. Burning the stuff might be the best solution, but she would check the burning regulations first. Any pieces that she thought could possibly be saved, she moved into another unit. She was about to start ripping up the ratty old carpet when Frank drove up with the kids.

She waved and went outside.

"Hi,'' Frank said, getting out of his car. "What's going on?''

"Demolition. I'm starting to clean out the mess in the manager's apartment."

"Need some help?"

Mary Beth glanced at his neat khakis and crisp blue shirt. "No, thanks. It's a filthy job."

"I promised to take the kids out for a hamburger. Mind if Katy comes along?"

"Please, Mommy. Please, please, please."

"Please, please, please," the twins said, joining in.

"Sure, if you don't mind."

"I don't mind at all. In fact, why don't you come with us?"

Mary Beth looked down at her grimy, paint-spattered jeans and shirt. "I'm filthy."

"We'll wait for you to change," Frank said. "How long since you've eaten somebody's cooking except your own—even if it is only a hamburger?"

"Ages." A big juicy hamburger suddenly sounded mouthwatering. "You're on. I'll be fast."

She longed to be able to take a shower, but she made do with a spit bath in the ladies' room and slipped into a knit dress and sandals. One of the nicest things about having an apartment would be having a shower of her own. Ellen had been good to let her use hers a couple of times a week, but the rest of the time, she bathed Katy in a washtub she'd found and managed the best she could for herself. After a couple of swipes at her hair and a dash of lipstick, she was ready.

"That was quick," Frank said, smiling as she came out the door.

"I'm speedy." She grinned. "Especially when I'm hungry. Does this place have onion rings?"

"And home fries. Both hot and greasy." He held open the door for her and yelled to the kids to come.

"The best kind."

BY THE TIME J.J. left the hospital, he felt lower than a polecat with a toothache. Not only had Mary Beth shot him down, but he'd spent most of the afternoon dealing with the disaster a couple of kids had caused with their reckless driving. One of them had lost an eye and had broken both legs. The other one was being transported to Dallas with serious burns.

The highway was clear and traffic was running smoothly again, but he was wrung out. He climbed into the blue SUV and headed for Ephraim's car lot to switch it for his truck.

The vehicle did have a nice ride. Hollis had taken good care of it, and it would be good, dependable transportation for Mary Beth. After the blistering she'd given him this afternoon about him interfering too much in her business, he hoped to hell that she didn't find out about the deal he'd made with Ephraim. If she discovered that he'd kicked in a hefty down payment for her, his ass would be grass.

But damn, that woman was hardheaded. He couldn't let her go running around in some old rattletrap that belched smoke and was held together with baling wire.

He ought to just let her go, leave her alone to do whatever stupid thing she came up with, but he could no more do that than he could fly. He cared about her, dammit he *cared*. It wouldn't take too much of a push to fall crazy, head-over-heels for her again. He had to watch out for that. He didn't want to go down that road again.

One thing for sure, he'd have to watch trying to run her business. She'd made that plenty clear—and not for the first time. He hadn't realized that he'd been domineering with her, but obviously she'd thought so. Maybe they simply weren't suited to each other. Maybe Mary Beth needed a gentler, more low-key kind of guy, somebody more like his brother Frank. He was steady as a rock, easygoing, and they had the kids—

Not no, but hell no! Even the thought of her with anyone else hit him in the gut like a mule kick, and he clenched the wheel as if he could wring somebody's neck.

He was in worse shape than he thought.

After he'd traded cars at the lot, he decided that he was hungry. He'd meant to take Mary Beth and Katy out to dinner somewhere tonight, but after all that had transpired, his plans sort of got left by the wayside. He'd stop by the Burger Barn and grab a bite before he headed home. God, he had a whopper of a headache.

He saw Frank's car when he pulled into the parking lot. Chances were his brother was there with the twins. They often ate hamburgers on Sunday night. The kids liked the playscape and the video games about as well as the burgers. Probably better.

He climbed out of his truck and ambled to the front door. At least he wouldn't have to eat dinner by himself.

Stopping inside the door, he looked around the room. The place was smoky from sizzling burgers and noisy with the shriek of kids and the wail of Faith Hill on the jukebox.

He spotted Frank at a corner table. Mary Beth sat beside him. They had their heads together, laughing.

Fury flashed over J.J.

He wanted to stalk across the room, jerk his brother out of that chair and beat him to a bloody pulp.

Instead, he turned and strode back out the way he'd come in.

He was nearly to his truck when he heard someone yell his name. He kept walking.

A hand clamped on to his shoulder, and he whirled around. There stood Frank grinning like a cat in the cream crock.

J.J. drew back his fist and punched his brother's lights out.

Chapter Eleven

Frank was gone for a long time after he'd spotted J.J. at the door, and when he returned, he looked a little strange. "Is anything wrong?" Mary Beth asked.

"No, no. Not a thing. I—uh, talked to J.J. in the parking lot. He couldn't stay. He was just trying to locate somebody. Where are the kids?"

"Where else?" She laughed and pointed across the room where a row of junior-size mechanical broncos stood. "I gave them each another quarter."

"I often wish I had their energy."

"Me, too," Mary Beth said. "Mine's flagging rapidly. I think we're going to have to call it a night after this ride. Thanks for inviting us along. This has been a real treat. Drop by the tearoom one day next week and have lunch on me."

"I may take you up on that. I've heard great things about your cooking. The Grill is convenient to the courthouse, and their food isn't bad, but it's cholesterol city. Let me round up the kids and we'll head home."

Mary Beth watched Frank as he talked to the children. He was such a nice man—and a terrific father. A shame about his wife; they'd talked about Susan a lot. He'd said her name almost with reverence, and his love for her still shone in his eyes. Susan had been a couple of years ahead of Mary Beth in school, but she remembered her—a beautiful girl with light brown hair and laughing eyes. They had been a perfect couple. Frank was a handsome man—all the Outlaws were good-looking—and he favored J.J. quite a bit, though J.J.'s features were more rough and angular.

During dinner, Mary Beth had discovered that, while Frank and J.J. resembled each other physically, their personalities were very different. She liked Frank very much. But being around him didn't ignite the spark that being around J.J. did. A pity, really. They had a lot in common, especially the children, but the sexual chemistry simply wasn't there.

But it was there with J.J. Boy, was it there. That was the problem.

"Ready?" Frank asked.

She glanced up from the straw she'd been mangling to find Frank and the kids waiting for her. She smiled. "Ready."

J.J. SAT IN HIS DARK apartment sucking on a beer and feeling lower than a snake's belly. Hitting his own brother. What devil had possessed him?

Mary Beth Beams Parker. She was the devil. No, she was an angel; he was the devil. But devil or angel, she possessed him just the same. He had never had a lick of sense when it came to her.

His doorbell rang.

He ignored it.

It rang again. And again. Somebody was sitting on it. Cursing, he got up, strode to the door and jerked it open.

There stood Frank.

"You want to tell me what the dickens is going on with you?"

J.J. raked a hand through his hair. "Oh, God, Frank, I'm sorry. I punched you before I thought. And I didn't mean to take off like that." He turned around and stared into the darkened room. "Are you okay?"

The light went on and the door closed.

"Yeah, I'm fine. What provoked you in the first place?" Frank asked, his tone more reasonable than J.J. had a right to expect.

"I'm ashamed to say."

"Say it anyhow. I want to know if I've done something to make you mad. If I have, I sure didn't intend to."

"Want a beer?" J.J. asked.

"No, I don't want a beer. I want an answer."

"Oh, hell's bells," J.J. said as he ambled over to his chair, slumped down in it and slung one leg over the arm. "I saw you and Mary Beth together and went a little crazy."

Frank laughed.

"Dammit, it's not funny."

"Yes, it is. J.J., there's nothing going on between Mary Beth and me. The twins wanted Katy to go get a hamburger with us, and I invited Mary Beth along. You know I couldn't be interested in a woman except as a friend. Susan—well, you know how it is with me."

"I know, Frank. But I swear, Mary Beth hasn't been back in town any time, and I'm already obsessed with her all over again. Love is a bitch."

"I think you've got a problem, little brother. I'm not sure love and obsession are the same thing. Love is a wonderful thing when it happens between two people. Obsession is one-sided, and it's repressive and destructive. Sounds like you ought to do some soul-searching to decide how you really feel about her.''

''Sounds like you'd make a good judge. Have you ever given it any thought?'' J.J. managed a halfhearted smile.

''Once or twice.'' Frank grinned. ''Are you going to be okay?''

''Eventually, I imagine. But you're right. I need to give things some thought.''

''If you want to talk, give me a call.''

J.J. nodded. ''I really am sorry about hitting you. How's your jaw?''

''A little sore, but I'll live. You pack quite a wallop, kid.''

J.J. laughed then. He got up, threw his arm around his brother and walked him to the door. ''Thanks for coming.''

BY FRIDAY AFTERNOON, Mary Beth was getting concerned. She hadn't seen J.J. all week. Both Wes and Frank had been by for lunch—on the house she insisted—but neither of them mentioned J.J. Of course he might have been having a busy week. She certainly had. She'd picked up the SUV on Monday afternoon and arranged for insurance with Jack Russo. The tearoom had been full every day, and she'd had two new waitresses to train. Again she thanked her lucky stars for Buck Morgan. He was a fantastic assistant. She often wondered what she would have done without him.

Dean Gaskamp had come by on Wednesday and looked at the motel roof. The news wasn't good. He said that the apartment unit needed a whole new roof to be livable, but the other units could make do with a few patches until she was ready to renovate them. His estimate nearly sent her into cardiac arrest. Roofs were expensive.

Every afternoon after the tearoom closed, Mary Beth worked on the apartment unit. She'd used the crowbar J.J. had left to tear out all the old plasterboard walls. She added the trash to the growing pile in back, which now included the gross carpet. She was waiting for a windless day to burn it.

Ripping up the carpet had been a chore but under it, along with years of dirt, she found that the flooring was generally sound. Thank God for small miracles. The bathroom was another story. There were some rotted spots under the curling linoleum. They weren't dangerous, but they needed patching.

She had hoped that the old claw-foot bathtub could be salvaged. Friday afternoon found Mary Beth and Katy wrestling the old tub's fittings. Katy held the flashlight while Mary Beth wielded a wrench and pliers. It was a tougher job than she'd expected, and she was getting more and more exasperated.

"Uh-uh, Mommy. That's an ugly word."

Mary Beth swiped her face with her T-shirt. "You're right, sweetie. And I apologize."

"What are you two doing?"

Mary Beth glanced up to find J.J. standing in the doorway.

"We're trying to get this dad-blasted tub out," Katy said.

"Katy!"

"But, Mommy, you said it."

"Yes, and I apologized. It's not a polite word."

J.J. just grinned.

"Stop smirking and help us," Mary Beth said. "I've skinned every knuckle I have."

"Then move back, ladies, and let a pro handle it."

"Gladly." They moved.

And wouldn't you know that with a couple of bangs and twists, he had the tub unhooked. Then he helped them carry it to the back of the restaurant where there was a working water faucet.

"What are you going to do with this?" he asked as they set it down.

"I'm hoping that I can clean it up and use it in the bathroom when I get it redone. If not, I guess I'll plant geraniums in it."

"Mommy, can I go watch *The Little Mermaid?*"

"*May* I? And, yes, you may. J.J., would you like a cup of coffee?"

"Think I'll pass on the coffee, but I wouldn't mind a cold glass of tea. Sheriffing is hot, dry work sometimes."

"Been working hard?"

He nodded. "Had a missing child two counties over. I was gone for a few days looking for her. We combed half the woods in the county."

"Did you find her?"

He nodded.

"Was she okay?"

He shook his head. "She was only two. Her mother left her napping alone and went to the grocery store. She woke up, wandered off and got lost. We found her drowned in a stock pond three miles from her house."

"Oh, that's horrible! J.J., I'm so sorry."

"Me, too. Makes you realize what's important, and what's not." He cupped the side of her face and rubbed his thumb along her cheekbone. "I did a lot of thinking while I was searching for that child. You're important to me, Mary Beth."

She didn't quite know what to say. Finally she settled on, "You're important to me, too."

"Good." He took her in his arms and held her, simply held her. "How about that glass of tea?"

She led him inside and fixed frosty glasses for them both. While they drank, she filled him in on the report from Dean about the roof and the progress she'd made in cleaning up the place.

"Appears that you've stripped it down pretty good."

"I have. Ellen helped me one day and Buck insisted on carrying out the old carpet. I even checked out some books from the library on remodeling. I think I could repair the tiles in the bathroom and put up drywall if push came to shove."

He grinned. "Good for you. I'm proud of you."

She smiled. Those words of praise from him made her feel better about herself than anything else had in a long time.

"Say, would you and Katy like to drive over to Travis Lake for pizza and a movie tonight?"

"We'd love it. What time?"

"About six?"

"You're on."

"Well, I'd better be moving along," he said. "I've got a stack of paperwork a mile high waiting for me." He stood, then leaned over and gave her a quick kiss on the forehead. "Bye, Katy," he called as he walked out the door.

Mary Beth didn't exactly know what to make of J.J.'s visit. He seemed different somehow. Subtly different, but different all the same. She couldn't quite put her finger on it, but she'd noticed a change.

"Katy, I'm going to be out back cleaning the tub," she called.

"Okay, Mommy."

She scrubbed on that tub for nearly two hours, but by the time she'd finished, it looked almost like new—at least on the inside. The outside was hopelessly stained, but a coat of paint would handle that.

"That looks much better," said Katy, who'd wandered out to watch her progress.

"Doesn't it?" Mary Beth said, dumping her bucket of wash water. "How would you like to take a bath in it?"

Katy's eyes widened. "Outside?"

"Sure. With those bushes on both sides and the trees and bushes in the back along the fence, it's very private. We can fill it with bubbles. Want to try it?"

Katy was game, and they used a flat rubber stopper for the drain, then carried warm water from the kitchen to fill it up. Katy had a wonderful time in the big old tub, laughing and splashing in the bubbles with her bath toys. Mary Beth practically had to drag her out. How wonderful it would be to have it hooked up in her very own bathroom. Never again would she take a bathroom or a bathtub for granted.

When she stood Katy on a wooden box to dry her and towel her fine hair, Katy said, "Are you going to take a bath, too, Mommy?"

Mary Beth hesitated, looking longingly at the frothy water where sunlight caught in multicolored prisms that shimmered and enticed her to enter. How good a long, hot soak would feel. But here, in the open? It was one thing for a four-year-old to bathe outdoors, but quite another for a grown woman to do it.

"Are you, Mommy?"

A sudden impulse made her think, *What the heck. Live dangerously and enjoy life.* She would be in and out before anybody came along. And as she told Katy, with all the bushes and trees around, she wouldn't be visible from the road. She grinned. "Yes. Yes, I am. Let's get your hair fixed, and you can put on the clothes I laid out for you while I take a quick dip. J.J. will be here in less than an hour to take us for pizza and a movie. Okay?"

"Okay. Can I have pepperoni on mine?"

"*May* I? And yes, you may."

"Mommy?"

"Yes, sweetheart?"

"Is Sheriff J.J. going to be my new daddy?"

Startled, she froze. "Where on earth did you ever get that idea?"

"I heard Miss Florence telling Miss Mabel that he was sweet on you, and she wouldn't be a speck surprised if y'all got married. And if you got married, wouldn't he be my daddy?"

"You already have a daddy, Katy, and Sheriff J.J. and I aren't getting married in any case."

"But my daddy's in the—" Katy clamped her hand over her mouth. "Sorry."

"Very well."

"I wish Sheriff J.J. could be my daddy."

"He can be your very good friend, like he's my very good friend. We're *not* getting married, so don't listen to gossip and think otherwise."

"What's gossip?"

"It's when people talk about other people and sometimes have the facts wrong."

"But Miss Florence said—"

"Ka-ty."

"O-kay." Katy sighed dramatically, but she didn't pursue the subject.

After brushing Katy's hair almost dry and leaving her to dress and watch another video, Mary Beth pinned up her own hair and carried more buckets of warm water outside to the claw-foot tub. She added more bubble bath and filled it as high as she could, then stripped off her grimy clothes in the kitchen and wrapped a big bath towel around her.

She poked her head out the door and looked around. The only living things she saw were a couple of butterflies and a mockingbird sitting on a fence post. She scurried out to the tub, which wasn't more than ten feet from the door, kicked off her thongs and climbed in. After checking all around again, she dropped the towel on the wooden box nearby and sank down into the water.

Heaven. Pure heaven. She hadn't realized how tired and achy her body was.

Lying back with her head on the rim, she let her whole body relax in the wonderful foamy water that smelled of bubblegum. The warmth of the water, the open air, the bit of a breeze that teased her skin and hair felt…well, it was an incredibly sensuous experience.

She thought of J.J. and her body reacted. Her nipples were hard. The tops of her breasts cresting above the water became supersensitive, and the playful fingers of cool breeze and warm suds on her skin heightened the erotic feelings. She closed her eyes and savored the sensations, relaxed and let her fantasies flow.

YOU'D HAVE THOUGHT that it was his first date. J.J. was as nervous as a woodshed waiter. Maybe that was why he arrived fifteen minutes early.

He knocked on the front door of the tearoom, then

stuck his head in. The proper way of calling was a little awkward when a person lived in a restaurant. Katy was sitting in a booth, her attention glued to the TV.

"Hi, peanut," he said.

She glanced at him and smiled. "Hi, Sheriff J.J. Mommy said I can have pepperoni on my pizza."

"Good. I'm partial to pepperoni myself. Where is your mom?"

"She's outside asleep."

"Asleep?"

"I think so. Her eyes are closed, and they didn't open when I whispered her name."

J.J. became alarmed. Had Mary Beth had an accident? Was she unconscious? Trying not to scare Katy, he asked calmly, "Exactly where outside is your mom?"

"In the back outside the kitchen door. It's very private there. Is it time to go?"

"In a little while, sweetheart. Let me check on your mommy."

His heart pumping ninety miles an hour, he strode through the kitchen, threw open the back door and rushed outside.

What he found stopped him dead in his tracks.

She really *was* asleep.

Sound asleep in that old claw-foot tub they had carried from the motel. A few thin patches of foam floated on the water's surface along with a little yellow duck bumping against her breasts.

Wow.

They were beautiful breasts, full and coral-tipped, and her arms draped over the tub's rim made them jut wantonly from the water. He wanted to kiss them, lick them, take them into his mouth and taste every inch.

Hell, he wanted to climb into that bathtub, boots and all, and make love to her until next Tuesday.

But at the same time, her total and innocent nakedness exposed her vulnerability and touched him deeply. She was so lovely, so perfect that she took his breath away. From the first minute he'd noticed her when she was little more than a gawky kid, he'd known that she was his, that they were meant to be together. He'd also known that it was his job to take care of her. For the life of him, he couldn't explain how he knew that, but he knew it as surely as he knew that the sun would rise in the east.

She hadn't been more than thirteen or fourteen when he'd seen her fall on her roller skates. Kids fell on roller skates all the time, but for some reason, he'd stopped to help her. She'd gotten a nasty scrape on her elbow and her knee, and when she'd looked up at him with tears in those big soulful eyes, something had happened inside him that changed his life forever.

Somehow he'd screwed up before and lost her. Maybe it was because she was too young or maybe it was because he'd been a little heavy-handed with his caretaker role. Whatever the reason, that was over and done with. Now he had another chance. This time, a lot older and a little wiser, he hoped to do a better job of seeing after her.

Love for Mary Beth swelled in his chest until it was almost painful. He'd never stopped loving her and he would love her until they put him in the ground. Sometimes he wondered if he'd been put on this earth to love Mary Beth. Maybe so, he didn't know. But he did know that it was as if he'd come alive again when she stepped off that bus.

J.J. had given a lot of thought to what Frank said

about obsession and love. He still wasn't sure that there wasn't a fine line between the two, especially when feelings ran strong. He guessed he'd made lots of mistakes with Mary Beth before. From what she'd said, he figured that one of them was holding on too tight and trying to do too much for her. It was important for her to feel that she could do stuff on her own. And he had to give her credit—she was a hard worker and gutsy as the dickens. Not many women could go through all she had and keep on plugging.

This time he was planning to go slow and easy with her—give her time and give her room. He could be patient.

For a while.

Yet observing the rise and fall of her breasts as she breathed made him wonder how long his patience would last. God, he wanted her.

Should he wake her? Should he go back inside? He didn't know quite what to do. But in the end, he realized that he could no more leave her here than he could sprout wings. He sat down on a wooden tomato crate by the tub, dipped the tip of his index finger into the tepid water and watched her for a moment before waking her.

J.J. took in every feature, from her close-cut toenails to the dark shadow below the water to her blue-veined eyelids. He could see her eyes move beneath her closed lids and figured she was dreaming.

He studied her face and her arms and her hands. There was a scratch on the knuckle of her right thumb, and before he thought, he bent and kissed it softly.

Her eyes opened slowly, languidly. When she saw him, she smiled and stretched. "I was dreaming."

"About me, I hope."

"Yes, I—oh, my God!" She sat straight up in the tub, water sloshing and splashing. She started to rise, then caught herself and drew up her knees and crossed her arms over her breasts in an attempt at modesty. "J.J., I'm in the bathtub!"

"I noticed."

"And I'm *naked!*"

"I noticed that right off, too." ·

"Turn your back."

"I think it's a little late for that, darlin'."

"You *looked!* Jesse James Outlaw, you sat right there and looked at me naked and asleep in the bath."

"Guilty as charged. It's a wonder you didn't drown. You shouldn't sleep in the tub."

"This isn't the time to discuss household safety. Hand me that towel!"

"Which towel, darlin'?"

"The one you're sitting on. Hand me that towel and turn your back this instant, or I'll never speak to you again."

It was obvious she was getting riled, so he played the gentleman. He handed her the towel and turned his back, fighting a grin as he did so. It wouldn't do to laugh, and he knew it.

"J.J., don't you dare tell a soul about this. Promise me."

He heard a lot of sloshing behind him. "You'll have to make it worth my while."

"Exactly what did you have in mind?" she said in a tone that singed his neck hairs.

He turned around to find her covered by the towel, glaring at him. He couldn't help but grin. "I was hoping that you might loan me your rubber duck."

Chapter Twelve

Mary Beth threw the blasted yellow duck at J.J. and nailed him square in the chest.

"I'll strangle you if you mention this to a soul, J. J. Outlaw! I swear I will." Then she turned and flounced away, slamming the kitchen door behind her for good measure.

Never in her entire life had she been so mortified.

Her face was still burning as she grabbed her clothes and makeup bag and hurried to the washroom to dress.

Long after she was ready, she stood inside the ladies' room dreading her exit. Finally she squared her shoulders, lifted her chin and opened the door. J.J. sat in the booth beside Katy watching TV.

He glanced at her and smiled. "You look very nice."

"Thank you," she said stiffly.

"I let the water out of the tub and locked the back door."

"I appreciate that."

"You did a good job of cleaning that old relic," he said.

"Thank you. The outside could stand a coat of paint."

"Have any particular color in mind?"

"I haven't decided yet."

"I'm hungry," Katy said. "When are we going to have our pizza?"

"Right now, peanut," J.J. said. He turned off the TV, picked up Katy with one arm and offered Mary Beth his other. "Shall we go?"

She took his arm, and he escorted them outside. Thank heavens he wasn't making a big deal out of the bathtub scene. She locked the front door while J.J. belted Katy into a booster seat in the rear of the extended cab pickup.

"Where'd you get the booster?" she asked as he helped her climb into her place.

"Bought it," he said, mentioning the name of the local superstore. "They had a sale going on."

"I hope you didn't buy it just for tonight. We could have used mine. Ellen loaned it to me. Her kids have outgrown it."

"Not a big deal. I figured we might get some more use out of it from time to time."

"Sheriff J.J. said I could ride his horse again tomorrow," Katy piped up from the back seat. "Can I get a cowboy hat like his?"

"*May* I? And we'll see."

"'We'll see' yes, or 'we'll see' no?"

J.J. grinned. "She's got you there."

"Frightening, isn't it?" she replied to J.J. "Katy, that's a 'we'll see' depending on how good you are between now and your birthday."

"But, Mommy, my birthday is *forever* away." She sighed theatrically.

BY THE TIME they returned home, Katy was sound asleep, her new straw cowboy hat askew. As luck would have it, there was a Western wear store in the same shopping center as the pizza place, and Katy had danced a jig when she saw a child mannequin wearing a hat that was a miniature version of J.J.'s.

J.J. had insisted on buying it for her. She'd worn it through dinner and the movie.

J.J. carried Katy inside and held her while Mary Beth made her bed and slipped off her sandals. She had balked at J.J. buying Katy boots, which her daughter had pleaded for, as well.

"You need to put on her pajamas?" J.J. whispered.

Mary Beth shook her head. "Her T-shirt and shorts are okay to sleep in. They're soft." She eased off Katy's new hat and laid it on a chair near the bed, then covered her daughter with the little quilt.

She and J.J. moved away quietly to the front door. "Thanks so much for the evening," Mary Beth told him. "We both really enjoyed ourselves, but I'm going to have to watch you or you'll spoil Katy terribly."

"She's a good kid. A little spoiling won't hurt her. Or you either. You both could use a little pampering, and I enjoy it." He circled his arms behind her waist and smiled down at her. "You wouldn't deny me something I enjoy, would you?"

"I suppose not—if you don't get too carried away."

"I'm making no promises," he said, then his mouth covered hers.

Her knees turned to banana pudding, and she clung to him, kissing him back with a fervor that matched his. If Katy hadn't been lying a few yards away, she would have been tempted to do more than kiss him.

He must have read her mind for he tore his mouth away and hugged her close. "If it weren't for Katy..." he whispered, his breath ragged.

She didn't trust herself to say anything.

"I'll see you in the morning, darlin', and we'll get started on that roof."

"But, J.J., I can't afford to pay for a new roof yet. The price Dean quoted may have been reasonable, but it's way beyond my means for now."

"You let me worry about that."

"No, I will *not* let you worry about it. You're not going to buy me a roof, and that's that."

"Hold your horses, Sugar Beth." He kissed her nose. "It just so happens that I have several squares of shingles left over from roofing my place. They're just sitting in Frank's barn gathering dust. I'm sure there are enough to do the apartment at least. I figure we'll only need a few sheets of plywood to do the job. I've even got some extra nails."

"You'll have to promise to give me the bill."

"What bill? I'm not going to charge you for roofing your place."

"I mean the bill for the plywood and other materials."

"Honey, I don't even remember what those shingles cost. I bought them at a surplus place a year or two ago. Got such a great deal that I took all they had. I've roofed everything from my house to the cow shed and I still have a stack left over. If I don't use them here, they'll just go to waste."

"Are you sure?"

"'Course I'm sure."

Mary Beth wasn't positive that she believed him, but short of calling him a liar, she didn't know what else to say except, "Thanks, J.J."

"You're welcome." He gave her another quick kiss and left.

THE HAMMERING WOKE HER UP. Hammering and the whine of a power saw. She glanced at the clock. It was only seven-thirty. Katy was still sound asleep. Mary Beth dressed quickly, tied her sneakers and, after a couple of swipes with her hairbrush, hurried outside to see what the commotion was.

It seemed that half of Naconiche was either on the roof of the apartment unit or in the yard picking up trash and tossing it onto a trailer hooked to J.J.'s pickup. She greeted several men nearby, then looked around until she spotted J.J. on the roof ridge, without a shirt and with his torso already shiny with sweat.

He spotted her about the same time and waved. He said something to Pete Lowery, an old classmate of hers who was on the ridge near him, and made his way to a ladder and climbed down. Taking off his straw cowboy hat, he wiped his face with a handkerchief from his back pocket and reamed out the inside band of his hat before replacing it on his head.

He looked darned sexy without his shirt, tanned and muscular. She tried not to gape.

"'Mornin'," he said with a big grin.

"Good morning. You're up early."

"We've been here since five-thirty. Did we wake you?"

"*Five-thirty!* Holy cow. Why so early?"

"Roofing is hot work. The idea is to get as much done as you can early in the morning, then knock off when it starts heating up in the afternoon. We've already got the old roof off, and we're putting down the plywood now. It goes fast when you have a big crew."

"Looks like at least half the former football players in my class are on the roof."

"Nope. I believe most of them were baseball players. The football players can't climb ladders anymore."

"I heard that," Chuck Brock said from nearby. "And I resent the hell out of your insinuation. I'm still in fine shape." He grinned and patted his ample belly. Chuck must have weighed at least three hundred pounds.

"Me, too," said Buddy Slokum, who had Chuck beat by a few pounds. "How you doin', Mary Beth?"

"Great, Buddy. Good morning, Chuck. It's wonderful of all of you to get up with the chickens to help."

"We're glad to," Buddy said. "Especially when J.J. promised us one of your special meals."

J.J. looked a little sheepish. "Hope you don't mind twenty or so extra for lunch? I didn't figure on so many takers."

"It's the least I can do. I'll go start some bread baking and get out the spaghetti pot. And from the looks of things, I'd better rustle up a midmorning snack, too."

"I don't think any of us would turn it down," Chuck said, "but we're glad to lend a hand anyhow. A good part of the football team wouldn't have passed algebra if it hadn't been for you tutoring us. Buddy was just saying that we probably owed you at least half of our district trophy."

J.J. loped back to the ladder and climbed up while Mary Beth made the rounds speaking to old friends, asking about their families and thanking them for coming. This was Naconiche neighborliness at its best. Coming home had been the right thing to do.

Katy was waking up when she returned to the tearoom. "What's that noise?" she asked, yawning and stretching.

"J.J. and some friends are putting a new roof on part of the old motel."

"The part where we're going to live?"

"The very one. What would you like for breakfast?"

"Popcorn."

Mary Beth smiled. "What's your second choice?"

"A grilled peanut-butter-and-banana sandwich."

She shuddered at the notion. "Buck has been teaching you some bad habits."

"That's what the king ate. They're delicious."

"Which king?"

"Elvis. Buck said he was the king."

"Well, I suppose if they were good enough for Elvis, they're good enough for you. I may even try one."

She sent Katy to brush her teeth while she folded up their beds and stashed them away. Then she went to the kitchen and put the ingredients for sourdough bread into the machine. She also made a couple of peanut-butter-and-banana sandwiches. While they were grilling, she heated the oven and started mixing a big batch of bran muffins and another of blueberry.

Katy sat on the counter and ate her sandwich along with a glass of milk. Mary Beth grabbed bites of hers between putting muffins in the oven and chopping onions for spaghetti sauce.

"You know, these are good," she told Katy.

"Fit for the king."

"I'll bet you don't even know who Elvis Presley is, do you, sweetie?"

"Uh-huh, I do. He was the best rock-and-roll singer in the world, and he lived at Graceland. Buck told me."

Then Katy started belting out a rendition of "You Ain't Nothin' but a Hound Dog" that had Mary Beth laughing and tapping her toes. She didn't know anybody had come in until she heard clapping in the doorway.

"That was mighty fine, Katy," J.J. said.

"Buck said I was good enough for the Opry. What's the Opry?"

"It's a big stage show they have in Nashville." He turned to Mary Beth. "Frank called to see if Katy was up and to ask if she could spend the day with the twins. Might be a good idea. I wouldn't want her to get hurt around all the construction."

Katy looked anxiously at Mary Beth waiting for her answer.

"I agree. Are you sure Frank doesn't mind?"

"Positive. He says the kids play well together."

"Oh, goodie, goodie, goodie." Katy held out her arms for J.J. to help her down from the counter.

She was about to scoot out the door when J.J. caught her by the waistband of her shorts. "Hang on just a minute, squirt. I'll have to call him back. Don't go outside yet. There are nails and other stuff on the ground."

Katy left to get a game she wanted to take with her while J.J. called Frank on his cell phone.

Mary Beth started browning meat for the sauce, poking clumps apart with one hand while she ate half of her sandwich with the other. J.J. leaned over and took a big chomp from the sandwich.

"Hey," she said. "That's my breakfast."

"It's good. What is it?"

"An Elvis special—grilled peanut-butter-and-banana sandwich."

"You ought to make some more. The guys will love them." He nibbled on her neck, then said, "I gotta go. I don't trust Pete to get that felt straight."

"What felt?"

"The felt you put between the plywood and the shingles."

"Be sure that it's on the bill."

"No bill. There were some extra rolls of felt in the barn with the shingles." He took another bite of her sandwich and left.

"Wait!"

He stuck his head back in the door. "Yes, ma'am?"

"Would you please carry a table outside?"

"Your wish is my command," he said, sweeping off his straw hat as he bowed. "Which one?"

"Any one will do. It's for the snacks."

As soon as the four dozen muffins were done and the sauce was simmering, she brewed a couple of pots of coffee and a big jug of tea, then made a dozen peanut-butter-and-banana sandwiches. After they were grilled, she cut them into quarters and carried the sandwiches and muffins outside and put them on the table. When she returned with coffee, tea and paper cups, the platters were clean and twenty men were licking their fingers.

"That was really good, Mary Beth," Pete said.

"Yeah," Chuck said, "especially those little peanut butter things. I could eat a dozen of them."

"I think you did," Buddy said. "I sure didn't get one."

"I'll make some more," Mary Beth told them.

She had to slice the bananas a little thinner to go around, but she put together another dozen sandwiches and carried out a big bowl of grapes as well. By the time Frank arrived ten minutes later, nothing was left on the food table except grape stems.

She decided they'd simply have to wait until lunch before the next feeding or she'd run out of food. To be on the safe side, she doubled the meat sauce, put on another loaf of bread and took two extra from the freezer to thaw. After she assembled a huge bowl of salad and stowed it in the fridge, she dumped several restaurant-size cans of ranch beans in a pot, added a few extra touches and started them simmering. Then she filled pots with water to boil and went outside to survey the work.

Wes Outlaw had arrived and was standing by the table drinking tea from a paper cup. "'Mornin'," he said, smiling and touching his hat brim. "Looks like the boys have been busy. J.J. tells me that he believes you'll have a roof by afternoon—or near about."

"It's unbelievable. I almost feel I'm at an old-fashioned barn raising. All I have to do is provide the food."

"That's quite a chore for this bunch." His eyes twinkled as he chuckled. "Think you can handle a couple of more for lunch?"

She laughed. "Sure. What's a couple of more? I'm making spaghetti in a washtub."

"That's what Nonie used to say when the boys brought their friends home with them. Swore those kids had bottomless pits for stomachs."

"I was asking 'cause a couple of friends of mine are coming by to check out the plumbing and electricity. J.J. sort of promised them lunch every day next week at your place for their time."

"That's wonderful, but Sheriff Wes, I'm afraid J.J. is moving a little too fast. I don't know that I can afford too many plumbing and electrical supplies."

"Well, they can at least take a look at things. May be that you won't have to replace a lot. And some things, like bathroom fixtures, you can pick up at the salvage yard for a little of nothing if you know what to look for."

"I wouldn't have a clue what to look for."

Wes grinned. "Yeah, but Will does. He and Curtis are retired and don't have much to do these days except play dominoes and swap lies. Like me, they're a little slower than they used to be, but they can still get the job done. Good men. You going to paint the outside of the units or put up siding?"

"I'll have to paint. I can't afford siding. I was thinking that I might paint the front of the whole row. That way, even though the insides of the other units are still a mess, the place will look more presentable and less like the Bates Motel."

Wes frowned. "The Bates Motel?"

"You know, the one in the movie *Psycho.*"

"Oh, yeah. I saw the original. 'Bout scared the pants off me when that woman screamed. It's pretty tame by today's standards. Say, if you're planning to paint the outside, how about I start doing some scrapin' and sandin'? I'll get some of these boys that are just standing around to make themselves useful and help me."

"I really appreciate it, Sheriff Wes."

"Glad to help. Makes me feel good. And I told you to drop that Sheriff before my name. J.J.'s the sheriff now—and doing a fine job. I'm right proud of that boy. And he's got a new spring in his step and twinkle in his eye these days. I 'spect that's your doin'." He winked and ambled off.

BY THREE O'CLOCK THAT afternoon, Mary Beth had a new roof. The holes in the other units were patched, the trash in the yard was cleaned up and the entire motel's exterior had been scraped and sanded and was ready to paint. There wasn't a strand of spaghetti or a bean or a leaf of lettuce left in the pots. Only two pieces remained from the three large bundt cakes Mary Beth had baked, and she sent them home with Wes for Nonie.

Everybody had gone home except J.J., and he sat in the tearoom, shirt unbuttoned and reared back in a chair, drinking a second glass of raspberry tea with Mary Beth. "I believe that in a couple of days," he said, "Will can get the plumbing hooked up so that you can at least take a bath in the apartment bathroom."

"But we still have to put down a floor in there, and the tile has to be replaced, and the wallboard as well."

"I figured that I would refloor it tomorrow afternoon. Maybe we could do the tile Monday afternoon. The wallboard can wait until we do the rest of the rooms."

"Having a real working bathtub would be wonderful."

"Oh, I don't know," he said, a slow grin spreading over his face. "I kind of liked your outdoor location."

"J. J. Outlaw! I thought you weren't going to mention that."

"Didn't promise that I wasn't going to mention it. Just said I wouldn't tell anybody. And I won't. You think I want some of the guys in this town sneaking a peek of you in the tub?"

"*J.J.!*"

He laughed. "Oh, Sugar Beth, don't get all bent out of joint. I'm sorry I teased you."

Sugar Beth. He'd used that old nickname a couple of times lately. That's what he'd called her when they were younger.

"I won't be taking any more baths outside."

"How much would it take to get you to change your mind?"

"A lot more than you have, buster," she said with a saucy grin.

"Mary Beth, if you want it, you can have everything I've got. Everything."

"Be careful what you offer," she said playfully. "Or I might just take you up on it."

"I wish you would. I'm serious, Mary Beth. It just about kills me to see you working yourself to death on this place and having to sleep in a corner of a restaurant and take a bath in an old tub in the yard. Why don't you marry me and let me take care of you?"

Fury over took her. "Take care of me? *Take care* of me?" she said, her voice getting shrill. "Do you know how insulting that is, Jesse James Outlaw? I don't need you to *take care* of me, thank you very much. I can take care of myself."

"Now don't go getting all in a snit, Sugar Beth, I—"

"I'm *not* in a snit! And don't call me Sugar Beth. It's juvenile, and I'm a grown woman. J.J., I appreciate all that you've done for me, but I've told you a dozen times that I can take care of myself. It may take me a little longer, but I can manage. I'm not some helpless little wimp who has to have a husband to tend to her and make all her decisions. Been there, done that, and I'm not going there again. Get that through your thick head."

J.J.'s feet hit the floor. "Forget I mentioned it," he ground out.

"I'll do my best."

"Okay, then." He crammed his hat on his head. "I'll see you tomorrow."

"J.J., you don't have to spend your whole weekend—"

"I'll see you tomorrow." He stalked out the door.

Mary Beth started after him. That man could do more

to infuriate her than anyone else she could think of. Yet at the same time she was undeniably drawn to him. Sparks of one sort or the other flashed between them constantly. What a muddle her emotions were in!

And *marriage?* Where had that come from? She couldn't believe he was serious. What on earth had prompted him to say such a thing? Did he feel so sorry for her that he was willing to *sacrifice* himself for poor little her? There was a *huge* difference between being a helpful friend and "taking care of her." Did he think that she didn't have a brain in her head or any gumption at all? All her life she seemed to have been smothered by control freaks—her father, Brad and now J.J. again. She felt like a two-year-old fighting for autonomy.

Men! Damn them all! They just confused things.

Chapter Thirteen

When Mary Beth and Katy arrived home after church, J.J.'s pickup truck was parked in front of the motel, and she could hear hammering. She sent Katy inside to change into play clothes, walked over to the apartment and went in.

J.J. was hammering plywood to the bathroom floor, and he'd already worked up a sweat. His shirt hung on a nail by the door.

"Hello there," she said, stopping outside the small room. She felt a little awkward after their exchange the day before.

He glanced up and smiled as he looked her over. "Hello yourself. You look awfully pretty."

"Thanks. It's good to be able to wear high heels again. We've been to church. I didn't see you there."

"Went to early service. I wanted to get this floor down before it got too hot. It's supposed to be a scorcher today. Given any thought to how you want to heat and cool this place? The old window units are shot, and I wouldn't trust those wall heaters come winter."

"I hadn't even thought about heating and cooling. I was more concerned with walls and a roof. I suppose that it will be expensive."

He nodded and stood up, dragging a handkerchief from his back pocket as he rose.

Sweat beaded his skin. One particular drop caught her attention as it rolled down his throat and moved slowly down his chest. Her eyes followed its leisurely descent until it puddled in his navel. Another drop followed. His bare navel seemed suddenly very erotic, and she ached to run her fingers over it. And over his damp chest, and—

"Mary Beth," J.J. said, his voice soft and husky.

Aware that she'd been caught staring, she immediately yanked her attention to his face. His dark eyes had gone darker still, and naked hunger marked his face.

Unsettled by what she'd seen, she turned away, suddenly aware that perspiration was popping out on her as well. She fanned herself with the small handbag she carried. "It's very warm in here, isn't it?"

"And getting warmer by the minute." His tone was blatantly suggestive.

Marshaling her composure, she turned and tried to remember what they'd been talking about. Heating and cooling. Ductwork. She smiled nervously. "Texas summers are always hot. What do you suggest?"

"It's always been my feeling that if you've got an itch, you ought to scratch it." He swiped his handkerchief over his chest. And over his navel.

Aware that her gaze had followed the handkerchief's path, she jerked her attention away again, her face fiery. "I was talking about heating and cooling the apartment, about ductwork and such," she said sharply.

He chuckled, blast him. "Uh-huh."

"I was! What do you suggest I do about air-conditioning and heating for this place?"

"You can always pick up a couple of used window

units to use at least temporarily through the summer, but come winter, you'll have to think about keeping warm.'' He gave her a lopsided grin that told her that he'd be happy to provide the warmth.

''*J.J.,* stop that.''

He sobered. But his eyes still danced with mischief. ''Of course you could use space heaters, but a heat pump to do for both would be my recommendation.''

A heat pump? Was there such a thing or was it another of his double entendres? Dare she ask? No, she wasn't walking into that one. She simply nodded and said, ''I see.''

''I'd also suggest you have the place wired and set up for ducts before we put up the drywall.''

She sighed and nodded. ''It sounds like it will be a while before Katy and I can sleep here.''

''Mary Beth—''

She held up her hand to prevent him saying more. Sometimes it was hard to keep up her spirits when things seemed so overwhelming. ''Let me go change clothes. Ellen and I went to the superstore last night and found some ceramic tile on a closeout sale. It was a real deal. I bought a couple of boxes and the stuff to stick it up with. I've been reading a book I got from the library, and I think I can put it up.''

''You think a couple of boxes will be enough?'' he asked.

''Oh, sure. Lots of tiles are still up, and I saved all the old ones that had come loose and cleaned them. I knew I couldn't match the old and new, so I thought I'd combine them in a checkerboard pattern or maybe do alternating rows.''

''Did you get a trowel?''

''Uh, what kind of trowel?''

"The kind with the little teeth notched in it for spreading the thin-set."

"Oh, one of those doohickeys. Yes, I got all that in a kit, including one of those chalk-line snappers. Handy little tool."

"Uh-huh. You have a level?"

"I have a yardstick."

He grinned. "It's not the same. You have to make sure all the rows of tiles are level and plumb or you'll have a mess."

"Right." She must have skipped that part when she was reading. She wasn't about to admit that she didn't know what a level looked like or what plumb was.

"Want to borrow mine?"

Why did everything that came out of his mouth sound suggestive? "Your what?"

"My level."

"Sure. I'd appreciate it."

"What are you going to attach the tile to?"

"Those two walls," she said. But as she pointed to them, she realized that the old walls where the tiles had been were gone. Nothing remained but the studs. Dismayed, she said, "What happened to the walls?"

"I tore them out before I started on the floor. Honey, they were a mess."

"But there were good tiles still up, and I was planning to—" She hushed before she started bawling. That morning, she'd hardly listened to the sermon for planning how she would put up the tiles. She could already imagine how it would look and she was excited about doing it herself.

Despite her best effort a tear must have escaped, because J.J. looked as if he'd just run over a family pet.

"Oh, hell, honey, I'm sorry." He gathered her into his arms.

She pushed him away. "It's fine, really it is. Maybe I can salvage some of the tiles. Where are they?"

"In the back of the pickup. But I don't think you'll be able to use any of them."

"I'll go see." She hurried outside, keeping her fingers crossed.

Not more than a dozen of the tiles had survived intact. What hadn't been broken or cracked when the walls were torn down didn't survive being tossed into the pickup bed. She wanted to weep.

"Oh, God, Mary Beth, I feel like a dirty dog. I didn't know you wanted to save those old tiles."

She lifted her chin. "I tore down all the other walls. I left those deliberately."

"I know that now. Look, I think I've got enough cement board in the barn to cover those walls. And I've got some tiles, too. Maybe enough. If not, I'll get you some more."

"J.J., you're doing too much as it is."

"No, I'm not doing enough." He put his arms around her again. "I'm sorry that I screwed up your plans, but trust me, those walls needed to go. They were bowed and disintegrating in spots. Cement board is a better choice. Besides, you need new insulation in that outside wall. Go change your clothes and let me finish up the floor. Then you and Katy and I can grab a bite to eat, then go over to the barn and rummage through all the stuff I have stored there. I think I have a scrap of vinyl that will fit the bathroom floor here. I wanted you to look at it anyhow. Okay?"

Clutching the few undamaged tiles, she nodded and went to change.

"HOLY SMOKE! Where did you get all this?" she asked as she picked her way through the stuff in the barn.

"Here and there. Some of it was left over when I built the fourplex, some when I remodeled Frank's house, some of it I'm using in my house."

"Which you haven't worked on since I've been in town."

He shrugged. "I told you it could wait."

"You haven't shown me your house. When do I get to see it?"

"It's not much more than a frame and a roof yet. When I get a little further along, maybe you can help me with the decorating. I'm not much good at that part."

"I'd be happy to. What is cement board?"

He rapped a knuckle on some sheets of material leaning against a wall. "This stuff." He pulled it out and looked it over. "I think there's more than enough here."

"Need any help?" Frank asked, joining them in the barn.

"Yeah, grab one end of this," J.J. said, "and help me put it in the truck. We're fixing Mary Beth's bathroom at the motel."

"Got it," Frank said. "Say, isn't this—"

"Yeah, it's that cement board I had left over from building the fourplex. And I think I have several boxes of tile, too. Mary Beth is going to look at it to see if she likes it."

"Can I help?" she asked.

"No, we've got it," J.J. said. "You might look in those boxes behind you. I think there's some tile in them."

While the guys carried out the cement board, which

simply looked like gray wallboard to her, she poked through the boxes that J.J. had pointed out. There *was* tile inside. Beautiful tile. Several boxes held a creamy yellow tile with a texture like slate. There was also a box with some slender trim pieces of the same soft yellow with terra-cotta, white and muted green designs.

"You like those?"

"They're lovely, but they look much more expensive than the ones I bought."

"You want 'em, you got 'em."

"But J.J.—"

"Honey, they're just sitting here gathering dust. You might as well have them. Besides, I ruined your other tiles. I owe you. There ought to be plenty to do your bathroom at the apartment. And check out this piece of vinyl. What do you think of it for the floor?" He untied a roll of floor covering and opened it.

"It's perfect." And it was. A pale terra-cotta, it looked like intricately laid Mexican tile instead of vinyl. "I hope it fits."

"If it doesn't, I have another piece or two of scrap that might," J.J. said, "but I think this one might be the better match for the tile."

Frank and J.J. laid it out and measured. It would fit with a foot to spare in one direction and three inches in the other.

"Good deal," J.J. said. "Frank, would you load this up while I get some more supplies?"

"Will do. You need help installing any of this stuff?"

"I think I can get it, Frank. We're going to wait on putting up the walls until the plumbing's done, right?" J.J. asked Mary Beth.

She glanced at her watch. "Right. And I have to get

to the store before it closes to pick up fruit and vegetables.''

In the end, it was decided that Katy could stay and
play with the twins under the eagle eye of Frank's
housekeeper, Matilda. Frank and J.J. would unload all
the material and finish patching the floor in the other
rooms, and Mary Beth would do her shopping for the
tearoom menu. They loaded up the pickup and went
back to the motel.

By the time she returned with her groceries, Frank
and J.J. were sitting under a tree in front, laughing and
sipping beers.

''You guys don't look hard at work to me,'' she said.

''We just finished,'' J.J. said. ''The floor is now
sound. I'll take your stuff to the kitchen.''

''I'll help.'' Frank got up and dusted off his jeans.
''Sorry I missed the roofing yesterday. I had to work. I
heard that your peanut-butter-and-banana sandwiches
were worth a day's work.''

Mary Beth laughed. ''They ate me out of bananas
and nearly out of peanut butter. I've replenished the
supplies. Want one?''

''Sure,'' Frank said.

''Don't leave me out,'' J.J. said.

Both men ate two.

''Want another?'' Mary Beth asked.

''I would,'' Frank said, ''but I don't want to ruin my
dinner. Matilda made pot roast. You guys want to join
us? She cooked what looked like enough for fifteen or
twenty people.''

''Thanks, but I'll pass,'' Mary Beth said. ''I have to
do prep work for tomorrow's menu.''

''And I have to finish up that paperwork that I'm

behind on," J.J. said, "but thanks. Mary Beth, I'll drop off Frank and bring Katy home."

"I seem to be thanking you all the time and thanks don't seem enough. I can't tell you how much I appreciate all you've done," she said.

"No problem. I'm enjoying myself."

ON THE WAY TO Frank's house, Frank said, "J.J., wasn't that cement board and those tiles what you'd bought for your house?"

"Yes, but Mary Beth doesn't know it. She doesn't know that I bought the shingles either, and for God's sake don't tell her or my ass is grass. As far as she's concerned all that material is scrap or she'd never use it."

"You think lying to her is a good idea?"

"I haven't exactly lied. I've just skirted the truth a little. I did have a piece or two of cement board left over from when I remodeled your house, and there was an extra square of shingles, too."

"There weren't enough shingles left to roof a doghouse," Frank said.

"Nobody knows that except you and me, and I'm sure as hell not telling her. Are you?"

Frank shook his head. "I'll keep my mouth shut, but I still think you're making a mistake. From what little I've been around Mary Beth, I'd say she's a proud woman. If you take away her self-respect, you're in trouble, little brother."

"I know that. She's always on my case about my butting into her business and trying to run her life, but hell, Frank, she and that kid are sleeping in a *restaurant* for God's sake. And the other day I found her outside— well, never mind what I found her doing, but I'm going to bust my butt trying to at least fix her a decent place to live.''

Frank grinned. ''Why don't you just marry the girl, J.J.?''

''Don't you think I've thought of that? She turned me down flat.''

''That so? Well, I guess maybe she's not interested in you in that way, though that's not the impression I've been getting. Seems like there's a lot of sizzle between the two of you.''

''Well, we haven't—I mean, well, the way she kisses me...''

''Sizzles.''

''I guess you could say that.''

''Maybe it was the way you asked her. Women like to be romanced, you know.''

''Oh, hell, Frank, I'm not much good at the romantic stuff.''

Frank laughed. ''I'd say it's about time you learned if you want Mary Beth.''

''I want her. I'll give it some thought.''

And he did. He gave it a lot of thought. He also worked at getting that bathroom fixed for her. He ''found'' some insulation batts in the barn. He goosed Will and Curtis a mite, and they got right on to the plumbing and wiring. They both did a good job, and the expense wasn't too bad. J.J. slipped them both a little under the table so that the bill for the materials that Mary Beth saw was a manageable amount for her.

In fact, Mary Beth commented on it when they were hammering up the cement board at the end of the week. ''I was pleasantly surprised at how little it cost to do the plumbing and wiring. Curtis said he got a deal on the wire, and it didn't take that many plugs and switches. He said he had a lot of the stuff just sitting around his garage from when he was in business. And Will said that he'd found a steal on a hot-water heater. It had a dent in it or something."

That evening, J.J. went to Frank's barn and whacked the new hot-water heater with a monkey wrench.

J.J. had been with Mary Beth just about every afternoon and evening that week. They'd spent a couple of days refinishing the old bathtub and painting the outside of it yellow to match the tiles. They'd moved it inside one of the gutted rooms of the unit to do their work, but it wouldn't be hooked up until the tile was done and the vinyl laid. They'd also put up drywall on the ceiling and the rest of the area not being tiled.

Business was still brisk in the tearoom. On Friday afternoon, after the lunch rush and when Mary Beth had time to catch her breath, J.J. dropped by and helped her snap guidelines for the tile. She was ready to start slapping thin-set on the walls right then, but he stopped her.

"How about we knock off for the day?" he said.

"But it's still early."

"I know, but I thought you and Katy might like to go to the rodeo out at the fairgrounds tonight."

"A *rodeo?*" Katy said from where she sat astraddle a sawhorse pretending it was a pony. "With horses and cowboys?"

"You betcha. It's a junior rodeo, and all the entrants are kids."

"Can I be in it?" Katy asked.

"*May* I?" Mary Beth said, "And certainly not. It's dangerous. I imagine the kids are a lot older than you."

"Right," J.J. said. "Want to go?"

"Oh, Mommy, please, please, please. I've never been to a real rodeo."

She raised her eyebrows at J.J. and said, "Why do I feel like I've been suckered into this?"

KATY WORE HER STRAW HAT like J.J.'s, and her eyes were like saucers the whole time. They ran into Ellen and her two boys as well as Frank and the twins. They all sat together and ate hot dogs and peanuts and cheered for the calf ropers and barrel racers.

Mary Beth enjoyed herself almost as much as Katy did.

On the way home, Katy yawned and said wistfully, "I wish I had a pony."

Mary Beth remembered that she, too, had wished desperately for a pony when she was a little girl. Little girls didn't understand about the practical aspects of a large animal, so rather than explain that they couldn't afford it and didn't have a place to keep it, she simply let it pass. "The rodeo was fun, wasn't it? What part did you like best?"

"When the girls rode around the barrels," Katy said, "I could do that. If I had a pony."

So much for distractions.

By the time they pulled through the grove of trees at The Twilight Tearoom, Katy was asleep. Again, J.J. carried her in and held her while Mary Beth made her bed. Setting aside the small straw hat, she slipped off Katy's sneakers and jeans, and J.J. tucked the quilt around her. Katy didn't even stir.

"She won't rouse until morning. I wish I slept as peacefully," Mary Beth whispered as she walked J.J. to the door.

"You don't?"

She shook her head. "I suppose I have too much on my mind. I worry about what would happen if people stopped coming to the tearoom. Everything has happened so fast that it seems like a dream. What if it doesn't last?''

J.J. eased the front door shut, and they walked together out to his pickup. "As long as the food is as good as it is, I don't think you have to worry about that. Business hasn't fallen off, has it?''

"No. We've had a full house every day so far, and I've booked a couple more special luncheons.''

"There you go. You've worked hard, and your place is a big success.'' He leaned against the truck fender and pulled her to him. Soft moonlight filtered through the trees overhead and shone in his eyes. "I'm very proud of you, Mary Beth.''

"Thanks.''

He lifted her chin. "I'm also crazy about you.''

His mouth covered hers in a kiss so potent she could have sworn shooting stars filled the sky.

The kiss went on and on, and she grew more frenzied with every rapid heartbeat. She couldn't get close enough to get her fill of him. His hands were all over her, and she reveled in the sensation of his touch.

"Oh, Lord, Mary Beth, I want you.''

"I want you, too,'' she moaned between kisses.

He began unbuttoning her blouse, kissing her throat and moving his mouth downward as the fabric fell open. She wanted to touch his bare skin, too. She ached to run her fingers over the chest her eyes had coveted, so she tugged his shirt from his waistband and allowed her fantasies to become reality.

Touching wasn't enough. She wanted more, longed to have him fill her. When she told him so, he went wild.

"J.J.,'' she said between ragged breaths, "we have

to stop. We're outside. Somebody might pass by and see us."

"I'll kill anybody who looks."

She laughed, but she didn't push him away. At that moment, she was so hungry for him that she didn't care who saw her.

"I'd give a million bucks for a bed right now. Wait." He pulled away and opened the pickup door. He rummaged through the glove compartment, then grabbed a tattered quilt from the back. "This will have to do." He tossed the quilt into the truck bed, then let down the tailgate and lifted her up onto it.

They didn't make it to the quilt. Clothes went here and there, and he barely had time to slide on protection before he took her as she sat on the tailgate.

It was glorious. She wrapped her legs around his waist and surrendered to raw sensations. It was hot and hard and fast.

She came first, then J.J., seconds later.

She could only hang on for dear life. He uttered her name over and over. When their breathing had stilled, he whispered, "I'm sorry, darlin'. This isn't the place I wanted to make love to you. I wanted it to be special."

"It doesn't matter."

"And I wanted it to last longer. A lot longer."

She smiled. "Do you have a curfew?"

He laughed. "Not hardly. I can spend all night right here. But that quilt might be softer for what I had in mind." He withdrew and unzipped his jeans, then climbed up himself and spread down the quilt. He yanked off his boots and pulled her into his arms again.

This time was slow and easy but just as passionate.

As they lay back on the quilt and looked at the stars through breaks in the canopy of trees, he held her close against him and stroked her gently. "This is about as close to heaven as I've been in a long, long time."

"Me, too, I haven't felt quite this way since—"

"Since we were kids?"

She nodded. "You were my first, you know."

"I know. I should have been your only. I love you so, Mary Beth. I've loved you since I was sixteen years old and I've never stopped. Nobody could take your place. I tried to find somebody else, believe me I tried, but the memory of you was always there."

His words brought tears to her eyes. She cared for him deeply, and the passion was there for sure, but did she love him in the same way? Could she say "I love you" and mean it? Suddenly she knew.

"I love you, too, J.J."

He clutched her to him so hard he almost squeezed the breath from her. "God, how I've wanted to hear those words from you. Marry me, Mary Beth."

She looked up at him and stroked his face. How easy it would be to say yes, but there were a dozen reasons why she couldn't. One of the major ones, of course, was her ex-husband, but she was ashamed to tell him about Brad Parker. No way would she subject J.J. to the embarrassment of marrying the ex-wife of a convict. If the truth ever got out, small-town gossip would rip him apart. But there were other reasons why they shouldn't marry.

"J.J., I love you, no question about it. I suppose that I have forever. You've always been my knight in shining armor, but right now I don't want a knight in shining armor. I need to learn to fight my own dragons."

"I don't know what in the hell you're talking about. I love you. You love me. I'm crazy about Katy, and I'll be a good father to her. Let's get married."

She shook her head. "It's impossible. There are things you don't know, things you don't understand."

"If you're talking about your marriage, I don't want to know. That part of your life is over and done with. I'm only concerned with our future. Don't cut me out again."

"I don't want to cut you out, but I'm sorry, J.J., if you're insisting on marriage, the answer is no. There are too many problems, and I don't want to go down that road again."

"But damnation, Mary Beth, we—"

She kissed him to stop his argument. At that moment, she didn't want to think about all the reasons they couldn't get married. She only wanted to savor the intimacy.

Chapter Fourteen

On his way home, J.J. wanted to beat his head against the steering wheel. He'd rushed her and gotten an answer he didn't want to hear. Would he ever learn? Slow and easy, he told himself. Give her room. Romance her for God's sake! Making love in the hard bed of a pickup truck wasn't romantic in anybody's book.

But it was so fine.

He grinned remembering.

They spent all day Saturday and most of Sunday working on the new bathroom. By the time she and Katy left on Sunday afternoon to pick up fresh vegetables for the tearoom menu, the tiles were up and the new vinyl was installed.

The minute Mary Beth's SUV pulled away, he worked like a son of a gun to wrestle the tub into place and hook up the plumbing. After making sure that everything was working right, he brought in the big sacks of stuff he'd stashed in the truck. Ellen had helped him by picking out some of the things...well, all of the things. He didn't know much about bubble bath and towels and candles, but he did his best.

He hung the new towels over the towel racks and set the candles in their holders all around the room. Seemed like an awful lot of candles to him, but women were supposed to like that kind of thing. They smelled good, he thought, sniffing a couple of the two dozen or so.

A little white wicker table went beside the tub, and he put the fancy bottles of bubble bath on it. The bubble stuff smelled good, too. He raised the window and hooked up the electric fan he'd bought the day before so she wouldn't suffocate in the heat, then checked his watch.

She should be back any minute.

He opened the last sack and hung the new white terry-cloth robe on a wall hook and set the matching slippers beside the tub. When everything was ready, he started the water running and dumped in some of the bubble stuff. While the tub was filling, he lit all the candles.

Just about the time he got the last one lit, he heard her SUV pull up. He hurriedly turned off the water, added one last touch, then wadded up all the sacks and went outside to meet her.

"Hi," he said, smiling. "That didn't take long."

"No, now that the wholesaler delivers, I only have to pick up fresh veggies and fruit and a few personal things. Did you get the tub hooked up?"

"I did," he said. "Why don't you go take a look at it while Katy and I put these groceries away?"

"I'll look at it later. I'd like a glass of tea. I'm parched."

"Go ahead, look at it now. I'll fix your tea."

"I want to see the new bathtub!"

J.J. caught Katy as she streaked by. "I have a surprise for you, young lady."

"You do? What?"

Frank's car pulled up and honked. Janey and Jimmy leaned out the windows, waving and calling.

"There it is. Hamburgers and miniature golf with the twins. Now scoot."

"Yippee!" Katy yelled, running to the car without even looking back.

As Frank's car left, Mary Beth laughed and said, "Why do I think that you might have suggested the evening out for them?"

"Can't imagine." He grinned and winked. "Let me get these bags to the kitchen. I'll put everything in the refrigerator while you check out the tub."

"I'll help. It won't take but a couple of minutes."

Oh, hell, the bubbles would be pooped out and the candles burned down if she lollygagged around much longer. "Go see the damned bathroom!" He grabbed armloads of sacks and hightailed it to the kitchen.

He put away the groceries in record time, then fixed a glass of tea and hotfooted it out to the apartment unit.

Her clothes were in a puddle by the door, and she sat in the tub, hair clipped up, chin deep in bubbles. He couldn't see the little yellow duck, but he knew it was in there somewhere.

"You dear, sweet man," she said, her smile more dazzling than the flickering candles.

"Like it?"

"I love it."

"Good." He grinned and handed her the frosty glass of tea he held.

She took a sip. "Ahh. This is almost perfect. Only one thing is missing."

He sobered. *Oh, hell, he'd forgotten something.* "What?"

"You."

He shucked his clothes in nothing flat. He didn't even stop to take off his hat.

MARY BETH SMILED at the four old-timers playing dominoes under the shade of the big oak tree out front of the restaurant. Will, Curtis, B.D. and Howard had moved their game temporarily to The Twilight Tearoom and Motel the week before when Will and Curtis were working on plumbing and wiring, and they all stayed on to work for their lunch and have a few games afterward. She had invited them inside the tearoom to eat, but they claimed they were too grimy and asked for a table to be set up outside. The table had stayed.

Curtis was still working on the wiring for the apartment, and the others had pitched in to do some outside painting. They all worked a couple of hours a day, and the place was shaping up.

The clapboard outside was about to get a second coat of a light buckskin color that was a couple of shades lighter than the stucco walls of the restaurant. The trim would be white, and she hadn't decided what color to paint the doors. Black maybe. Or perhaps Williamsburg-green.

Even though the insides of the other units were still a mess, at least the outside was beginning to look presentable. She was hoping to clear enough at the tearoom this week to buy some insulation and drywall for the apartment. If not this week, then maybe next. She'd just do things a little at a time as she could afford it. Until then, she planned to spend her afternoons cleaning out the next of the motel units.

"You fellows want another glass of tea?" she asked as she passed.

"We're doing just fine, Mary Beth," Curtis said.

"But much obliged anyhow," Will added. "We'll be quitting directly. It's getting a mite warm."

"You're welcome to move inside," Mary Beth said.

"Thanks," B.D. said, "but it's about time for Howard's nap."

"*Whose* nap?" Howard said with a snort. "*I'm* not the one that takes a snooze in the middle of the day."

They all laughed, including Katy, who was sitting in Mr. Will's lap. The old fellows had taken a shine to Katy and were teaching her the finer points of dominoes. She loved sitting very quietly with them and watching. Will often let her play his domino when it was his turn.

Mary Beth unlocked the second unit and propped the door open to catch the breeze. The electricity didn't extend to the other units yet, and it was dim inside, even with the plywood removed from the front windows. Each unit was one large room with a kitchenette in one rear corner and a small closet and bath partitioned off in the other.

She made a quick survey of the items in the room. The mattresses on the twin beds would have to go. Some of the furniture possibly could be salvaged. With some sanding and painting, the bed frames would do, maybe even the nightstands. The table and chairs were iffy. The little fridge and stove looked as though their best days had come and gone. When she could afford to fix up these units to rent, a microwave and mini-fridge were a better choice for the small space.

She dragged the first old mattresses outside and started around to the back.

"Need any help, Mary Beth?" Curtis called.

"Thanks, I'm doing fine."

Just as she hauled the second stained and rotted mattress out, Wes Outlaw drove up in his pickup. She waved, then started carrying her load around to the burning area in back.

"Hang on there," Wes called. "Let me give you a hand with that."

"It's not heavy. I can manage."

"Maybe so," he said, taking over the job, "but I'd feel terrible standing around watching you strain yourself. Got something for you. Go take a look in the back of the truck while I get rid of this. Will, you take a look, too."

"I'll be right along. Katy and me are fixin' to score big, and that'll be the game."

"You wish," Howard said.

"Thanks, Wes." Mary Beth smiled at the good-natured ribbing among the old friends and went to peek in the back of the truck. Perched there, twinkling in the sunlight, was a toilet. And not just the standard model. This was a really nice toilet. A white one. And there was also a beautiful pedestal sink with brass and glass handles. Was she crazy to be excited over the pristine bathroom fixtures?

She was admiring the toilet when Will and Katy joined her. Will hoisted Katy up to the fender so that she could see, then he said, "Very nice. Where'd you pick these up, Wes? I can't see that they've been used."

"Haven't been hardly. I fixed an old clock for a lady over in Cherokee and I went to deliver it today. Mrs. Hale's got more money than she's got sense. Lives all by herself in a big fine house, and she was redecorating her powder room to some fancy flowered stuff. She was about to throw these out, so I offered to buy them from her. Paid her ten dollars for the sink and the commode."

"Ten dollars?" Mary Beth exclaimed.

"Boy, you got a steal," Will said. "Come 'ere, y'all and look," he called to the other players.

Everybody gathered around and eyed Wes's find, mumbling admiring comments.

"Let's haul 'em in," Howard said. "Will, you got your tools?"

"Got my tools, but I'll need a wax ring before I seat the toilet. We'll set them inside, Mary Beth, and I'll hook them up first thing in the morning." He winked at her. "What's for lunch tomorrow?"

"Beef stroganoff and spinach salad."

"Hoo boy," Will said. "I can taste it already."

"I think you got a tapeworm," B.D. said. "You haven't been done with your dinner more'n an hour or two and already you're talking food again." He gave Mary Beth a big grin, showing off his perfect dentures. "What's for dessert?"

"What would you like?"

"Well…I'm right partial to that chocolate cake you make. You know, the one with that thick chocolate icing and pecans on top."

"I'll make one."

He grinned even wider and went to help unload the toilet.

Mary Beth thanked them all, then repaid Wes the ten dollars he'd spent on the fixtures.

When all the men had gone, Katy helped Mary Beth carry some of the smaller furniture to another unit for storage. "You're a good helper, Katy," she said as she removed the door of the old refrigerator. "How about we stop for a snack and a cold drink? It's getting hot in here."

"Okay. What's this, Mommy?" She pointed to an old humpback trunk in the closet.

"Hmm. I don't know." With great effort, she dragged it out of the closet. It was heavy. And it was locked. "I'll see if I can find something to open it with later. I'm thirsty."

"Me, too. Can I have a Popsicle?"

"*May* I? And yes, you may. In fact, a Popsicle sounds good."

Ellen dropped by about the time they were going inside the tearoom and she joined them. By the time J.J. arrived a few minutes later, all three were sitting at a table slurping on orange Popsicles.

"Want one?" Mary Beth asked.

He laughed. "I haven't had a Popsicle since I was about twelve."

"Then it's been too long. I have orange or grape," Mary Beth told him. "Pick one."

"Grape."

"I'll get it for you."

"Keep your seat. I'll find it."

"We have a new toilet," Katy said. "Mr. Will is going to hook it up tomorrow. Mr. Wes stole it from a rich lady in Cherokee."

J.J. frowned and looked at Mary Beth. "Is that true?"

She grinned. "More or less. The Popsicles are on the second shelf behind the chicken tenders."

"I'll show you," Katy said.

"Do I want to find out more about my dad stealing toilets."

"And a sink," Katy said. "Are you gonna put him in the pokey?"

"Probably not with him being kin and all," J.J. said seriously, "but I may have to consider a time-out." He winked at Mary Beth, then headed for the kitchen freezer.

Ellen rose. "Well, no rest for the wicked. I have to go. The boys have a swimming lesson in twenty minutes. You and Katy want to come over for hot dogs later? We're grilling in the backyard."

"Sure, we'd love to."

Ellen fluttered her fingers. "See you about six-thirty."

J.J. came back in licking a grape Popsicle. "Say, these aren't bad. Where are you going about six-thirty?" He leaned over and casually kissed her. "Your lips are cold."

"So are yours. And your tongue is turning purple. Think the criminals of the county will ever take a purple-tongued sheriff seriously?"

"Ah, but it's a wicked tongue. Want me to show you?" He came at her, flicking his tongue as if he were a snake.

Mary Beth squealed and tried to duck. "Don't, don't! J.J., don't." She was strangling with laughter as J.J. held her and licked her lips. "Don't!" she squealed again.

Katy came running out of the kitchen and started beating at J.J. "Don't you hurt my mommy! Don't you hurt her. Leave her alone."

J.J. stopped immediately. He squatted down beside Katy. "Honey, we were only playing. I would never hurt your mommy."

Katy glanced at Mary Beth.

"It's true, honey," she said to her daughter. "He was only teasing and trying to lick me with his cold purple tongue."

"Let me see your tongue," Katy demanded.

J.J. stuck it out.

Katy giggled. "It *is* purple."

"And it's cold, and I'm going to lick you with it," he said, making a swipe on her cheek.

She squealed with laughter. "Don't! Or I'll lick you with my cold orange tongue."

"No, no," he said, feigning a horrified expression.

Katy giggled again and went after him.

"Enough of the licking," Mary Beth said. "You two are dripping all over the floor. Guess who's going to have to mop if you don't cut it out? And it's not going to be me."

"Yes, ma'am," J.J. said, taking a seat at the table when she sat.

"Yes, ma'am," echoed Katy, sliding into another chair.

"Well, if you two are going to go out on the town," J.J. said, "I guess I'll have to batch it tonight. You going to tell me the story about the toilet?"

Mary Beth stood. "Come see the new fixtures for the apartment."

While Katy stayed behind to wash her hands and watch cartoons, they walked over to the apartment.

After J.J. admired the new acquisitions and finished eating his Popsicle, he turned to Mary Beth, a troubled expression on his face. "I know that I said I didn't want to know anything about what went on with you and... him, but dammit, something's worrying me."

"Him?"

"What's-his-name, your ex."

She went queasy. Had he heard something about Brad? Was he about to launch into some jealous inquisition? She braced herself. "Brad. His name is Brad."

"Whatever." J.J. scowled. "Did Brad ever abuse you?"

She really didn't want to discuss her ex-husband with

her ex-boyfriend. Although he seemed to have changed, she recalled how very jealous and possessive J.J. used to be. Brad had been even worse. He used to grill her for hours about every man she'd ever dated or even spoken to.

"Why do you ask?"

"Because of Katy's reaction when we were horsing around. I wondered why she thought I might be hurting you. I figured that she must have seen something before. Did he ever hurt you, Mary Beth?"

"Not physically. I mean, he didn't beat me, but he was emotionally and verbally abusive. Especially before he—before we separated. I tried to shield Katy from it, but sometimes she saw and heard him harangue me or witnessed us arguing. She was only a toddler, but it upset her terribly." Merely remembering agitated her, and she turned away, fighting back tears. "It was bad." Her voice broke in spite of her effort.

J.J. took her in his arms and held her close. "Shh. Don't think about it anymore. Nobody's gonna ever say a cross word to you while I'm around. You can count on that."

She smiled and sighed. "There you go with that knight-in-shining-armor bit. J.J., I'm not so fragile that I have to be protected from every cross word. I can handle normal disagreements. It's—it's—"

"Being ragged on from daylight till dark that you can't take."

She pulled back and searched his face. "How did you know?"

"Honey, I've done a lot of studying and had a lot of experience with abuse in the last several years—it's part of my job as sheriff. It's a problem more common than you think. I had a couple of graduate seminars in domestic violence and abuse.''

''Graduate seminars?''

He grinned. ''You didn't know I had a master's degree in criminal justice, did you?''

''No, and I'm impressed. I'm also very proud of you.''

''Thanks.'' He kissed her. ''I'll miss you tonight.''

''I don't imagine Ellen would mind if you came along.''

He shook his head. ''You need to have time alone with your friends. I'll catch up on some paperwork or start installing the ducts in here. Did I tell you that a buddy of mine got all the material for me at wholesale prices? His brother-in-law owns a heating and cooling outfit in Tyler. When we're ready, we can get the units from him as well.''

''How much was the duct material?''

''Not much.''

''*How* much?''

When he told her, she was relieved that it was an amount she could easily afford. The insulation and drywall could wait a while.

She was relieved, too, that he wasn't upset that she was spending an evening with Ellen. Brad would have gone ballistic; he'd done his best to cut her off from all her friends. She'd learned later that keeping their wives alienated from friends and family was typical of abusive husbands.

There had been a time when J.J., too, would have been unhappy with her for going to Ellen's instead of being with him. Had he changed?

Perhaps so. After all, he'd matured in the twelve years since they'd been kids in love. J.J. wasn't like

Brad, she reassured herself. Brad, the consummate charmer, the consummate liar.

BY THE END OF THE WEEK, the ducts were in place and most of the insulation batts were in the walls. J.J. came by every afternoon and spent several hours working on the apartment. She worried that he was spending too much time helping her at the expense of his job.

When she'd mentioned it, he'd simply kissed her and said, "Don't fret about it, Sugar Beth. The county gets their money's worth out of me. I haven't taken a vacation since I've been in office."

The following Tuesday, Mary Beth was replenishing the glasses under the bar when she overhead Florence and Mabel talking by the cash register. All the patrons had gone, and they were having a last glass of tea. Neither of the women realized that Mary Beth was around.

"I swear," Mabel said, "I could pinch that Delbert Watkins's head off."

"What's Delbert done now?" Florence asked.

"Finding fault, as usual. I heard him at the VFW hall last night, during the break at the bingo game. He was blasting J.J. this time, telling anybody who would listen that our sheriff was so wrapped up in Mary Beth and this place that he was shirking his duties. Said criminals were running loose in the county, and J.J. wasn't turning a finger to apprehend them. Delbert stood right there by the coffeepot and declared as big as David that he was going to run against him in the next election."

Mary Beth's heart almost stopped. Horrified by what she'd heard, she slapped her hand over her mouth and sat down hard on the floor. Dear Lord, she didn't want J.J. to lose his job over her.

"Oh, Mabel, nobody pays any attention to Delbert Watkins," Florence said.

"I surely hope not," Mabel said. "And I hope Mary Beth doesn't get wind of his hateful tales. She's such a sweet thing, and such a hard worker, and I'm very fond of J.J., too. Nice boy. I do believe he has his eye on our Mary Beth. Let me just total out this register and I'll be ready to go."

Mary Beth sat cross-legged on the floor and waited until they had left.

"What are you doing down there, boss lady?"

She glanced up to find Buck looming over her.

"Meditating."

He shrugged. "Whatever floats your boat. I cut up the squash for tomorrow and started another loaf of bread. Katy's out with the domino gents. Need anything else before I leave?"

She shook her head.

"See you in the a.m., M.B." He touched a finger to his forehead and left.

She sat there for the longest time, worrying. If Delbert Watkins ever learned about Brad being in prison, he'd have a field day smearing J.J. Oh, what a mess. What should she do? After giving the matter a lot of thought, she realized there was only one thing she could do.

J.J.'S HAMMER STOPPED in midswing. He turned around and looked at Mary Beth as if she were slightly demented. "Say that again."

"I said that I think we should stop seeing so much of each other. It would be…wise."

"Wise? What the hell are you talking about, Mary Beth?"

She flinched. This wasn't going to be easy. She didn't like confrontations. If she could have thought of another way to get the same results, she would have tried it. "Well, the fact is, I feel terrible about monopolizing your time. You're here almost every day. And you've spent the whole weekend working on this place. You should be out…playing golf or something."

"Playing *golf*? I hate golf. I don't even like to watch it on television. Besides, I like being here with you. Helping you." He turned back to ripping out the old wallboard.

"J.J.?"

"What, darlin'?"

"Listen to me. You're going to have to quit coming here so much and spend more time in your office or out looking for criminals. People are talking."

He stopped and looked at her again. "Who's talking?"

"Delbert Watkins for one."

J.J. roared with laughter. "Honey, nobody pays any attention to that old blowhard."

"It's not funny, J.J.," she said, growing distraught that he wasn't taking this seriously. "Listen to me. He's saying awful things."

"What things?"

"That you're neglecting your job because of me, that criminals are running loose in the county, and that he's going to run against you in the next election."

J.J. laughed again. "Sugar Beth, as far as I know, we don't have a single loose criminal in Naconiche County—if you don't count the lawyers—and Delbert has been threatening to run against one official or another for the last forty years. It's nothing to worry about. In the first place, Delbert is too stingy to come up with a filing fee, and in the second, nobody would vote for him if he ran for the bus.''

''But he was gossiping about us at the VFW hall, and people were listening. You know how small towns are and how small-minded some people can be. What if— what if—''

''Whoa, whoa, darlin'.'' He put down his hammer and led Mary Beth to the old humpback trunk in the middle of the room. He sat down on top of it and drew her down into his lap. ''You're getting all worked up over nothing. My job's not in jeopardy. Trust me.'' He kissed her forehead. ''And there's not a thing I'd rather be doing right now—except maybe one.'' He wiggled his eyebrows and grinned lasciviously. ''What time is Katy due home from that birthday party?''

''J.J., listen to me, darn it! I think we should back off a little. Maybe you could date somebody else for—''

''Date somebody else? Woman, are you nuts? I'm crazy in love with you and I'd marry you this afternoon if you'd say yes. Why would I want to date somebody else? What's going on?''

She burst into tears and buried her face against his shoulder. ''Oh, J.J., it's awful. It's just awful. And if Delbert Watkins or anybody else finds out about it...''

''What's awful?''

She mumbled against his shirt, dreading even to say the words aloud.

He lifted her chin and kissed her nose. ''I missed that.''

''Brad, my ex-husband Brad Parker, is a criminal, a common *criminal*. Well, maybe not so common. He embezzled three million dollars from the savings-and-loan where he worked. He's in jail. Federal prison. The pokey. My ex-husband, Katy's father, is a *convict.*''

"So?"

"So?" she shrieked. "So, if word gets out, my reputation will be ruined. And by association, your reputation will be ruined. Folks won't approve of the sheriff keeping company with a convict's ex-wife. The gossips will crucify us.''

He smiled. Damn him, he just sat there and smiled like a blooming idiot.

"Don't you have anything to say, Jesse James Outlaw?''

"Thank you for telling me.''

"Thank you for—don't you *get* it?'' Her voice rose an octave. "Brad is in *jail.*''

"I know.''

"What do you mean you know?''

"I mean that I know. I've always known. I imagine about everybody in town knows.''

She felt herself blanch. *"Everybody?"*

"I 'spect so. It was in the paper.''

"Oh, God.'' She dropped her face in her hands.

He pulled her close. "Honey, don't worry about it. You didn't help old Brad embezzle that money, did you?''

"Good Lord, no! I had no idea what he was doing.''

"There ya go. Folks around here don't blame you for something somebody else did. They know you've had a tough time. You're one of ours, Sugar Beth, and I'm not the only one in town who loves you.''

She started crying again and she couldn't stop.

J.J. just held her and rocked her and patted her back until she was through. Then he offered her his hand-kerchief to blow her nose.

Chapter Fifteen

Mary Beth couldn't sleep that night for worrying about the things J.J. had said. Maybe Delbert Watkins was a blowhard and a chronic malcontent, but if he had noticed how much time J.J. was spending working on the motel, maybe others had, too.

And, even worse, she thought, was the notion that everybody in town knew about Brad being in prison. How humiliating. Here she'd been trying to be so secretive about it. Were people helping her out of pity? Were they whispering behind her back?

She checked the clock. One twenty-six. She didn't dare call Ellen or Dixie at this hour, but she needed to talk to them.

After wrestling with her pillow for another three hours, and doing no more than doze, she rose and went to the kitchen. First she put on bread to bake, then she made two large sheet cakes, one carrot and one chocolate, and started the soup of the day.

By sunrise, everything was ready for lunch except for the last-minute items. By the time she woke Katy for preschool, she'd made pancakes with smiley faces.

"Is it Saturday?" Katy asked.

"No, sweetie, it's Monday. Why do you ask?"

"We have pancakes on Saturday. On Monday, I have cereal."

Mary Beth hugged her. "This is a special Monday breakfast for a special girl."

Katy didn't argue. She adored pancakes.

As soon as Katy climbed on the church bus, Mary Beth made a beeline for the pay phone and called Ellen. She was already at the office.

"What's up?" Ellen asked.

"I need to talk to you."

"So talk."

She debated about whether to ask to see Ellen in person, or whether it would be easier to discuss the whole thing over the phone and not have to face her. Chicken that she was, she plunged in on the phone.

"Ellen, do you know about Brad?"

"Who's Brad?"

"My ex-husband."

"Oh, that Brad. Has something happened to him?"

"No. I mean, I don't know. I don't have any contact with him. I mean, do you know where he is?"

Ellen hesitated, and Mary Beth knew then. An awful feeling soured in her stomach. All the embarrassment that she had endured in Natchez came rushing back in.

"I see. You do know. Well, Ellen, I've got to go. Talk to you later." Mary Beth quickly hung up the phone.

She sank into a nearby chair and put her head in her hands. She'd thought she had escaped that part of her past, but she hadn't escaped anything. Everybody knew of her shame. Katy was older now, and sooner or later some mean-spirited kid would tease her. And—

Her first instinct was to pack her bags and run. But to where? Everything she had, which wasn't much, was tied up in The Twilight Tearoom and Motel. She couldn't afford to leave.

With a whirlwind of thoughts tumbling in her head, she quickly dressed, stowed the beds and was rolling silverware in napkins when Ellen rushed in. An enormously pregnant Dixie arrived not three seconds behind her. Both looked distressed.

"We need to talk," Ellen said.

"Yes," Dixie agreed, "we do."

"Would you like some coffee?" Mary Beth asked, suddenly feeling very nervous around her two best friends. "Or some breakfast?"

"I'm always ready to eat," Dixie said.

Ellen glared at her. "No, we don't want breakfast or coffee. We want to talk. Let's sit down." She took Mary Beth's hand, and they all sat at one of the tables with its neat blue cloth and pot of lemongrass. "What's happened?" Ellen asked. "Why did you ask me about your ex-husband?"

"J.J. said it was in the newspaper, and that everybody knew about him."

"That idiot!" Dixie huffed. "Men complain about women, but they're the ones who can't keep their mouths shut."

"No, no, it wasn't like that," Mary Beth said. "I—I'd told him about Brad, and he said he already knew. Is it true? Does everybody know about his being in prison?"

Ellen sighed and nodded. "Some snot-nosed kid down at the newspaper picked up the story about the trial and published it. We all felt really bad about it at the time, and I tried to get in touch with you."

"So did I," Dixie said, "but your phone had been disconnected. We didn't know how to reach you."

"I lost the house and had to move in with a friend. Katy was only two, and we didn't have a penny left. It was terrible."

"Oh, honey," Ellen said, squeezing her hand. "I wish you'd called us. We would have helped."

"Of course we would have," Dixie said, squeezing Mary Beth's other hand. "That's what friends are for."

"I was too humiliated to let anybody know. I simply hid out for months. The publicity was awful, and knowing that it was in the paper here just makes me sick. I'll bet the gossips had a field day."

"There was some talk," Ellen admitted, "but it soon died down when something else came along. Now it's old news. Nobody much cares about it anymore."

"I'll bet it got stirred up again when I came to town."

"Not really," Dixie said. "Nobody blames you for what your sleaze of a husband did. After all, you didn't steal anything."

"That's what J.J. said."

"He's right," Ellen said. "And you divorced him, didn't you?"

"As soon as I could afford it. And I have full custody of Katy. He didn't even argue about it. He was never much of a father to her. Or much of a husband to me."

"Good riddance to bad rubbish," Dixie said. She fished in her purse and came out with a granola bar. "Want a bite?" she asked as she peeled open the wrapper.

Mary Beth smiled. "No, thanks. I guess I don't have to worry about keeping secrets anymore."

"Puddin'," Ellen said with a wink, "don't you know that there are no secrets in Naconiche? Everybody in town already knows what color your tile is in the new bathroom.''

Mary Beth felt herself blush. ''I hope they don't know everything.''

Dixie laughed. ''Wally down at the feed store is getting up a pool to bet on the day you and J.J. get engaged.''

Mary Beth was horrified at the notion. ''You're kidding, right?''

''Nope.''

She dropped her head into her hands and groaned. ''It's not going to happen. I have no intention of ever marrying again. Certainly not for a long, long time.''

''Why ever not?'' Dixie asked.

''A question only a happily married woman would ask,'' Ellen said.

Dixie patted her stomach. ''I should hope I'm happily married. But why not consider marriage, especially to J.J.? Surely he's not like your ex-husband, Mary Beth.''

''In most ways, no, but in some very important ways, they're more alike than I would want.''

''Oh, fiddle,'' Dixie said, ''J.J. is as honest as the day is long.''

''I know that and that is very important to me, I'll grant you that, but both J.J. and Brad are strong, domineering men. Brad liked to keep me helpless and dependent to make him feel powerful and important. I don't think J.J.'s motives are quite the same, but I think he'd be happy to take over my life if I would let him. And believe me, sometimes it's tempting. I'm afraid I'd lose myself again if I married someone like J.J.''

''Do you love him?'' Dixie asked.

Mary Beth hesitated, then said, ''I think I do, but sometimes love isn't enough. I'm beginning to wonder if coming back here wasn't a big mistake. Katy and I probably would have been better off to have made a fresh start somewhere else—picked a place where nobody knew about the past.''

"But you have friends here," Ellen said, "and having friends can make all the difference. I couldn't have made it through Bobby's leaving and the divorce if it hadn't been for friends and family."

"I understand," Mary Beth said, "and I agree. I couldn't have survived without my friends in Natchez or my friends here after I came. After all, if not for you two and Florence and Wes and J.J. and *everybody,* I wouldn't have a business or a place to sleep. I'm so grateful, believe me, I am.''

"We love you," Dixie said. "Don't forget it. And I hate to break up this get-together, but I do believe that I'm in labor.''

"In *labor?*" Mary Beth shrieked. "How far along?''

"Far enough to go to the hospital.''

"Why didn't you say something sooner, for gosh sakes?''

"I thought it was gas.''

"Shall I call an ambulance?''

Dixie laughed. "Good Lord, no. But I would appreciate it if one of you would drive me there. Quick. I spit out the last two like watermelon seeds. I don't think I have much time.'' She grabbed her belly and grimaced.

Mary Beth jumped up. "We'll both drive you. Come on.''

Ellen grabbed Dixie's purse and her own, and ran to open the door while Mary Beth helped Dixie to her feet.

"We'd better hurry," Dixie said.

"Pant," Mary Beth said, "and hold on.''

B.D. and Howard arrived ready to do their morning's painting on the motel just as the women were getting into Ellen's car.

"We're taking Dixie to the hospital. The baby's coming," Mary Beth told them.

"Need any help?"

"Call Jack and tell him to meet us there. Tell Buck and Mabel to handle things at the tearoom till I get back."

"Hurry!" Dixie yelled.

As luck would have it, J.J. pulled up about then.

"Dixie's having the baby!" Mary Beth shouted, then climbed in the back seat with Dixie just before Ellen gunned out of the lot.

J.J. roared out after them, then, siren screaming and lights flashing, passed Ellen's car and led the way to the hospital.

Ellen threw her cell phone to Mary Beth. "Call Dr. Kelly."

"Drive faster!" Dixie yelled.

"I'm doing eighty!"

"What's the phone number?"

Dixie managed to recite the number, then let out an awful groan.

Mary Beth got through to the doctor's office and yelled, "Dixie Russo is in hard labor, and we're taking her to the hospital right now. Hurry!"

"*Please,* hurry!" Dixie groaned again. Sweat beaded her skin.

Mary Beth ripped off her chef's apron and blotted her face. "Pant! Blow! Something!"

"It's coming!"

"Dammit, hold on," Ellen said. "We're almost there. Oh, hell, that light's turning red."

"Run it! Keep on J.J.'s tail."

They screeched to a stop at the emergency entrance of the hospital. J.J. must have called ahead because two nurses waited at the curb with a wheelchair.

"It's coming!" Dixie yelled as the nurses opened the car door.

They got her into the chair and took off running.

J.J. came to the car. "I'll park the car for you, Ellen. Y'all go with her."

They didn't argue. They left the car and ran after Dixie.

LESS THAN TWO HOURS LATER, Mary Beth, Ellen and J.J. stood in front of the nursery window looking at Robert Alan Russo. He was beautiful. Mother and son were doing fine.

The doctor barely made it, and Jack arrived ten minutes after his son's speedy delivery. He was with Dixie now, calling Florence and the rest of their family.

Mary Beth glanced at her watch. Five till twelve. "I hope Buck and Mabel are holding the fort. I need to get back and help."

"Want a ride?" J.J. asked.

"Please. I'm not sure I could drive if I had a car. Ellen, what about you?"

"I'm still kind of shaky, too, but I think I can drive. I'm suddenly very hungry."

J.J. hooked arms with the two of them. "Come on, ladies, I'll take you both to lunch at a little tearoom that I hear is great. Ellen, I'll drop you by later to pick up your car."

Mary Beth could have kissed him. Sometimes he was a handy guy to have around.

MABEL AND BUCK and the others had done a great job running things, and everybody was eager to hear about the new baby. She finally posted on the chalkboard: *Robert Russo, 7lbs. 4oz. Perfect.*

"Buck," she said to her kitchen helper, "you've been a lifesaver. When Dixie went into labor, I didn't even stop to worry about serving lunch to folks. And it looks as if you did fine without me."

"Thanks for the vote of confidence, boss lady, but there wasn't much for me to do. Almost everything was ready. You must have been up cooking early."

"I couldn't sleep. Maybe I had a premonition about Dixie."

"Or maybe," he said with a wink as he ladled a bowl of soup, "you had your mind on a certain guy with a badge. If you two decide to tie the knot and you get out of the tearoom business, keep me in mind as your replacement."

"I've no doubt you could handle things but don't plan on my leaving."

"Mmm-hmm," he said in a way that meant he didn't believe a word of it. "You want me to start making crepes for that luncheon tomorrow?"

"Yikes, that is tomorrow, isn't it? Sure, you make prettier crepes than I do anyhow. How'd you learn to do that?"

"Kept company with a French girl for a while when I was in the navy. She taught me quite a bit." He wiggled his eyebrows.

Mary Beth laughed. "I'll bet. Was her name Monique?"

"It was. How did you know?" He set four crepe pans on the stove and started mixing a batter.

She pointed to the name inside the tattooed heart on

his upper arm. "You have a permanent reminder. Haven't any of your other lady friends given you grief about it?"

"Nope, I've got a system." He pointed to a similar heart on his other arm. The name in it was Sue. "I only date women named Monique or Sue, and I put a bandage over one or the other."

Mary Beth laughed. "You're full of it. Have you ever considered laser removal?"

"Only briefly. Here," he said, handing her the sandwich and bowl of soup he'd fixed. "Go eat your lunch and leave the crepes to me. You look about ready to drop."

She couldn't argue with that.

By the time the tearoom closed, Mary Beth was ready for a nap, but she knew that she dared not take one or she wouldn't sleep again that night. She didn't feel as if she had enough energy to swing a hammer, so she abandoned the notion to work on the units and took Katy downtown to the Double Dip to visit with Nonie and indulge in a banana split.

Nonie beamed when they walked in. "How are my girls? And how is Dixie? I heard about the baby from J.J., but he didn't know any of the details."

Mary Beth related the adventure and gave her all the facts about the baby while Nonie concocted a banana split for Mary Beth and a strawberry ice-cream cone with chocolate sprinkles for Katy.

Katy browsed carefully in the gift section while they talked. "Look, Mommy. Nana Nonie has a trunk almost like yours." She pointed to a humpback trunk used to display gift items.

"Yes, I see."

"Maybe she has a key," Katy said.

"What's this about a key?" Nonie asked as she handed Katy her ice cream.

"We found an old trunk in the closet of one of the motel rooms," Mary Beth told her. "Problem is, it's locked. J.J. said that the locksmith could open it, but I simply haven't had the time or wanted to spend the money for it."

"I'd be dying of curiosity if I were you," Nonie said. "There might be something valuable inside."

"Not likely." Mary Beth dug into her banana split. It was heavenly. "Nobody would have left behind anything valuable. It's probably filled with junk. Heavy junk."

"Why don't you take the key to my trunk and try it? And I'll bet Mattie and Fred next door have two or three trunk keys. One of them might work. I'll just run over and ask them while you finish your ice cream." Nonie bustled out and headed for the antique store next door.

She was back in a flash, dangling keys. "Here are several keys that might work. Mattie said that those old locks aren't that complicated, and you could probably get it open with a hairpin. These are just extras they've collected. She said there was no hurry in returning them."

"Thanks." Mary Beth stuck the keys into the pocket of her shorts. "I'll let you know what I find."

"If I didn't have to mind the store, I'd go with you right now and take a look."

Two customers came in, and Nonie went to help them while Mary Beth finished her banana split and Katy crunched the last bit of her cone. After chatting with Nonie for a few more minutes, they waved goodbye and walked down the square to the dollar store.

Mary Beth bought a lipstick for herself and socks and

a new coloring book for Katy. Funny, she thought, once she'd thought nothing of paying ten or fifteen dollars for a tube of lipstick. Now she saved her pennies for buying drywall and floating tape. Even though things had gone quickly, it would take a while just to get the apartment in usable shape. Heaven only knew how long it would take to remodel the entire motel.

She sighed and, tired to the bone, hustled Katy into the back seat of the SUV and strapped her in. How nice it would be to spend the afternoon in a bubble bath.

THE SHERIFF'S CAR WAS sitting out front when Mary Beth and Katy arrived at the tearoom. J.J. was leaning against the front fender.

"Hi," he said. "Where've you been?"

His question chafed a bit. Brad used to grill her endlessly to account for every minute of the day. "Out and about," she said.

"We went to see Nana Nonie and got ice cream," Katy piped up. "And I have a new coloring book. Wanna see?"

"Sure," J.J. said. He admired the new acquisition.

"And Nana Nonie gave Mommy some keys to open the trunk."

"What trunk?"

"You know," Mary Beth said. "That old trunk in unit two. I'm sure there's nothing more than junk inside, but your mother was very eager for me to look inside."

"Mom's the curious type."

"I gathered."

"Let's go look in the treasure chest," Katy said, her eyes bright.

"Sweetie, it's not a treasure chest. It's merely an old trunk. People used to store their clothes in them in the olden days. And I'm not even sure any of these will fit.'' She pulled the handful of assorted worn and tarnished keys from her pocket.

''Please, please, please,'' Katy begged.

Mary Beth sighed. ''Okay, let's check it out.''

The three of them walked over to the second unit and went inside.

''Want me to try?'' J.J. asked.

''Sure.'' Mary Beth dumped the keys into his hand.

J.J. pulled off the drop cloth that had been thrown over the old trunk and squatted down in front of it. The first key he tried didn't work, nor did the second. The third one did the trick. A musty smell wafted up as he lifted the top to reveal a wooden tray filled with various things—what looked like papers and old photographs. He opened a worn leather coin pouch to reveal three silver dollars and a small gold piece.

''I wonder who this belonged to?'' Mary Beth asked.

''I don't know, but I suspect you can find something in these papers.'' He lifted out the tray to see what was underneath.

''Look!'' Katy exclaimed. ''A cowboy hat!'' She grabbed the battered hat and plunked it on her head.

''Katy, don't! We don't know where that thing has been.'' Mary Beth divested her of the musty black hat.

Several smaller boxes were in the bottom. J.J. opened one and unwrapped a gunky-looking rag from an object he found there. He let out a slow whistle. ''Man, oh, man, would you look at that baby.''

Chapter Sixteen

"What is it?" Mary Beth asked, frowning at the nasty-looking thing.

"If I'm not mistaken, it's a Colt single-action pistol," J.J. said. "Dad could tell us for sure. He's the gun expert in the family."

"What's that stuff on it? It looks like molasses."

"Let me see," Katy said.

"Don't touch it, Katy," Mary Beth told her. "It's gooey."

J.J. rubbed a smidgen of the dark substance between his fingers, then sniffed it. "I'd guess axle grease."

"Why in the world would anybody put axle grease on a gun?"

"It's a common way of preserving the metal. And it did a good job. It looks almost new."

"How old do you think it is?"

J.J. shrugged. "Hard to tell, but from my limited knowledge, I'd say it's at least a hundred years old."

"A hundred years?" Katy said. "That's a long, long time. That's older than Mommy."

"I don't know," Mary Beth said with a chuckle. "I feel close to a hundred after the day I've had."

J.J. picked up another object rolled in a blue rag. "Oh, man."

"It's a knife," Katy said.

"A bowie knife," J.J. added. "Looks like the genuine article, too."

"What's a bowie knife?" Katy asked.

"An early Texas hero named James Bowie first made a knife like this over a hundred and fifty years ago. They became popular around these parts after that." He carefully rewrapped the knife and put it back in the wooden box with the gun.

"What else is in there?" Mary Beth asked.

He opened a second wooden box. Inside was another cloth-wrapped object. Unrolling it revealed a leather gun belt and holster. "This is in remarkable shape considering its obvious age. And here is the maker's mark."

Stamped on the leather was H. A. Holtzer, Llano, Texas. Also inside was a leather tobacco pouch, well used, and a silver badge. J.J. picked up the badge and looked at it.

"Now we know who this stuff belonged to."

"Who?"

"A Texas Ranger."

"But what's it doing here?" Mary Beth said.

"I don't know. We'll need to go through those papers to see if we can figure it out. The rest of it seems to be clothes and assorted personal items. Here's a shaving mug and brush and a razor. And that looks like an old rifle on the bottom. I'll leave it be for now."

"It's hot in here," Mary Beth said. "Let's take the photographs and the papers over to the tearoom to look at them."

"I'm with you," J.J. said. He locked the big trunk

and handed Mary Beth the key that worked, then hoisted the wooden tray containing the other material.

Mary Beth fixed tea for J.J. and her and juice for Katy. Katy lost interest in looking through the old stuff and begged to watch cartoons instead. After Katy was settled in the TV booth, J.J. and Mary Beth started sorting through the material.

"This may explain something," Mary Beth said. She held a fragile piece of paper that she'd pulled from an envelope. The envelope was addressed to Edward Prescott, Esq., Naconiche, Texas. "This is a letter from a Captain Hughes of the Texas Rangers, dated June 7, 1894. It says that Sergeant Austin Prescott died from wounds received when he was shot fighting a band of bank robbers and murderers outside of El Paso. Edward was his brother. Austin was buried in El Paso with honors, and the effects in the trunk were being shipped to Edward."

"Well, this is quite a find. I wonder who Edward Prescott was?"

"I have no idea. Could he still have relatives living around here?" Mary Beth asked.

"I know one way to find out. I'll call Millie down at the library. She knows the genealogy of everybody in town." J.J. called from his cell phone and talked to the librarian for a few minutes. "She's going to call me back," he told Mary Beth.

"Look, here are some photographs of Texas Rangers. This group picture is dated 1888. And here's another of Austin Prescott and a man named Wood Pierce with the same date. I wonder which is Austin?"

J.J. picked up another yellowed photograph, then glanced at the back. "This one was taken in 1891 and is of Austin Prescott and Walter Pickney." He put the two pictures side by side to match likenesses. "This one on the left must be Austin. And that looks like the cartridge belt and gun we found. And the knife."

"He was so young."

"Most of the Texas Rangers were young men. Did I tell you that my baby brother Sam is a Texas Ranger?"

J.J.'s cell phone rang before she could answer. From his conversation, she gathered that the caller was Millie at the library. J.J. stayed on the phone with her for several minutes.

After he hung up, he grinned. "The mystery is solved. According to Millie, Edward Prescott was a lawyer in town at one time. He and his wife Sarah begat Esther who married Leonard Bartlett and begat Marjorie."

"My father's cousin, who owned the Twilight Inn."

"Correct. And Leonard Bartlett's older sister Beatrice was your great-grandmother. So, as far as Millie can tell, you're the closest surviving relative. All this stuff belonged to Marjorie Bartlett and is now yours. If I were you, I'd get it appraised."

"Do you think it's valuable?"

"Probably worth a fair amount. I don't have any idea what. Fred Twiller down at the antique store next to the Double Dip is an authority on Texas memorabilia, especially guns and such. Give him a call." He handed her his cell phone and checked the phone directory by the pay phone for the number.

She briefly described to Mr. Twiller the things she'd found in the trunk, and they made an appointment for the following morning at eight-thirty for him to examine the items.

"IT'S WORTH *WHAT?*" Flabbergasted, Mary Beth stared at Mr. Twiller.

Fred Twiller, who reminded Mary Beth of Santa Claus without the beard, looked over his half glasses. "Twenty-five thousand. That's just for the Colt single-action. If you make a collection of, say, the Colt, the bowie knife, the holster and cartridge belt, the Winchester, the badge and the hat, and throw in a photo of Prescott wearing all the regalia, I'd estimate that you could get four or five times that. Depends on how anxious a collector is to get his hands on it."

For a moment Mary Beth could only gape. "Four or five *times?* You're joking."

"Nope. And I haven't even gotten to the coins yet."

"The coins?"

"I'll have to check with somebody more experienced in the field, but I believe at least a couple of those Morgan dollars are rare. And the gold piece, too."

"Good Lord! There's more?"

Mr. Twiller smiled. "Yes, indeed. The coins may be worth more than the ranger memorabilia. It looks as if you've come into a bit of a windfall."

"I'm going to have to take some time to digest this. If I want to sell the items, how do I go about doing it?"

"There are shows for such things, and there are serious collectors that you can contact on the Internet. Fact is, there's a show in Dallas next week that I'm planning on attending. If you'd like for me to, I can either take the items or photographs of them, or we can put the collection up for auction."

"Let me think about it."

Mr. Twiller nodded. "In the meantime, I'd suggest that you move these items to a more secure location, and I'll check on those coins."

Still numb, Mary Beth gathered up the antiques, leaving the coins with Mr. Twiller, and said goodbye. Returning to the motel, she replaced the items in the trunk, locked it, and tossed the drop cloth over it. After she locked the door to the unit, she walked slowly back toward the tearoom.

She was rich!

Well, maybe not rich, but she had stumbled onto a nice chunk of change. She and Katy could pack up the SUV and take off for—

For where?

Now that she wasn't broke, she could go almost anywhere. With the tearoom fixed up, she could probably lease it or sell it. Or Buck and Mabel could run it and provide her with additional income. She could go back to Natchez and open her own aerobics studio or buy into the one where she'd worked before. The possibilities were endless. She wasn't tied to Naconiche through lack of alternatives.

But did she want to leave?

Did she want to leave the friendships she'd rediscovered? The tearoom? The dream of a remodeled Twilight Inn? The wonderful memories and laughter and love?

Did she want to leave J.J.? That was a big one. In some ways, she wanted to run like crazy and avoid dealing with her feelings for him.

When she was young, she could hardly wait to get out of the stifling small town, especially after seeing J.J. with that waitress. She'd loved living in a larger world and never wanted to return to the place where she'd grown up. Only desperation had drawn her back.

Now she had choices. What did she really want? What would be best for Katy and her?

She sat down in Katy's tire swing and pushed off.

With the idle back-and-forth motion, she tried to sort
out her emotions from good sense.

The domino foursome arrived and went to work
painting and wiring and such. If she stayed, she could
afford to buy all the materials she needed and fix up the
old inn. She and Katy could have the apartment finished
and move into it in a couple of weeks. She could even
afford to buy Katy three beds if she wanted to.

Katy loved Naconiche. She had blossomed here with
so many loving people around and with friends to play
with. Katy would be heartbroken to leave Janey and
Jimmy. She'd even adopted Nonie and Wes as her
grandparents, calling them by a version of the twins'
pet names—Mr. Pawpaw Wes and Nana Nonie.

Mary Beth missed Isabel, her dear friend from
Natchez, but Dixie and Ellen more than filled that void.

And then there was J.J.

That was a problem.

Buck roared up on his Harley, and Mary Beth
glanced at her watch. Yikes! She had to get a move on.
Not only did they have to feed their regular crowd, but
the ladies from the Tuesday Book Club were having a
luncheon at one o'clock. She had work to do.

MARY BETH STAYED SO BUSY for the next several hours
that she didn't have much time to think. By the time
the tearoom closed, she was numb. She sat in one of
the booths sipping a glass of tea and trying to regroup.
Katy had gone swimming at the twins' house and J.J.
was out of town until Friday night. He had some sort
of meeting in Dallas—which was just as well. She
needed some time alone.

Mr. Twiller had phoned earlier, and she needed to
return his call, but she wanted to make a decision about

the memorabilia in the trunk before she talked with him. Should she sell it or keep it?

Actually, it was a no-brainer. Sentiment was all well and good and keeping the items she'd found might be a nice thing to do, but the cold hard facts were that she had a child to support and she needed the money. Wherever she ended up, she would sell the contents of the trunk. It wasn't as if Austin Prescott had been her great-grandfather. She wasn't even related to him. He was from Marjorie's maternal side of the family.

Her decision made, she called Fred Twiller.

"I've good news," he told her. "One of the silver dollars is worth a good amount of money, as is the gold piece." When he named the price that a similar silver dollar sold for recently, she almost swallowed her tongue.

"The other two dollars will bring a nice sum, as well, but not as much as the first," Mr. Twiller said. "Have you given any thought to selling the other things?"

"Endless thought, Mr. Twiller. I'd like to keep one of the photographs, but I'm going to sell everything else. The sooner, the better. Would you act as my agent? I'll leave the details up to you."

They settled on what she thought was a fair commission for him, and he said that he'd pick up the trunk the following morning.

As soon as she hung up the phone, she felt a hundred pounds lighter.

To celebrate, she was going to town to buy herself a new dress and a pair of stylish sandals at the most expensive shop in town. Except for a cheap pair of sneakers, she hadn't bought any new clothes in over two years.

But first she called her old classmate Lester Hawkins,

who was now a building contractor in town. Luckily, he was free, and he agreed to come out right away and look over the motel. She wanted a detailed estimate of the cost of restoring all the units as well as the apartment. She'd get the new dress tomorrow.

THE MORE LESTER TALKED to her about the cost of various materials needed for the job, the more she frowned and made notes. Either Lester was trying to gouge her, which she doubted, or J.J. had misled her about the "deals" he'd gotten on various items.

"Now, in the units," Lester said, "there's no need to put the high-end tile that J.J. bought. A cheaper grade will look nice and wear well. You can save some money there."

"Which high-end tile are you talking about?"

"The yellow in the apartment bathroom. It looks real pretty in a house like the one J.J. is planning, but folks don't expect something that fancy in a motel room."

"I see," she said. But she didn't see. J.J. had told her that those tiles were left over from earlier work.

After they had talked a while longer and walked the property some more, Lester said, "Let me take a few measurements, and I can get back to you on Thursday or Friday with some more accurate figures for the renovations."

"Fine. It will be a while before I can proceed—if I decide to. Lester, let me ask you something about building materials. If we order too much of something, say bathroom tiles or cement board, can we return it to the supplier for a refund?"

"Oh, sure, if it's in good shape, but that doesn't happen too often. Builders usually figure pretty close so there won't be any waste. Materials are expensive these days. Why, in the last three months alone, plywood has gone up fifteen percent.''

''Really?'' A thought struck her. ''About what is the going price for plywood decking like what was used on that new roof?'' She pointed up to the apartment roof that J.J. and the other men had put up so recently.

He named a price that was three times what J.J. had told her it cost.

Had he lied?

She had a terrible feeling in the pit of her stomach. The plywood, the tile, the insulation, all the other things, all were suspect. She couldn't stand it if J.J. had been lying to her.

Above all things, she hated deceit. She despised being lied to and made a fool of. Brad had done enough of that to last a lifetime.

She told Lester goodbye and went to pick up Katy.

A thousand things went through her mind as she drove to Frank's house. Most of them concerned J.J.

When she went to the door, she hid her concern behind a smile for Frank. ''Have the kids been running you crazy?''

''Not at all. But I have to admit Matilda gets credit for that. I haven't been home long. It's almost dinnertime. Why don't you stay and have meat loaf with us? There's plenty.''

She begged off, telling him that their dinner was waiting at home. And it was—leftover chicken crepes. Luckily, Katy loved chicken crepes and wasn't too keen on meat loaf.

As soon as Katy was buckled in, Mary Beth decided that she couldn't wait any longer. Instead of turning right and heading back to the tearoom, she turned left toward J.J.'s part of the Outlaw property.

"Aren't we going the wrong way?" Katy asked.

"No, I wanted to drive up this way for a sec and see something. Did you have a nice time with the twins?"

She nodded. "I love swimming. I wish we had a pool."

"Well, you never know what might happen," Mary Beth said, adding a pool to the wish list.

She turned off on a dirt road, then drove past the stable and corral. She'd never seen the house J.J. was building, but it ought to be—

There it was in the clearing ahead. She pulled to a stop and looked at it. It was nothing more than a slab and a framework of two-by-fours. There was no roof, no shingles.

Her stomach twisted inside out. She knew where the shingles were. They were on her apartment.

"What's that?" Katy asked.

"It's where someone is building a house." She turned around and headed home.

"Who?"

"Someone I used to know." Mary Beth clamped her teeth together to keep from crying.

What else had he lied to her about? What other things were people snickering about behind her back?

A sudden and terrible possibility struck her.

The SUV.

Oh, no. Surely not.

Chapter Seventeen

As soon as Katy left on the church bus for preschool, Mary Beth went straight to the pay phone. She already had the number of the used-car dealer in Travis Lake that she planned to call. She pulled the scrap of paper from her pocket, took a deep breath and punched in the numbers.

It only took a few minutes to confirm her worst fears. According to something called a "blue book," even the lower end of the range of prices for an SUV like hers was several thousand dollars more than she'd paid. *Several* thousand. When she recalled how surprised some people had seemed when they had heard about the deal she'd made on the car, she felt incredibly foolish and wretchedly gullible. No wonder. Why hadn't she noticed the strange looks she'd received?

Just to be sure, she called another dealer in Travis Lake, described the vehicle to him, and asked what he would pay her for the SUV. He, too, named a price several thousands dollars above what she'd supposedly paid to Ephraim Hobbs.

"Of course, I'd have to see it and check it out," the dealer said, "but if it's anything like you describe, I'd buy it in a flash. Vehicles like that are hot items. I could probably have it sold three or four times before the day is out.''

Sick at heart, she told the man she'd think about it and hung up. No question about it, J.J. had lied to her— not once, not twice, but many times. It would serve him right if she sold the SUV, paid off Ephraim Hobbs, and let J.J. whistle for the money he'd plunked down for her car.

The more she thought about J.J. and his underhanded dealings, the more angry she became. She hated the thought that everybody in town knew that J.J. was footing most of her bills. And there was no doubt that everybody knew. In Naconiche, *everybody* knew *everything*. Simply being in the tearoom and overhearing a few conversations told her more about the town's goings-on than reading the local newspaper. She heard about everything from Alma Summers's hemorrhoid problems to how drunk Billy Joe Sowell got last Saturday night when his wife locked him out of the house.

Fury drove her directly to Ephraim Hobbs car lot. She strode into the small trailer that served as his office and demanded to know how much J.J. had paid on her car. Ephraim hemmed and hawed, but she cocked her chin and stood her ground. He finally mumbled the amount that J.J. had paid down on the SUV.

She slammed out of his office, drove home and began chopping celery and onions and green peppers with a vengeance. If she ever needed a reason to leave this town and Jesse James Outlaw, she'd found it. She was angry enough to chop off various vital parts of his anatomy.

When Buck walked in a few minutes later, he raised his eyebrows, slicked a hand over his bald head and said, "Boss lady, remind me never to get on your bad side. You're wicked with a knife."

Mary Beth stopped slicing and dicing then and surveyed the pile she'd created. "I've been taking out my frustrations on the vegetables. I think we have plenty for the jambalaya."

Buck laughed. "And for the next two weeks. What's got you riled up?"

"Personal problems."

Buck tied on his chef's apron and washed his hands at the sink. "Is there any other kind? You having trouble with your man?"

"He's *not* my man!"

"That bad, huh? Want me to break his legs?"

Horrified by the thought, her head jerked up. Buck was grinning.

"Careful what you offer. I might take you up on it."

"I'd probably have to give up my job and leave the county, but if that's what you want, I'll give it my best shot. I've grown right fond of you, M.B., and I don't take to anybody giving you grief. What's the sheriff done?"

"Lied to me. Several times."

"Serious lying or soft lying?"

"Soft lying? You mean like a little white lie? No, these lies weren't in that category. They were big. *Big*."

"Nope. Serious or soft isn't about size. It's about intent. Some of the biggest whoppers I've ever told were soft. When my mama lay dying and asked for my brother and sister, I told her that my brother was out of the country on a business trip and I couldn't reach him. Told her that my sister Tammy and her whole family was sick in bed with the flu but that she'd sent the big bouquet of roses on the dresser. Even read her the card that came with the flowers saying how much Tammy loved her."

"And those things weren't true?"

"Not a one of them. My brother was in Huntsville prison for dealing heroin and my sister couldn't be bothered to take off work to come see her. I sent the flowers."

"But you lied to your mother out of love for her. I know you, Buck Morgan. Underneath that tough exterior, you're a pussycat. You couldn't stand to see her hurt."

"You got it in one. There's low-down, sorry-son-of-a-bitch serious lies, lies that are mean and hurt people or cover up rotten, sneaky or selfish things the liar has done. And then there are soft lies where you bend the truth a little or a lot because you care a whole lot for the person you're lying to and want to make their lives easier or nicer or protect them from a truth worse than the lie. Somehow I can't see the good sheriff telling you low-down, sorry-son-of-a bitch lies. I got him pegged as too damned straight for that. And the guy's crazy in love with you. A blind dog could see that."

"Buck, when did you get to be a philosopher?"

"Hell, I've always been one." He grinned and started sautéing a heap of the vegetables she'd chopped. "Have you talked to J.J. about whatever has you so pissed off?"

"Not yet."

"Talk to him. Find out his intentions. And cut him some slack when you do. He's a good man, M.B. He'd make a good daddy for Katy."

"I'm not looking for a daddy for Katy."

Buck smiled. "I'd have said he'd make a good husband for you, but I didn't want you to come after me with that knife. Think about what I said, M.B., before you go after the sheriff with that blade.''

SHE THOUGHT ABOUT what Buck had said. During the following two days, she thought about it a lot. And she thought about the lies Brad had so glibly spouted when they had been married. Brad was a born liar. He'd tell a lie when the truth would have served better. He was a low-down sorry-son-of-a-bitch liar in every sense of Buck's definition. There had been times when Mary Beth had confronted Brad with facts that refuted his lies, and still he would try to lie his way out of things. Or turn on her with his vitriolic tongue to take the heat off himself.

Was J.J. different?

She'd like to think so. Still, despite Buck's philosophical discourse on the subject, Mary Beth hated lies. Lies eroded trust. And without trust, a relationship didn't stand a chance.

J.J. PUT THE PEDAL to the metal on his way home from Dallas. He'd missed Mary Beth something fierce and he was anxious to get home and see her. She'd sounded funny when he'd called her last night, but she'd claimed she was tired. Maybe that was it. She worked too damned hard, and it hurt him to see her do it. If he had his way, she'd sit—

There he went again, wanting to carry her around on a silk pillow. She didn't like that, and he was trying hard to give up the notion of babying her. Maybe she'd relax a little if she got a good price for the stuff they'd found in the trunk. Maybe she'd even consider marrying him if she had the security of her own money and didn't have to try so blamed hard to make it on her own.

He was looking forward to having the whole week-end with her. He'd called Frank earlier and asked him to invite Katy to spend the next couple of nights with the twins. That wasn't a problem, Frank had told him. He owed his brother big-time.

It was almost three o'clock when he drove into the parking lot of The Twilight Tearoom. The only car around was Mary Beth's SUV. The front door was un-locked, so he went inside looking for her.

He found her in the kitchen putting away pots.

"Hi, gorgeous."

She looked up and a smile flashed over her face. Then the smile immediately shifted to a frown. "You're not due back until tonight."

"I ducked out early. Come here, woman." He gath-ered her into his arms and kissed her. She tasted like pure honey.

At first she kissed him back, but then she went stiff as a post and pushed him away. "We—we have to talk."

He leaned against the kitchen counter, pulled her into the V of his legs and began nibbling on her neck. "You talk. I'll do this while you're at it." His hands stroked the sweet curve of her butt. "I've missed you."

She wiggled out of his hold and moved back. "I mean it, J.J. We have some serious talking to do."

A fist of dread squeezed his gut. He didn't like that tone. "Are you going to get a lot of money out of that stuff?"

She nodded. "Quite a bit. More than I ever imagined, but—"

"Have you decided to hightail it out of Naconiche now that you've come into some money?" His tone was sharper than he meant it to be, but he was suddenly scared, scared of history repeating itself and her leaving him again. The fear had always been there, hanging like a sword over his head. "Honey, I'm sorry. I didn't mean to say that."

"Didn't you?" Her words were frostier than a meat locker. "Actually, I haven't decided if I will go or stay, but that's not what I wanted to discuss with you."

"Darlin', don't even consider leaving. Don't you know how much I love you? It would kill me if you left me again. Sometimes I wake up in a sweat, dreaming that you're gone again. I guess that's why I'd like to handcuff you to me."

"Is that why you've lied to me?"

Oh, boy. What had she heard? "Lied to you? About what?"

She put her hands on her hips and glared at him. "Don't play innocent with me, Jesse James Outlaw. I'm on to your game. I've been talking to people."

"Which people? About what?"

"I've been talking to Lester Hawkins for one, and to the folks at the builder's supply store for another, and to Dean Gaskamp. I've learned a lot about the price of plywood and tile and shingles and insulation and ducts and hot-water heaters and PVC pipe." She advanced on him and began punctuating every word with a poke of her finger in his chest.

"I've also been talking to used-car dealers—three of them, including Ephraim Hobbs—and I went to the library and read the blue-book prices on SUVs for myself. Wanna know what I've found?"

He closed his eyes and prayed like the devil was on his heels.

"I'll tell you what I found," she said, giving him another poke. "I found that you're a dirty, low-down miserable liar. And above all things, I hate liars! Why did you lie to me?''

He opened his eyes and looked at her. Somehow he knew that a lot rode on his answer. He'd been caught with his pants down for sure. There was nothing to do but to own up to it.

''I lied to you, Mary Beth, because I love you so damned much. I lied to you because you were so damned proud that you would do without things that you and Katy needed if I didn't lie. It was killing me to see you going without, so I doctored the particulars some. I don't cotton to liars myself, and I've always taken pride in the fact that I'm a man of my word, but I tell you this, Mary Beth, and it's the God's truth, I'd lie again rather than see you suffer.''

Silence hung in the room like air inside a crypt.

Mary Beth didn't say a word. She just stared at him, but he could almost see the wheels turning in her head. Had he blown any chance they had?

''So they were soft lies,'' she finally said.

''I don't know what a soft lie is, but I'll tell you what I do know. I love you with all my heart and soul and spirit. I always have, and I'll love you until the day I die. If you leave me again, I'll follow you this time. We were meant to be together. You know it's the truth.''

''I want you to do something for me.''

''Anything. Name it.''

''I want you to sit down and make a detailed list of every penny you've spent on me and this place.''

''Now?''

''Now.''

''Mary Beth, I don't even know what some of that stuff cost—like the shingles, I already had those.''

"Estimate. And don't try to feed me another line of bull about those shingles being left over from roofing your house. I went to your house. It doesn't *have* a roof."

He grinned. "How'd you like it otherwise?"

She scowled. "J.J., you're on thin ice here. Don't try to charm your way out of it. I want that list immediately."

"I don't have a pencil and paper."

She plucked a ballpoint from his pocket, ripped off a length of paper towel and shoved them at him. "Go find a table and start writing."

"Yes, ma'am."

"Would you like a cup of coffee?"

"Coffee would be nice. Tea would be better. A beer would be wonderful."

"You'll have to settle for better. I don't have any beer."

"Yes, ma'am." He didn't dare argue. He marched himself into the dining room, sat down at a table and started writing.

She brought his iced tea and looked over his shoulder from time to time, but she didn't say a word.

After a few minutes, he tossed down the pen. "That's all I can think of."

She glanced over the list. "What about the vinyl in the bathroom?"

"That really was a scrap, Mary Beth. I swear. Go look in Frank's laundry room if you don't believe me. It's the same stuff."

"Very well." She added up the figures. "As soon as Mr. Twiller sells Austin Prescott's belongings, I will repay you every penny of this."

"Oh, hell's bells, Mary Beth—"

"J.J., put a sock in it! I will repay you as I will repay everybody who has loaned or given me money or other things. Is that clear?"

"Yes, ma'am. Perfectly clear."

"And if you ever, *ever* lie to me again, I'll have your balls for breakfast."

"Yes, ma'am. Does this mean that you forgive me?" he asked.

"I'm working on it."

"Does it mean that you love me?"

"I suppose that it does."

He grinned. "Does it mean that you'll marry me?"

"Absolutely not. And I would appreciate it if you would stop asking."

"I'd be lying if I said I would, and I promised that I wouldn't do that. I'll ask you at least once a week until you say yes."

Before she uttered another word, he jumped to his feet, pulled her up and kissed the daylights out of her. As soon as he finished kissing her, he planned to take her back to his apartment and spend the weekend doing some serious loving.

Chapter Eighteen

By the end of summer, the work on The Twilight Inn was almost complete, and soon the motel would be open for business. Mary Beth had hired Florence to do the decorating—with an eye always on the budget. It had taken a good chunk of her windfall to restore the old motel, but it was looking really good. She had refused to let J.J. so much as swing a hammer. She insisted that he needed to spend time finishing his own house. She and Lester would tend to the work at the motel, thank you very much.

J.J. accepted her decision with only a bit of grumbling. He was learning.

She did let him help her move into the apartment. Isabel had shipped the few items of furniture she had left in Natchez. With a little help from Florence, Mary Beth turned the front bedroom into a sitting room with her sleeping on a Murphy bed that was cleverly disguised during the day. Katy had the back bedroom, complete with bunk beds. They'd kept one of the rollaway beds to use as a third when Katy had both twins over for the night.

The domino foursome had moved a playing table into the small office. They got a heated and cooled place to play, with lunch thrown in, in exchange for a couple of hours' work each day. Will, Curtis, B.D. and Howard were in charge of the front desk as well as grounds and building maintenance. B.D. turned out to be a master gardener with a true green thumb, and there were now window boxes filled with flowers attached to each unit. Under his pampering, Mary Beth's herb garden was flourishing as well.

The unit next to the apartment had been turned into an aerobics studio. The beautifully framed photograph of Austin Prescott and Wood Pierce hung in a place of honor on one wall. She'd sold the other pictures with the collection. Mr. Twiller had set up an auction that brought in even more that they had hoped. The coins had fetched a nice price as well. Mary Beth had more than enough to repay J.J. and the others and completely renovate the property with plenty left over to establish a college fund for Katy and a nice nest egg for the future.

Even during the summer, the tearoom was full for lunch almost every day and J.J. was a permanent fixture. They spent a lot of time together. Ellen and Dixie dropped by for a late lunch on the last Friday in August. Dixie brought along the baby, but young Robbie slept the whole time. Mary Beth turned the kitchen over to Buck's capable hands and joined her friends for dessert.

"The motel looks super," Dixie said. "I like the red doors and the red geraniums in the window boxes. When are you going to open?"

"Next week," Mary Beth told her. "And Dr. Kelly okayed me to start teaching aerobics again. I'm going to begin classes in mid-September."

"Oh, great," Ellen said. "What's the schedule?"

"Regular classes will be at eight-thirty on Monday,

Wednesday and Friday mornings, as well as at seven o'clock on Tuesday and Thursday nights. I'm going to have a senior stretching class at eight-thirty on Tuesday and Thursday mornings.''

"Count me in for the senior's stretching class," Dixie said, polishing off the last of her banana-cream pie.

Mary Beth laughed. "In your dreams. You're going to have to sweat with the rest of us. I'm having a tough time trying to get back in shape so that I don't make a complete idiot of myself.''

"You look fantastic," Ellen said.

"Do you think if I do aerobics that I can fit into a size six by Christmas?" Dixie asked.

"Good Lord, Dixie," Ellen said, "don't expect miracles. You haven't worn a size six since you were in the eighth grade. I'll be happy just to be able to fit into last year's Christmas dress for the office party.''

"Say," Dixie said, "speaking of parties, you ought to have an open house, Mary Beth, to celebrate the grand opening of The Twilight Inn and Tearoom.''

"What a wonderful idea," Mary Beth said. "When would be a good time do you think?''

"Friday nights are out," Dixie said. "High-school football games. Saturday mornings are soccer games. You'll be teaching on Tuesday and Thursday nights. Wednesday night is prayer meeting, and Sunday morning and Sunday night is church, so I guess that leaves Monday night, Saturday afternoon or night or Sunday afternoon. No, wait, Monday is bingo night at the VFW, isn't it?''

"I thought that was Tuesday.''

Dixie shrugged. "Something is Monday night.''

J.J. walked up to their table. "What's Monday night?" he asked.

"We can't remember. We were trying to think of a good night for Mary Beth to have a grand opening party."

"Isn't that a lot of trouble?" J.J. asked.

"Spoken like a man," Ellen said. "Of course parties are trouble, but they're also fun. We'll all pitch in and help. Dixie, we've got to get on the road. I have to meet a client in a few minutes."

After Mary Beth said goodbye to her friends, she asked J.J. if he wanted some lunch.

"Am I too late?"

"I think we can still scare up a few scraps to feed you. I'll see what's left."

"I'm not picky. What time do you want me to pick you up this evening?"

They were going to a new dinner-theater production that was opening in Travis Lake. Katy was staying with Janey. It seemed that Jimmy had decided to go to his friend Mike's house—without the girls around.

"About six-thirty. I'll go rustle up some grub, pardner. Do you like quiche?"

"I'm crazy about quiche. Just bring the ketchup."

THE DINNER WASN'T BAD and the community theater's production of *Nunsense* was delightful. Both J.J. and Mary Beth roared with laughter throughout the play, then drove home in an upbeat mood. They decided to go to his place for a nightcap—and other things.

Although everybody in Naconiche seemed to be following the details of their love life, Mary Beth still felt funny about J.J.'s car being parked overnight at the motel. As long as his car was at his place and hers was in the carport beside the apartment, nobody really knew if they were together or not.

Except Maud O'Riley.

"Evenin'," Maud said as they climbed the stairs to J.J.'s apartment. She sat rocking in the shadows of the veranda on the second floor.

"Evenin'," J.J. said, tipping his hat. "Nice night."

"Good evening, Miss O'Riley," Mary Beth said. "We're just going up to have a cup of coffee."

"Uh-huh."

Mary Beth stifled a giggle until they were behind closed doors, then she fell against J.J.'s chest and the laughter escaped. "I don't think we fooled Miss O'Riley."

"I don't think so either. If you would marry me, we wouldn't have to sneak around to do what everybody in town knows we're doing anyhow."

"J.J., now don't start. You've proposed at least twice a week this entire summer and you promised not to rush me."

"I know, darlin', but it's awful hard."

She giggled. "Don't tell me. I can feel it."

He kissed her then, and all thought of Maud O'Riley and marriage and everything else was forgotten. Oh, how she loved this man. How comfortable she'd grown with him. He was damn near perfect.

But marriage?

No, not yet.

TWO WEEKS LATER, on a Saturday evening, they held an open house at the tearoom to celebrate the grand opening of The Twilight Inn and Tearoom. Mary Beth wore a new dress for the occasion with strappy high heels and an expensive perfume she'd treated herself to with some of her newfound money.

Tables were set up both inside the tearoom and outside under the canopy of oak and pine trees. J.J. and Buck had strung up lanterns in the trees and torches had been lit to both repel little flying critters and provide festive atmosphere.

There were three kinds of punch and tons of finger foods. It seemed as if most of the citizens of Naconiche showed up, from the mayor to the farmer down the road who sold tomatoes for the tearoom salad. Dean Gaskamp and two of his buddies entertained. Turned out that Dean was a really good country singer, and the friends had formed a small band.

Nonie and Wes Outlaw arrived, and Nonie hugged Mary Beth and said, "I'm so happy that things are going well for you. Everything looks beautiful. I peeked into one of the unoccupied units, and it's really nice."

"Tell Florence," Mary Beth said. "She's here somewhere. Didn't she do a wonderful job of decorating?"

"Absolutely. The room seems restful and a bit rustic, just as you would expect a country inn to look."

"And you already have some tenants," Wes said.

Mary Beth nodded. "We're booked almost full. Luckily, the guests have been warned of the party tonight. Some of them are here. Have you eaten yet? There's a punch bowl over there and food everywhere. Help yourselves."

She left the Outlaws and greeted other guests, seeing that folks had food and answering their questions. All the staff from the tearoom and inn, including the domino players who were all wearing red bow ties, had pitched in and were serving food or guiding people around the property.

Ellen was there with her two boys; Dixie and Jack had brought their six. Many old high-school friends were there. Even Ephraim Hobbs and his wife stopped by for a few minutes.

Dwight Murdock, the lawyer who had handled the dispersal of Marjorie's estate, arrived when the festivities were in full swing. "I'm impressed with the excellent job you've done with the property," he said. "I never would have imagined that it could look like this in only a few short months."

"It took a lot of help and a lot of work."

"Has your foot healed, then?"

"Yes, thank you, Mr. Murdock. Please help yourself to refreshments and enjoy the music." She moved on to greet Vera Whitehouse, the waitress from the City Grill, and Mrs. Carlton, her old neighbor who made the chefs' aprons, and a dozen more who had arrived.

Katy, the twins, and several other children were laughing and playing tag and generally having fun, but if they got too rambunctious, one parent or another would calm them down.

A sense of warmth and community flowed through the tearoom and the grounds. Mary Beth's heart swelled, both with pride in her accomplishment and with love for this town and its people. How could she ever want to live anywhere else? This was where she belonged.

As she stood by the oak tree that held Katy's swing, J.J. came up behind her and put his arms around her. He nuzzled her neck and nipped at her ear. "You're wearing a pretty smile, Sugar Beth. What were you thinking about?"

"I was thinking about how much I love this town

and the people here. I've finally accepted that this is where I truly belong." She leaned back against him.

"And does that love include me?"

"Of course."

"Enough to marry me?"

Mary Beth hesitated. She'd been giving marriage to J.J. a lot of thought. She loved him, no question about that. And she knew that he would be a wonderful father for Katy. And she also knew that he was nothing like Brad. J.J. was a man of strong character and commitment who respected her as a person. And if they had problems, they could talk about them. Why was she denying herself the man she loved?

"Yes," she said quietly.

Silence.

Then J.J. let out a yell that turned every head at the party. "She said yes!" He grabbed Mary Beth, lifted her off her feet and kissed her.

The news spread like wildfire, and the partygoers broke into applause.

The kiss went on. And on.

Wally Gaskamp, who was holding the bets on the day Mary Beth would say yes, pulled a plump envelope from his pocket and studied a piece of paper tucked inside.

"Wes," Wally said. "Appears your day came the closest. Believe you won the pot."

Wes Outlaw beamed and hugged Nonie to his side. "Appears we won more than money. We get two new additions to our family."

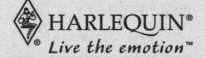

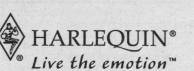

Falling in love...with a little help from Mom!

Mother, Please!

Three original stories by

BRENDA NOVAK
JILL SHALVIS
ALISON KENT

What's a daughter to do when her mom decides to play matchmaker?

The three heroines in this collection are about to find out that when it comes to love, mothers do know best!

Coming in May to your favorite retail outlet.